The Call of Angels

James T. Durkin

authorHOUSE®

AuthorHouse™
1663 Liberty Drive, Suite 200
Bloomington, IN 47403
www.authorhouse.com
Phone: 1-800-839-8640

First published by AuthorHouse 7/21/2008

ISBN: 978-1-4343-9629-7 (sc)

Printed in the United States of America
Bloomington, Indiana

This book is printed on acid-free paper.

Dedication

This second novel by James T. Durkin, *The Call of Angels*, is dedicated to every family affected by Deep Venous Thrombosis, commonly known as DVT. This health issue kills more than 200,000 Americans each year. Here, a blood clot forms in the deep vein of the leg. If it travels to the lungs, heart, or brain it may result in a pulmonary embolism, a heart attack, or a stroke, respectively.

According to various websites, symptoms of DVT may include sharp pain or swelling in the leg, normally starting in the calf. The skin may be tender, discolored and / or is warm to the touch. Sadly, about half of all cases of DVT have minimal or no symptoms at all.

Like any other public policy or health issue, the key is being informed as to the symptoms and causes of this serious medical condition. If you fear that you (or a loved one) may have DVT, please contact your family doctor. You may learn everything is fine. However, you may be referred to obtain an ultrasound of your leg. The first step of contacting your doctor may help save your life. Don't be afraid to make the phone call.

A special note of thanks to the medical professionals and staff at the DuPage Medical Group, Woodridge Family Practice, Edward Hospital in Naperville, Illinois and The Lord for keeping watch over me in December of 2000 and beyond. They frequently remind me what is truly undervalued in our life---our health.

My first novel, *In My Dreams*, was dedicated to everyone I had ever met. It was published as a second edition in 2005. More information is available at the website for the novel at http://www. in-my-dreams.com

Table of Contents

Chapter 1:
Back to the Future

"Bob, come on. Hurry up or you'll miss the bus," Mrs. Hamlin states while looking at her watch. "I love my son to death, but sometimes he just…doesn't understand the importance of what needs to be done now!" she mutters under her breath to herself.

"Yes, son, we have to get going. We may miss the bus and no, I'm not driving down to Cullerton to take you back to school. Did that once before, with the emphasis being once!," his father, Peter Hamlin, declares.

Both his parents grow tired of waiting for Bob. They stepped outside to get some fresh air. While outside they each light a cigarette. A few moments later, their eldest son approached them.

"Where have you been?," his mothers asks of Bob. He is wearing a travel bag over his shoulder while rubbing his head.

"I was making great time and then this happens. Well, let's just say I forgot to duck when entering my room again. The same mistake I've made hundreds of times. As you can guess, I was on the ground in pain…after I fell," Bob states in absolute frustration. "I'm really tired of this happening. Ah, my damn head…." Bob declares to those present.

"How many times have we told you to duck when approaching your room?…No, the number must be around 1000 times now", his mother states. Let me get a washcloth. You can use it in the car", Mrs. Hamlin shouts.

"Not again. We don't have time to make your head feel better son. As I said earlier, when you were wasting time back at the house, we're late…again. Be glad your mother has a lot more patience than I do. I don't feel like returning home tonight at Midnight because you don't understand the importance of being on time. Now, more importantly, what was that act you put on this morning about majoring in politics?" Hamlin sarcastically asks.

"Ok, I have the cloth. Let's get moving" Mrs. Hamlin says. She interrupts herself in noticing that blood is pouring out from the right side of Bob's head. "Did you know that you're bleeding?" she directly asks her son. "Don't tell me you didn't know."

"Come on. I'm not bleeding. How can that be? I've hit my head countless times….hell, I'd become too tired to guess how many," Bob replies as his father cuts him off.

"Don't swear in our home son!" his father sternly corrects him.

"With all due respect Dad, we're outside the home and I didn't swear. I said hell" Bob answers. After applying pressure to his head with the cloth, he discovers what his mom alerted him to: He was bleeding.

"Will you duck now?" his mother politely inquires of her son. "Promise me you'll start to bow when entering your room, ok?" she politely whispers in only a tone a mother could convey.

"If we miss the bus, your bleeding head will seem insignificant to the fun we'll have as we drive two hours back to school. Let's get going!" his father unequivocally yells.

"Peter, watch your temper," Mrs. Hamlin conveys. Bob smiles as his father is briefly humbled.

About five miles down the road while heading south on Interstate 57 near Country Club Hills, a suburb of Chicago, Illinois, Mr. Hamlin speaks up.

"Now son, I asked you a question back at our home that you haven't replied to yet. I was just wondering…When you're going to provide me with an answer?" Mr. Hamlin sarcastically inquires.

"I'm sorry Dad," Bob responds while applying pressure to his head, "what was your question again, " Bob patiently asks with a sigh.

"What prompted the idea about majoring in Politics. I mean, please help me comprehend how you, a very honest person, would have any interest in government? I'm sorry but….they're a bunch of crooks and liars. I truly thought we raised you better than that. More importantly, what would possibly motivate you to come up with such a stupid idea?," his father asks with a raised tone in his voice.

"Hey stop that. I have been pushing our son to decide what he would want to major in and you're belittling him. I've been asking him for, at least six months now, to begin thinking about some career path. Please don't be so rude as to put someone else down. Maybe Bob is genuinely being sincere with his answer but you're not giving him a chance," his mother states while cutting off her husband.

"Bob, we've invested a lot of time and money in you and your academic career. College isn't cheap. We're middle-class (people) son. Can you give us an answer to this one question? After all, we're paying for you to go to school and quite frankly…I feel we have a right to know," his father calmly asks after being silenced by Mrs. Hamlin.

"Well, I checked into the priesthood. Apparently, Central Illinois University had already met its quota for my sophomore class, so I was out luck, " Bob replied with a smile on his face.

"That isn't funny whatsoever. If we weren't running so late, I'd pull over and stop the car. We spent a lot of money sending you and your siblings to parochial school. However, since we may not make the bus, you'll just have to hear my reply from the driver's seat," Mr. Hamlin finally declares to him. To say he was angry would be an understatement.

"You know, Dad, I have usually been very serious…some would say too serious in my life. However, I want to assure you that I was joking. Actually, Mom has been asking me to question my career options for some time now. I've been putting some thought into this. Call me naïve but I really think most people in politics are honest, well-meaning, and well-intentioned people. I don't see any difference in honesty levels between politics, being a lawyer, or studying for the priesthood…there are bad apples in every profession. Most people, from what I have seen, want to do a good job. Whether you are a garbage collector, a correctional officer, a priest, or a Good Samaritan…there are good people in every career. There are fools in each career from teachers, attorneys, supervisors, and…peons. Just look at the news on any given day. Stockholders, CEO's and insider traders are frequently indicted. Someone new is criminally charged every day with misleading the shareholders, a government agency, or worse….the employees of respectful companies. I just want to try something that I feel I can make a positive difference in," Bob declares. He is being polite and respectful to his parents. From the tone in his voice, one can genuinely sense his candor and sincerity.

"Well, have you given any consideration to the priesthood?" his mother asks as both he and his father turn and look toward her. She replies, "I have two sons. From my generation, a mother was expected to convince one of her sons to pursue the religious life. It doesn't hurt to ask," she politely answers.

"Don't think that's going to happen. Let me just say this, skip me and go to Dan....Well, scratch that," Bob states.

"What do you mean skip Dan? Your brother is a good person. Don't be so hard on him," Mrs. Hamlin warns her son.

"If you can't see the lack of reasons why Dan isn't ready or qualified for the priesthood, then I can't explain them. Let's just say he lacks a genuine interest to be nice. Deep down he probably has a kind heart but he has a problem showing it. So, neither Dan nor I score high on 'the ministry meter'" Bob says with a smile on his face.

"Well imagine that. Just when we were seeing a return on our college investment we have arrived at the mall. In fact, there's the bus. We made it!" Mr. Hamlin sarcastically says while clapping his hands.

"Keep your hands on the wheel. Bob already has one cut on his head. We don't need another one caused from some rude celebration in the parking lot," Mrs. Hamlin clearly says.

"On a serious note, I wanted to say thanks. I had a really nice time at home with my family this weekend. The food was good. It was nice to see everyone again. Oddly, I had some really strange dreams last night," Bob offers to his parents.

"Oh yeah, what were they about?" his mom inquires.

"Let me guess....you ran for political office?" his father jokingly asks. Both parents begin to loudly laugh at the mere suggestion of a political campaign.

"No Dad, not that weird or foolish. Maybe someday after you safely park the car near the bus I'll tell you in the future," Bob replies. "Mom and Dad, I love you both. Thanks for motivating me to be a good person. Someone who likes to help other people and has fun doing it," Bob politely declares to his parents.

After retrieving the last of Bob's personal items, they kiss and hug their son good-bye. "Good luck Bob. Hope things go well in school," his father states.

"Yes, we're very proud of you. We're always here if you need someone to talk to. Call us tonight after you arrive at school, ok?" his mother lovingly asks. "Be careful around the girls at school," she adds.

"Yeah, right," Bob replies with a smile. "Besides, it would be hard to find one who meets your expectations," he replies teasing his mother with a polite response.

"What do you mean?" Mrs. Hamlin asks.

"Every Mom only wishes the best for their kids. You're no exception but you're the best!" Bob responds while tossing a school bag over his shoulder. "Looks like it's the last call for the bus. We barely made it. I'm going to load my bags. Don't want them to think I don't want to ride with them. Thanks again Mom and Dad for a great weekend. I got a lot done and did relax a bit. I have a lot of fun at school but it's always good to come home. I love you both," Bob states with a big smile on his face.

"We love you too Bob," his mom replies. His father nods his head in approval while smiling.

As Bob boards the bus, Mr. Hamlin says, "You know it's very easy to tease our son. Some of the things he does are just….odd, but he is a wonderful person. He genuinely does care about other people and the problems they face. Maybe of all the people we know, and of course, we're biased, but he would be a good elected official. We did good hon," Mr. Hamlin whispers as a tear forms and begins to roll down the side of his cheek.

"You know, that's very nice for you to say. Now, don't be afraid to tell him that tonight. You were a little hard on him," Mrs. Hamlin tells her husband.

"Perhaps I was. Remind me to tell him when he calls tonight," he says sadly. "Here, watch this," after seeing where Bob sat down, Mr. Hamlin taps on the window. He places the palm of his hand squarely on the glass and whispers "I love you" to his son. Bob smiles in approval as his parents wave good-bye.

"You know, maybe you should stay with them and go back home! This bus is for college students," a young man says to Bob to the amusement of most of the students present.

"That's great to know. Thanks for the heads up. By the way, if that's the case, then who let you on our bus?" Bob says with a serious look. The other student was clearly taken aback and asked Bob if he wished to discuss the issue in far greater detail in the parking lot. "Actually, I'm staying here but thanks for your concern for my well being. Why is it that when some people make smart-ass remarks and someone offers to discuss it with them, they suddenly get upset? Where's this anger coming from buddy? What prompted all this pent up tension? Please do us all a favor. Give your mind a rest and just sit down," Bob says. Many students clap and cheer to show their approval.

"Who the hell do you think you are?" the student asks.

"Hey, thanks for asking. My name is Robert A. Hamlin. We're returning to the Promised Land known as Central Illinois University. Take solace in the promise made by our ancestors that things are about to get better for us all," Bob says with his arms extended. Many openly laugh or sit there in disbelief.

"Who let Moses on the bus?" another male student asks his girlfriend.

"I'm just glad my parents enjoy my company. I love them very much," Bob gently replies. "Be excellent to each other on our journey home." Strangely enough the other student, identified as Kyle from his name embroidered on the jacket he was wearing, sits down. He was fearful that angels could appear from above to protect this individual.

After the bus left the parking lot it pulls onto Interstate 55 from Joliet, Illinois. The school is located 80 miles south in Cullerton, Illinois. "Interesting choice of words back there," a young female sitting next to Bob says about ten minutes into the ride. "I mean, are you some kind of religious freak?"

"No, I'm not. Sometimes there are people who swim in the shallow end of the gene pool. If they approach you with some hard ass attitude, giving such odd remarks are effective. He's better off keeping his mouth shut. I bet other people here probably think I'm nuts but its amazing how a jerk backs down when you stand up to him. It's not that complicated," Bob says. "They soon learn that it's better just to walk away - especially if they think that the other person is crazy. Some odd reply forces them to wonder if the person they're talking to is nuts. After all, have you heard any of his genius opinions offered since we left the mall?" Bob asks.

"No. It's been nice," she replies. "Interesting approach; I'll make a note of that. You know...I normally do not talk to strangers. Don't get me wrong, I'm not shy. I'm just selective about who I talk to. My name is Emily," she says.

"It's nice to meet you. My name is Bob. I'm a sophomore at Central Illinois (University). And you?" Bob inquires in response.

"I am a junior. I'll be 21 next week. Lucky me, right?" Emily asks with a smile.

"Well, congratulations. Don't blame you for being cautious. There are a lot of crazy people out there," Bob says with a smile. Do you have any plans for the birthday weekend planned yet?" Bob politely questions.

"Going to go out with the girlfriends' probably. No serious plans but I'm sure it'll involve some local bars....you know," she answers smiling.

"Yeah, I guess. Hope you have a fun time. Congrats. No birthday for me. I'm just looking to get back into my regular routine. Went home for this past weekend and relaxed a little. Caught up on some sleep....you know," Bob says.

"Yeah, it's always nice to get away from all that happens here. College is fun, but we all need a break. Did you do anything special?" Emily inquires.

"Nope; I had no plans at all. Just spent time with my family and did some laundry" Bob says with a smile. "What was really nice was that I did nothing. It was really cool. I'm not quite sure how I was able to chill out since I'm normally high strung and wound up. However, some things have me pretty anxious. I mean....never mind, it's not that important," Bob offers. His demeanor seems to become fearful as evidenced by his folding his arms and looking in the other direction, away from the person seated next to him.

"Hey, it's really none of my business, but are you going to be okay? I mean, two minutes ago you seemed fine and at ease. You really put that guy in his place about ten minutes ago," Emily says with a look of concern on her face. Bob's lack of eye contact, conversation and infrequent muscle movements (how his fingers were shaking) began to concern her.

"Is there anything I can do to help? Most people feel better once they get an issue off their chest. I'm here...if you need any help," Emily offers. While saying this, she places her hand on his arm to assure him. She was concerned and wanted to listen. Bob seemed to be oblivious to her gestures. He was, in fact, very anxious. For about two minutes, his physical response seemed to take control of his well being. His hands became clammy. His heart rate accelerated. He was on the verge of an anxiety attack. In fact, his thoughts completely drowned out the fact that Emily had moved her hand away from his arm and was now holding Bob's hand. Not as an overt gesture to take a pass at him. She found his comments to the other student on the bus interesting...A welcome change from a man standing up for himself without intentionally causing harm to the other person," she thought.

"Is there anything I can do for you?" Emily offers. Bob seems ambivalent to her genuine sense of concern for his own well being. "You seem like you have a sincere interest in how other people perceive you. Have you ever contemplated an issue and then... BAM, something occurs, or someone walks in, that just makes everything else seem insignificant?

"Yeah, like much of this weekend...when I was asleep," Bob conveys with a great deal of insecurity. He has not made eye contact for a few minutes now. Suddenly, he looks downward and realized that Emily had her hand clasped with his. "Why are you doing that?" he politely inquires.

"Doing what?" she innocently asks.

"Holding my hand," Bob whispers in response. He looks deep into her eyes. He wasn't scared, just unsure.

"I'm sorry, I don't know you. If it will make you more comfortable I'll stop," she states. Emily tries to pull her hand back, but Bob refuses to let go. "You know I can't withdraw my hand while you're holding it," she whispers in a low monotone while staring at him.

Bob senses her willingness to listen. For the first time he sees something he's not yet seen before. Emily interrupts his thought chain and says "As I stated earlier, most people become more relaxed when they just say what's on their minds. There is no right or wrong answer here. All you're doing is discussing what you're thinking about. I'm not here to make decisions or cast judgment. This may sound stupid but…it may be safer to tell a stranger your feelings after all. You'll probably never talk to me again anyway. I can't believe I'm asking you this. I never kiss on the first date. I'm embarrassed to hold hands, let alone in public, but here I am reaching out to you."

"Then what's there to gain by telling a stranger about some dream I had last night?" Bob asks.

"No one can help you if you don't permit them to. I really thought your comments earlier were very interesting. I never saw an example where someone replied to some jerk and politely, I might add, reminded them of how insignificant they are as a jerk to the rest of us and society in general," Emily says while leaning forward. She did not wish to violate his space so she moved her back to where it was a few seconds ago.

"Let's just say, I…um…had some weird dreams this weekend. Nothing tragic or bad, but they were clear to see and understand. Didn't need some fortune teller from a carnival offering to see my future and reveal it to me," Bob declares.

"Okay. Tell you what. If you wish to tell me what happened you can…" Emily says as she is interrupted by Bob laughing.

"There's no chance I'm going to tell you what I dreamed about yesterday. Let's just say this…Have you ever caught yourself daydreaming. You see or hear something and say something stupid like I've seen this before?" Bob questions. I think something was revealed to me about my future. I just didn't know how I would respond. I keep most of my feelings to myself. No need to share everything. Besides most people really don't care about other people's views or opinions," Bob calmly says.

"That's ridiculous and you know it. Everyone has that special someone. Sometimes it's someone who we're dating. Other times a co-worker or occasionally a close friend of the same gender. Everyone wants some safety blanket....someone who they can discuss their feelings thoughts or events with. Bob, sadly you know it. Tell you what, let me be your crash dummy," Emily says. Bob begins to laugh uncontrollably.

"I'm sorry, but you sound like me," Bob replies. Emily withdraws her hand from his and crosses her arms.

"You know, I didn't begin talking to you to be insulted. Nobody deserves to be treated like that," she states. Her face is looking straight ahead, not wishing to look at him.

In sensing he has hurt her feelings, he says, "Hey, I'm sorry. I didn't mean to offend you. I was wrong. A few minutes ago you didn't think talking to Mr. Wonderful in that manner was bad," Bob comments.

"Then why were you rude to me," she asks.

Bob does not answer right away. He glances at his watch and says, "Ok. I'll tell you about my dream for 15 minutes, but that's it. I've got some homework to do."

"30 minutes or even more...Why would you limit yourself to something you feel is important?" she asks with a renewed sense of optimism and a smile.

"15," Bob replies and just stares at her for a few seconds.

Eventually Emily breaks the tension by offering her reassurance. "Whatever time you want is fine. Just didn't want you to limit what you'd say by some arbitrary limit such as time."

"I know. I just wanted to see your response," Bob replies as she slaps him on his leg with a smile.

"How did I do?" she asks in a suggestive manner.

"You passed," he answers. "Just wanted to remind you I was in charge. You'd forgotten that the past two minutes."

"Not on your life," she answers while laughing. She pushes her finger into his chest and says "would you believe the B.S. you just told me? If you were anyone else, I'd tell you to go sit somewhere by some other fool on the bus," she says laughing. "And in fact, at this point, the only reason I'm letting you stay here is for my desire to find out what you dreamed about. How do you like them apples, buddy?" she teasingly asks him. Emily was forming a genuine interest in him. She liked confident men and Bob appeared as such. She could also give as well as she could receive.

"This morning I walked into the bathroom after eating my breakfast with my parents. I looked into the mirror and said, 'Let the future begin'...Bob offers.

Chapter 2:
A New Day is On the Horizon

"Good morning everyone! I'm Rosemarie Branch and we're here, *Live*, in Chicago. For those of you just waking up we'll begin with today's top story. In one of the closest presidential elections ever, Congressman Robert Hamlin was elected President of the United States last evening. Shortly after 2:00 (am), U.S. Representative Hamlin took the stage and declared victory in the race, which many political pundits are now calling one of the greatest upsets ever.

Hamlin, 29, defeated incumbent U.S. President Crowe by the slimmest of margins. In what was statistically a tie with a very narrow lead of approximately 400,000 popular votes, Hamlin won the states of Kentucky and Georgia to squeak out a victory in the Electoral College.

Most importantly we're pleased to be joined this morning with U.S. Representative Robert Hamlin. Actually his official title is President-Elect. Congressman Hamlin, we're pleased you could join us at this hour. Congratulations. To those people just waking up and now learning, perhaps for the first time you won, what's in the immediate future for you and your family and how is everyone?"

"Excuse me for using your first name, but Rosemarie I really am glad to be here this morning," Bob replies with a smile.

"Did you get any sleep last night?" she inquires in an upbeat manner.

"Um, no," Bob politely answers. "In fact, my wife Tracy is asleep and has been for about an hour now. Me, I've been up for about 2-3 days now," Bob says with a deep laugh.

"Two to three days?" she says. "How will you be able to faithfully execute the duties of your office with no sleep," she jokingly asks.

"You know," Bob says while smiling," I'm kind of used to this. Not winning presidential elections, but insomnia. While in college and much of my young life thus far, I frequently have been up at night or lay in bed thinking, just like other Type A personalities.

Don't really need much sleep, in the short term. I'm guessing from past experience that I'll crash in five to six hours," Bob offers with a tired look on his face.

"Congressman Hamlin, I know you're genuinely pleased with the results last night. Anything you want to say in your first public appearance this morning to the American people?" Rosemarie asks.

"To begin, there are so many people to thank and let them know of our appreciation. Aside from my wife and my immediate family, as you know, my parents were here last night as I spoke. I truly want to thank some specific people. Even though I'm very tired, I want to make sure I do this properly. First, my immediate thoughts go out to the people who voted for us last night. Yes votes were cast for Senator Touter from the state of Georgia and I" Bob says.

"Yes, a state that came in very late last night for you and according to many pundits, Georgia is the state that allowed you to win," Rosemarie says in an upbeat tone.

"Well, yes, it could have been any of the 50 states. However, I couldn't have won without a lot of things. First, Senator Touter comes from the state of Georgia. He is primarily responsible for our win and I do mean, our win," Bob offers.

"Yes, I wanted to ask that first. You have stated that for months now…to the chagrin of your opponents and those people who didn't vote for you. How is it *our* campaign? How it is our goal to improve the situation of the American people? For clarification purposes, Representative Hamlin, whose campaign was it really?" Rosemarie asks with a sort of cocky tone in her voice.

"You know, in my limited time here, I have been involved in a number of campaigns. I do know this: there isn't much I'll say now at 6:05 (am) Central Standard Time to those people who didn't or could never vote for me that will please them anyway," Bob replies.

"Isn't that kind of rude to say? Some people would say you're gloating," Rosemarie rudely asks.

"You know, Rosemarie, if you would stop interrupting me I think that I might be able to provide some insight here," he says with a keen but polite look on his face. "Last night the first call I made after the victory speech was to Mrs. Howard (the widow of Senator Al Howard of Louisiana. He had been nominated to run for president, but died during the campaign. After being elected as the Vice Presidential nominee, Hamlin moved up to fill the spot on the ballet from Howard's departure). "Before I could express my appreciation to her, she interrupted me. She said she was so proud of not just the race we ran, but how we ran on the issues.

In this campaign, she was amazing. She made countless campaign appearances as a surrogate speaker across the country for our campaign because she, as stated to me again this morning, told me how proud she was. More importantly I might add, she stated how Senator Howard would have been incredibly proud of what we did. She told me and please excuse me to anyone who may be offended by what I'm about to say, how we won because we stuck to the issues. She conveyed how proud she was that we promoted the policies that Senator Howard fought for in the 30 some years he represented the state of Louisiana in the U.S. Senate."

"That's really selfish to say," Rosemarie stated as Bob cuts her off.

"Rosemarie, I don't think the viewers here today really want to watch a debate between you and I. They've heard a lot of talk and watched a lot of commercials the past two months. I'm pleased to say that the American people issued their decision by casting votes yesterday. I'm most proud to say that Senator and Mrs. Howard, my family, Senator Touter, and most importantly, the American people won about four hours ago! Today, in fact begins the start of a new future for America, one that everyone can be proud of. We won't agree on every issue. You see, in a democracy it's okay and even expected that we'll disagree at times. I've stated many times that a democracy rests on the consent of the governed. I'm just...very pleased Senator Howard's family and those families who live across this great nation of ours that we stuck to the core issues of this campaign. We won because we expressed in a sincere, honest and forthright manner what we wish to accomplish," Bob declares.

"How can you think that? You have no foreign policy experience. Your win was a fluke. Quite simply, you have no business running this nation. Let's face it, if it wasn't for winning the lottery in college, you would be a nobody!" Rosemarie shouts. The studio crew members are sitting there in amazement from the exchange they are witnessing. More importantly, they wonder how the American people are viewing this exchange.

Bob sits there for approximately 30 seconds without saying a word. Eventually his silence ends. "I apologize for my delay in responding to your comment. I wanted to make sure I could gather my thoughts. You know, it's really easy to sit there and toss verbal grenades at someone else without offering any substantive proposals to address the serious problems facing the country. For the past two months, our staff has watched your daily diatribes. Sometimes they've been entertaining….other times they've been pathetic."

"I don't take offense with what you have stated about me personally. I have thick skin and it's generally accepted in the American political system that negative commentary is the rule, not the exception. As for my true opinions about you, I'd rather keep them to myself because I'm a gentleman. I have always tried to take the high road in this business. Having class is something you can't buy or inherit from your parents," Bob calmly states. She was the daughter of two very wealthy television executives. It was alleged she had received the current position from the lobbying efforts of her parents.

After hearing Hmalin's previous comment, she begins shouting in earnest. Bob Hamlin casually ignores her and resumes his reply. "Rosemarie, on many of the items you brought up, you are absolutely correct. I really had no formal training for this position. I never attended any private educational institutions. I've never taken a real interest in foreign affairs. In fact, if it weren't for winning the Illinois Lottery, I wouldn't be here today," Bob says as he pauses.

"However, there are some things that I have learned about how to interact with people. It's easy to put your arm around someone at a funeral when they've lost a loved one and say you care. It's tempting to position yourself to benefit when other people are truly suffering and it's easy to 'rant and rave' about shaking up the political system when you're truly working to shake it down for personal financial gains (Bob was alluding to some dated allegations about Rosemarie Branch's involvement in pyramid schemes. It was alleged she was increasing the value of stock in some financial corporations in her position while reporting financial news for another news network. The negative observations about these activities were old, but were announced to the general public about two months beforehand). Her reply, as Bob anticipated, was very vocal with her shouting a stream of four letter words in the screen. The nationwide audience viewing the interview at this early hour could not have paid any prominent comedians enough money that she was providing to the American people for free with her profanity-filled tirade. To put it bluntly, she was beside herself, yelling four letter words at the television. Ironically, Bob proceeded to ignore her and continued with his rebuttal.

"Most importantly, I'm certainly not the most qualified person for this position. I'm only 29 years of age. As I've discussed many times, I have truly been blessed. I have the most wonderful wife. I've had the honor of representing the wonderful people of the Fourth Congressional District in Illinois. I've traveled the nation meeting people, on their terms, at their homes, their jobsites, and in their communities."

"I've spoken many times about the luck I've enjoyed in my short life. More importantly, I try to live my life as a good citizen, good neighbor, and good public official. I've been in the most prestigious educational facilities in the world, yet I've spoken with people who live in the poorest communities. I've given countless speeches about my deep concern about the problems that face America. I've also been honored to meet with and listen to former prisoners of war, national religious figures, and other people whose deep convictions about moral issues we have all faced or have been tempted by is truly humbling."

"The long and short of this campaign is this…I truly believe that the events of the past few years and the good fortune I have been provided has prepared me to be a leader," Bob calmly explains. Meanwhile Rosemarie Branch is being escorted out of the newsroom by security personnel. She is absolutely beside herself and sadly doesn't realize her career has probably ended today.

"I'll close by saying this…I make mistakes every day. As my family and staff can attest to, I am not the most patient person. At times I use profanity and truly enjoy watching various sporting events like many of you do. In my first political campaign five years ago, I remember speaking at my event where I announced my intention to run for political office. I made only a few, brief, campaign promises. I earnestly felt that most people didn't believe elected officials kept their word. Therefore, I resolved to minimize what I would promise to do if elected. I did, however, offer two promises. One was to limit my time in office to a fixed period and the second pertained to give my wholehearted effort in everything I did to make a genuine difference in improving the quality of people's lives and earn their trust in doing so."

"I didn't have an answer to every problem facing our great country. I don't profess to know everything. I don't know the heads of other countries by their face or name and I don't wish to take too much of your time today especially since I haven't slept in two days," Bob says with a smile.

"I'll close by saying this: I'm not ever going to apologize for working hard, for caring, for remembering peoples names who I meet, and for wishing to help people. I thank God every day for the blessings I've received to date. In the political world I was never more proud the day I first endorsed Senator Al Howard for president. I really believe there were few people more qualified to be president than he was, certainly much more than I." I still seek his counsel and wisdom on many issues even those that pertain to politics.

Mrs. Howard has been an angel to me. She was there for me, in her time of need, to this campaign and our nation after having lost her spouse of 40 some years. I'll never fully comprehend why I was selected to be his running mate. I'm not here to lead cheers on the major issues of our time. Throughout this presidential campaign

I vowed to pursue the policies that he had so eloquently spoken about while in the U.S. Senate."

"Four years from now the American people will be selecting a new president. However, until that time, I'm going to work night and day, without sleep if I have to," Bob says with a smile, "We're going to help the country move forward, maintain its position as the leader of the free world, and try to improve the plight of our least fortunate - just as Senator Howard would have done with all his energy."

"Thank you, my fellow Americans, for the trust you have provided me. I'll do my utmost to show you by my words, actions, and the legislation we propose not to let you down. May God bless you; May He keep watch over you; May He protect you and our nation, the United States of America. Thanks for taking the time to listen today and over the past few months," Bob declares. There is no response at the television network. Rosemarie Branch has been escorted from the studio. Tommy Perkins, a noted political commentator, who was supposed to be interviewed by Branch next after Hamlin is sitting by himself, on camera. No one is there to direct the audience to the next topic.

"We have lost our transmission with President-Elect Hamlin," a voice declares.

Suddenly the colored bars appear on the screen. Two minutes later, the picture is restored and another reporter addresses the national TV audience. "As you can see, we've had a lively discussion and commentary regarding last night's election. As reported by the votes counted last night, Congressman Robert Hamlin of Illinois was elected President of the U.S. We've just been handed a bulletin: Apparently both President Elect Hamlin and his running mate, Senator Sam Touter of Georgia, will be holding a joint press conference at 3 (pm) Central Standard Time later today. From the events of the election decided yesterday and the discussion this morning, some interesting fireworks to discuss this week," Michelle Dempsey, veteran political reporter, states to the national TV audience.

Later that afternoon, the national political press corps gathers at the South Suburban Convention Center in Tinley Park,

Illinois. The room, filled with 300 plus reporters who covered the presidential election and news organizations from around the nation, is buzzing with excitement. Not only are they there to cover the results from the presidential election the day before, but they, not surprisingly, are very interested in hearing Hamlin's opinion about the discussion earlier that morning.

Initially it was planned to have the event in downtown Chicago or at a location near O'Hare Airport. However, Hamlin's staff determined that they wanted the nation to become more comfortable with the person who was just elected president. It was subsequently decided to have the event in the South Suburbs of Chicago, in the district he represented in the U.S. Congress. After some debate, it was agreed the South Suburban Airport located in Peotone, Illinois could accommodate enough charter flights from most of the large press contingent anticipated. Also, since the victory celebration was in downtown Chicago last night, much of the press corps was already in town for the event.

At 3 (pm) Central Standard Time, Robert Hamlin and Sam Touter, accompanied by their spouses, entered the room. Many of the media representatives were disturbed with Hamlin. Not because he had won in a stunning upset. They were more concerned about how their colleague, Rosemarie Branch, had been treated earlier this morning. (She had not been seen since her participation in the interview that morning that had been terminated by the news network). Most news commentators had been reporting throughout the day that it was Ms. Branch who had clearly been the aggressor in the discussion and was at fault for how the interview quickly went downhill. Most news reporters and pundits had been very complimentary of Hamlin's performance with her, particularly since he had not slept the two days before. However, some reporters were of the opinion that one of their peers had been slighted professionally.

After everyone was seated, Hamlin began the press conference by addressing the topic on many of the reporter's minds. "I doubt you're all here wondering if I wear boxers or briefs," Hamlin says to the amusement of those present. "Before we proceed to far more serious matters, I wanted to begin by offering an apology to the

American people. Earlier this morning I was being interviewed by Ms. Branch, a noted national news reporter. As many of you observed, things went downhill very quickly. After campaigning very hard the past few months and not getting enough sleep the past couple of days, I may not have had an A + performance this morning. I watched a tape of the interview several times and was advised by many that I was not to blame for what happened. Many of whom are here today with us from the national news media are friends of Ms. Branch. Nevertheless, I didn't want to begin our mission by making enemies. Therefore, if anyone feels that they were slighted by my comments or performance this morning, I apologize.

"I learned a long time ago by my parents, both of whom I am pleased to say are here with us today, to take the blame - even when you're not at fault. Doing so puts people at ease and begins the healing process a lot quicker. After all, it takes at least two people to have a fight. The bottom line is there is a desk plate in the Oval Office that says "*The Buck Stops Here.*" It's not time to make excuses or point fingers. It's time to move forward and get things done."

"Let me explain why. We've all seen a lot the past few months. We saw a great human being, my political hero, Senator Al Howard pass away unexpectedly. We saw an incumbent president who had a huge lead in public opinion polls lose an election. Both Senator Touter and I have seen the best of what America has to offer. We've been to world class hospitals here in Chicagoland and spoken with pioneers in modern medicine. We viewed miracles, firsthand, in what good health care can bring to bad medical situations, particularly in terminal illnesses for children and their families in offering them solace and hope for a cure.

"We saw countless examples of good people doing great things everyday, in the common display of their everyday routines. We went to a blood drive in Savannah, Georgia and watched hundreds of people, most for the first time, donate blood to help their fellow human beings. We went to Georgetown, Kentucky, and saw how advances in technology can help produce a car that competes and defeats foreign competition. We went to Rochester, New York, and viewed people filling grocery bags for the homeless and less fortunate at a food pantry. We witnessed *countless* positive stories, events and influences that help shape our lives. For that, we were deeply moved and most grateful.

"However," Hamlin says with a pause. He knows what he wants to say but wishes to have the attention of everyone present…"We also saw great difficulties. We went to Minnesota and witnessed the destruction of a few towns from an EF5 tornado where more than 50 people were killed. A storm that provided no warning since the emergency alarm system was destroyed by the thunderstorm that preceded the tornado. We went to Appalachia in parts of West Virginia and North Carolina. We went to the Bronx, New York. We went to South Central Los Angeles and we went to the west side of Chicago, the greatest city in the world," Bob offers with a smile on his face. Robert Hamlin was a lot of things, but he was never shy about his pride of where he was from and in his support of its sports teams or its people.

"Everywhere we went, whether it was to a joyous occasion or to some tragedy that only God would have an explanation for, there was one common element. Do you know what it was?" Hamlin asks the media representatives present, all looking intently at Hamlin. "The common element was hope. That regardless of how happy or torn or depressed they were at that time, the American people always have a sense that things are going to get better. Former President Reagan was notorious for having a positive mental attitude. He generally believed things would always be better. It may not happen overnight and there may be no pot of gold that can be seen or grabbed. However, the American people are at their best when they are pushed, some may say shoved. That's why we're here to say 'Let the future begin'.

"Before Senator Touter and I take your questions I wanted to share some things about myself. We spoke today, as we had during the course of the campaign while spending time talking on a plane or a bus, or…just shooting the breeze after an 18-20 hour day.

"To begin, we're both truly blessed and humbled. Winning any campaign is hard but demonstrating you have the right to govern is much more difficult. Neither of us was born wealthy, has millionaire backgrounds, or was 'stamped' with what would be the traditional seal of approval the American people demand and are entitled to. We spoke at length about being honest, reaching out, and giving 100 percent every day, over the past few months.

"Today, we're pleased to announce that we're going back out on the road. No, we're not running a political campaign again. Believe me, we saw the best of what the U.S., the greatest country in the history of the world, has to offer. We saw every reason to be optimistic and to be encouraged in what we can do as a society. We saw the best in a nation, a land of immigrants from around the world. As you all know my grandfather came here from Ireland with nothing more than the clothes on his back and a dream of making a better life for himself."

"What Senator Touter and I also see is difficulty. We fully anticipate that getting legislative approval from the Congress for the issues we discussed in the campaign and asked the American people to put their trust in us is going to be hard. However, it pales in comparison to the problems a starving child has who goes to bed hungry....pales in comparison to the news a family learns that the manufacturing plant, the sole employer in their town, is about to be closed and the jobs lost forever ...and it pales to the problem when a family with no health insurance has just learned their mother has Breast Cancer."

"We're going to visit with the American people...again... on their terms in the states and congressional districts of the chairpersons of key legislative communities in the U.S. Senate and the U.S. House of Representatives."

"Why are we doing this? Why is this important? Why are we using this approach, you may ask," Hamlin shares with the audience. At this point Hamlin stands up, removes the microphone from the podium, and walks into the section of the room where the media are seated. "We're going back out on the road to Americans' homes and to their cities and neighborhoods. We're doing this because what elected officials do is important. However, life has meaning, life has value and the problems the American people face are real. If Senator Touter and I don't try, then we don't have a moral right to lead this nation. Too many elected officials govern by reading public opinion polls. If we fail to try to address those issues that even a grammar school student can comprehend, then we have to ask ourselves why we even bothered to run. Both Senator Touter and I understand this: the American people voted yesterday for us to act upon the problems facing this great country. They have the right to demand the best of us and our national government. They, also, should expect our best effort from our God-given time, talents and treasures. We live in the greatest country in the history of the world. We're going to tap the financial resources and moral authority we have. We, in turn, will challenge the American people, our corporations, our churches and selves to be even better."

"The American people, yesterday, placed us here to help make an even better society, for all of us," Hamlin declares. Upon finishing his statement he walks back to the front of the room and places the microphone back in the podium stand.

"Now, we're available to answer any questions you may have," Hamlin declares. He has a serious look on his face that shouted determination. He was trying to be sincere and genuine. However, the first question he faced concerned his discussion earlier that morning with reporter again.

"Congressman Hamlin, how can you expect we in the news media to offer you a fair shake when you treated Ms. Branch, one of our peers, so poorly today," Tim Drummond from *ANN*, America's News Network asks. The crowd just sat there patiently. Many were in shock at the gall demonstrated by this veteran reporter. Many others, however, agreed with him.

"Well, nobody said governing was going to be easy or that press conferences were exciting," Hamlin says with a smile. "You know, if I was one of your peers, I'd probably agree with you and understand your opinion," Hamlin calmly says to those present. "But I'm not. You see, politics is not a simple game. You can't play touch football when everyone else is playing tackle. I began today's press conference by taking the responsibility for what happened. I'll let you reporters and citizens of our great nation determine culpability. I'm taking my share of responsibility for what happened. I don't really care if she does. The American people are tough, but fair. They're willing to forgive when someone is willing to say I'm sorry. It occurs, everyday, when couples try to sort out problems in their marriage. It happens, everyday, when citizens look at how their elected officials have voted on bills and spend their tax dollars. The buck stops here…I began by saying I was sorry. You as a reporter and you as an American citizen can decide, for yourself, if you wish to accept it. If not, then I can't help you much more. I remember a passage from the New Testament where it was written 'He without sin can cast the first stone.'

"As a follow-up, Congressman Hamlin, have you apologized to her?" Tim Drummond stunningly asks. Many present, even Ms. Branch's supporters, are amazed by the reporter's strength of conviction or naiveté in asking again. Many others cannot believe his indignation or disrespect.

"I'd be glad to apologize to her personally. However, last I saw in watching the videotape she was being escorted from the newsroom by network security personnel. If you could tell me where she is and what her phone number would be, I'll call right now," Hamlin says. Many in the audience are now laughing. Many others begin to clap in support of Hamlin because he was trying to bring humor to a very embarrassing event.

"Yes, Russell, go right ahead. How can we help you?" Hamlin asks with a genuine look of sincerity. He was referring to Russell Thomas, a correspondent with *BDN*, the Black Discussion Network, a company owned by prominent minority individuals.

"Congressman Hamlin, millions of African Americans voted for you yesterday. They gave you their votes, some pundits have described, one being your efforts of campaigning throughout all of America to reach out to segment in society. Having met with you, myself, several times on the campaign, I would have to disagree. I know it's because you have a diverse staff and always treated everyone covering your campaign with dignity" Mr. Thomas declares.

"Thanks. That's very kind of you to say" Hamlin says in acknowledgement and nods his head in appreciation for a kind compliment.

"More importantly, I saw that you do care. You were in Charlotte, North Carolina and listened intently to the people describe their concerns about the textile mill that is scheduled to close. Families of both black and white citizens described their fears and their children have about losing their jobs. However, they were more afraid that racial problems would worsen in the future with fewer good-paying jobs. My question is this: What are you going to do to help the African American community that gave you 92% of their votes yesterday?"

"First, Russell, thanks for your kind remarks. Having met me you know I do care about both our wealthier and our poorer communities for both African-Americans and whites. It doesn't mean we all love one another or join hands and sing at various religious services or that we don't care about poor people or different ethnic groups. Yes, quite frankly, we received the support of approximately 92 percent of African-Americans that voted. In addition, there was, which was not as actively reported, a record turnout for citizens of your community. It's difficult for all of us, to trust and reach out to people who are different from our own religious and social backgrounds. I try to lead by my actions, not just words, so once again I thank you for your polite remarks to acknowledge our efforts."

"That said, our efforts did not end yesterday. In fact, they just began. I really believe we can create an economy that stands up for working men and women. I know in my heart that being president not only means signing treaties to enhance free trade, but enforcing applicable penalty provisions when our trading partners don't play by the rules if they do not open their markets to American businesses. Our society has always valued the premise of work and fair play. I have always supported affirmative action programs , many times offending some of my white constituents. Have always felt that everyone should have an opportunity to succeed and be part of the American dream. But don't misunderstand me: those people who believe they should keep their jobs due to political clout or because their name sounds nice in their respective geographic areas or that they feel they're being appointed to appease some voting constituency need to be made aware of this: as easily as you were brought in, you can be removed."

"In the weeks ahead, we're going to put together a task force simply titled '*Americans.*' The goal of this group will be to improve the plight of everyone here. It doesn't mean everything we do will create some pot of gold at the end of the rainbow. However, I can guarantee you, Russell, and everyone else here in the room today this: we're sure as hell going to try," Hamlin replies. He recognizes Cheryl Ferguson, a female reporter from the newspaper *USA Tomorrow*. "Yes, Ms. Ferguson, go right ahead."

"President-Elect Hamlin, I am proud to be the first to address you as such today," she says. A few members of the media applaud from her comment. "I, for one, am pleased you put a member of my profession in her place today, but let me tell you why. As you know, I have been a correspondent for a long time. It has been incredibly difficult for many minorities to break into various professions here in the U.S. However, I would also add women to the category of minority. Even though we are numerically a majority of our citizens, we still are a minority group when you consider our lack of presence in our corporate boardrooms and holding certain political positions, if you know what I mean, Congressman Hamlin," Ms. Ferguson says. Hamlin claps along with many present to acknowledge her accomplishments as a reporter, regardless of her gender. They were also showing their approval of her analysis that women are not equally represented.

"I'm very pleased, Congressman Hamlin, that you put her in her place today. She, in just a few minute's time, went out of her way to embarrass herself, but, more importantly, made all women look like rude, power-hungry people. She had been "taunting" you for weeks now on the morning broadcasts. You could have found a cure for a horrible disease and she would have ripped you for not finding it fast enough. She had absolutely no business being in that position whatsoever, period. As a fellow woman I proudly ask that you disregard her actions. Please do not stereotype all of us women as second-class citizens. We're good at what we do and we've earned the right to be here. I'm proud to stand here and say you won because you deserved it," Ms. Ferguson shouts to her peers. Many of the women jump to their feet to show their solidarity with her view of the election and women's contributions to society. Many of the media also clapped in recognition of her and other women's efforts.

"I wanted to say thank you for your kind remarks about me. More importantly you're right about the value of the contributions women make today and have always made. As for my opinion about Ms. Branch, I'll let my comment made at the beginning of the press conference stand by itself," Hamlin says. Many present cheer at his response, with most people present smiling.

"But if I can President-Elect Hamlin, I would like to ask two questions. One, what are you going to do to assist women's empowerment in corporations and the political process? Secondly, what is the likelihood we will see a woman elected as the U.S. President in the near future?" she inquires. The female reporters present all stand to demonstrate their solidarity with her prodding of Hamlin.

"The position and power the U.S. President has on many issues should not be underestimated, Ms. Ferguson. I thank you for asking. Simply put, we have a lot of work to do. There are numerous reasons why women are not equally represented in corporate boardrooms and in positions of elected office. We have to strive to continue to push women to pursue educational opportunities. After all, you can't become a lawyer unless you complete law school and pass the state's bar exam. You can't work on a road construction project unless you're accepted into the union. You can't be a police officer unless you graduate the academy. It should be pursued, quite simply, because it's the right thing to do," Hamlin declares. All the women present stand and demonstrate their approval.

After the applause stopped Hamlin resumes talking to the mass media gathered. "Let me be quite candid if I can. Afteral all the election is now overYou know, we all make mistakes. Part of the problem goes back to the days of the caveman...you know, Me man; me must hunt as the provider...Ugghhh," Hamlin says with a smile as many men present laugh. However, the women just sat there some having looks of anger on their face. "There have been a lot of mental blocks for men to overcome over the centuries and that includes me. I haven't always been the pursuer of good over evil and doing what's right. I'm a human being, just like everyone else. I, too, looked at people as objects - I think you know what I'm referring to because you're all smart people. Let me be even more candid: I finally came to the realization that I too had a mother. It didn't happen overnight. It took...a long time. Luckily, I had some friends and family members who offered, when needed, some tough love to me. Finally, after a few hundred hits to the head, long before I won the Lottery, I caught on to the importance of treating other people as I would like to be treated.

Women are human beings, partners in our quality of life," Hamlin affirms with the media members, many of whom are applauding to show their approval. "Notice, however, that I did not say 'equal partners'. Regardless of the effort undertaken, things are never going to be equal. We can't change how and what people think. We can, however, put forth our best effort to be nicer and more respectful toward each other. We have a moral responsibility to do what's right, including the need to give everyone a chance to prove their worth and value to society. I'm glad that I started a long time ago, but as evidenced firsthand this morning," Hamlin says with a grin, "I haven't reached the finish line yet."

"As a follow-up Congressman (Hamlin), I too was born and raised in Illinois. It's great that for the first time, we'll all have a president who was born and raised here and was elected to the office while still a resident of the great State of Illinois," she says with pause.

"I couldn't agree with you more. I've been thinking that for a few months now," Hamlin uncharacteristically replies while interrupting her.

"On a more serious note, when do you think we'll break what one prominent political journalist called the last glass ceiling, having a woman elected as our U.S. President?" she asks once again. As anticipated, the women present cheer enthusiastically.

"In fact, I am familiar with a book that has a very similar title. I honestly don't know when it will happen. After Senator Howard passed away a few months ago, I had the opportunity to select a female running mate, but I didn't. I picked someone, here with us today, who is not only a friend and is capably qualified to be president, if something unforeseen were to happen to me. Senator

Touter helped me get elected. Politics is about winning. It's not about doing your best or finishing close. Only one team can win the Super Bowl each year. We all know how important close is, like in horseshoes and hand grenades. The sad truth, however, is that being close doesn't help in national political campaigns. Simply put, if you don't win, you can't govern or lead. This isn't T-ball. Someday, I'm hoping I'll be there to help make history on that issue" Hamlin politely says. The women present are very quiet, some even angry with him.

"I asked Senator Touter to spend the entire last week in two states: his home state of Georgia and Kentucky. Now, don't get me wrong: I'm sure he enjoyed being able to sleep in his own house at home," Hamlin says as everyone present laughs. "Here I am campaigning non-stop 24/7 for the week. I called Senator Touter at 10 (pm) Eastern Standard Time, that's one hour ahead of where I was the other night and I'm told he's asleep. Here we are, the final week of a presidential campaign and his wife tells me his snoring sounds like sawing lumber," Hamlin says with a smile. Members of the media present laugh as Hamlin publicly was letting his guard down and showing his strong sense of humor that many reporters viewed firsthand when traveling with him and when he would meet with the public at campaign appearances. "The world could have ended and he would have missed it" Hamlin says as he gently prods his running mate to laughter from the audience.

"In all honesty, I truly value Senator Touter's contributions to our nation with the legislation he's sponsored and fought for over the years. He accepted his role in the campaign. You know, it's tough to run for the vice-presidency. I know firsthand what it's like. I briefly was in that role a few months ago when tragedy struck," Hamlin whispers. He begins to be overcome with emotion. The reporters all sat, silently in their chairs as Hamlin closed his eyes, took off his glasses and begins to blow his nose. Tears were clearly visible as Hamlin looked up and saw Senator Howard's widow.

"I haven't taken the time to say thank you to Senator Touter. You know, Sam, we would not have won yesterday without your contacts and campaigning in Georgia and Kentucky. Thanks...for everything," Hamlin gently and clearly says. Both he and Senator

Touter stand and embrace before everyone present. After what seemed like a minute, Hamlin turned to Mrs. Howard and invited her to join them. As she arrived on the elevated stage, everyone present stood to applaud as the three of them all hugged and embraced.

Hamlin and Touter took questions for the following hour. Hamlin sought to end the event by stating, "In closing today, I wanted to extend our offers of appreciation. First, our thanks go to people who travel as part of their jobs, particularly to the members of the media, especially you all here today. I don't think most people understand how tough it is to jump on a plane to cover our political events, leaving your families behind, eating unhealthy food, etc. Yes, the campaign was spirited and exciting, but you tried to help inform the voters of our various political positions. To that, I wish President William Crowe the best of good health and happiness in the years ahead."

"Lastly, I really miss Senator Howard. It was an honor getting to know him over the past few years and in the few weeks when I was his running mate. However, based on my faith, I am convinced that he is smiling today. I continue to seek his advice each night, just before I go to bed, just before I say my prayers each night. I, luckily, thank God for my health, my family and the best wife in the world a man could have. I can solemnly assure you...I didn't deserve to win the Lottery, to meet my wife, to be elected to the U.S. Congress and the presidency. But I'll promise you two things: I'll govern just like I campaigned; a workaholic for the next four years. Afterwards, I'll leave the presidency. My wife and I will begin life, together, after politics.

Thank you, the American people, for everything and believing in me when it would have been very easy not to do so. May God watch over and protect you, may he hear your prayers and thoughts, and may he forever guide and protect the greatest country in the history of the world, the United States of America. Thanks again for everything," Hamlin calmly declares.

Hamlin and Touter, accompanied by their wives, offer invitations to the media present to join them for a buffet set up in the lobby. They personally walk through the room and engage in non-political social talk with everyone who was there.

"You're an hour late," Thomas Pain of *WIN*, the political radio network says in approaching Hamlin. They had an interview that was now delayed because Hamlin and Touter were conversing, socially, with many of the hundreds of media representatives present "You know the two of you really do like the game of politics don't you!"

"I like people. More importantly, I like helping people. Even in our great nation, there are a lot of people who need help. However, today we eat," Hamlin replies while pointing to the buffer table. "More importantly, how are you and your family doing?" Hamlin asked.

Chapter 3:
On the Road Again

One week later, President-elect Robert Hamlin, his running mate Sam Touter accompanied by their wives and about 300 members of the media, gathered in Green Bay, Wisconsin at a local university. After they were introduced Hamlin approached the podium. "I am so glad you've made an effort to be here today. In fact, it's a little secret I have family members that live not far from here in Waupaca, a town about 30 miles east of Stevens Point. In fact, twice I have visited the city twice: once on a work trip and a second time with my wife - just to get away for the afternoon."

"I'm going to begin today with a comment that won't go over well in the papers tomorrow or the TV newscasts tonight. In hearing it, you'll know I'm not running for re-election in 4 years. However, there is a point to why I bring this up. You see, I don't like the (Green Bay) Packers," Bob says as the local media representatives begin to boo him. "Living near Chicago my whole life I've grown up rooting for my local sports teams. In fact, I love a sport recently introduced here in Green Bay, Wisconsin: Arena Football. You know what's a real irony in politics? All of us want an elected official to be honest and tell the truth. Yet here, I told you something personal about me and a lot of you didn't want to hear it. It's like we live our lives in some segment that used to be on a show on public television. We want honesty. We want the truth. We want our elected officials to be candid with us about themselves and what they'll do after being elected. Well, here's the truth, I'm not King Friday and this isn't the world of make-believe" Hamlin offers with a smile.

"No, I'm not here to tell you I'll sign legislation that will outlaw the Packers. Although, where I was born and raised, my friends in Illinois - from cities near the border of Galena to Waukegan from Zion to Rockford and from Dubuque to Lake Forest. You know, it sounds as if I'm running for public office again," Bob says while laughing.

"Deep down, here's what I'm talking about. We are so humbled, Senator Touter and I. That said, we all have a lot of work ahead of us. We have to put forth a vision: a plan for the future."

"In the weeks ahead, after we conclude the bus tour we're on now, we'll be sitting down with the legislative leadership in our Congress with a lot to do, including putting together a budget. Now, we have the luxury of having a lot more money than the typical family in deciding what to spend on what programs. However, it's your money when you really think about it. It's your income, but we will determine in tax dollars who will pay more or less" Bob says with a smile. "Now, I'm not grinning because we think we're all powerful and they'll be no consequences to us politically."

"Yes, it's true that I'm not running for a second term, but it doesn't mean the issues all get fixed and that nobody will pay more in taxes. Many of us, including me, will end up paying more. Hence, there's the conflict. There are, of course, the disagreements we have in a democracy over who will receive what benefits. You know, which government program will receive more or less money."

"Let me digress a little bit. In my short lifespan, I've learned quite a few things about the American political system. A lot of people think it's incredibly complicated. In this system, the pundits (some say cynics) believe that all the participants, whether you're a liberal, moderate, or conservative, can't agree on anything. Worse, we believe that the voters really don't have a clue and that it doesn't matter which party wins because it won't change anything. Many people, sadly, in America believe this.

"Here's what I've learned. Most voters when discussing the political system truly, want only a few things. Americans want their kids to go to good schools. They want to live in safe neighborhoods. They want to be gainfully employed - meaning they have a job. They want to put more money in their savings account each month, after paying the bills. They want to know that they are protected from all enemies, foreign and domestic. Lastly, they want to feel that they'll have a chance to express themselves. They want to feel assured that their voice means something. Political scientists refer to this as a higher level of political efficacy. In its most simplest term - that you feel elected officials at least, are listening. That you'll want to fulfill some basic civic responsibilities - like voting, serving on a jury when called to do so, writing a letter to the editor, giving your time to charity, etc."

"I've also learned firsthand that the American people are not stupid. They're not fooled easily. You see: our democratic system is not easy. We have a process which has evolved over 200 years. We place great value in allowing people the opportunity to give their input, whether testifying in the Congress or discussing issues, among our friends or co-workers. Sadly, we as elected officials, let down the voters when we get caught lying, cheating, taking bribes, and not playing by the same rules and laws we impose upon the American people. We are incredibly blessed here in the U.S. We enjoy the greatest freedoms here, as citizens, much more than any country in the world. We can express our support for or opposition to our elected officials without being executed or sent immediately to jail. We also have the greatest opportunity to, if we're willing to work, pursue our financial goals and dreams. *That's* why people risk their lives everyday now and our ancestors made the effort to come here in the quest to come to the U.S. Here, we enjoy the opportunity to express ourselves politically and further improve our economic fortunes."

"Why do I bring up these 'tough' issues? I can assure you that many elected officials in the past have brought them up long before Senator Howard, Senator Touter or I entered politics. It's not easy telling the truth or following the rules when the system rewards people for not being fair or acting in a manner that's trustworthy. Former President John F. Kennedy, once said 'One man (or woman) can make a difference and that everyone should try'. Nobody, including me, knows all the answers to the complicated problems we have today and in the years ahead. The purpose of the tour is not to repeat the past political campaign because the American people spoke and we won. The purpose is to lay forth some ideas we have and to continue growing a process of openness and communication with the American people. The goal is to reassure the economic markets that the world will continue, remind our allies that we intend to honor our commitments and to let everyone here know that we're going to try our best to give you a government you can be proud of. That statement, also, includes the people who did not support Senator Touter and I. Not everything we do will be easy or painless. However, with your help, we can work through our political and ideological differences" Hamlin says while smiling, "to create a better future for everyone."

"In concluding, I too love my athletic teams, as do you. I, also, was born and raised in the Midwest. I wanted to thank the people of Wisconsin for voting for us last week. We didn't earn everyone's trust and support. We do live in a democracy where it's ok to disagree. However, we have to put aside our differences and work toward building common ground. After all, when the game has ended, we're all on the same team - regardless of our economic, religious, ideological, social, or geographic backgrounds. Thank you for coming today and may God bless you all," Hamlin says with a smile. He stays to greet as many people as possible and even put on a Packers sweatshirt to finish his speech. "Remember, we're all on the same team," Hamlin shouts to the crowd, as they cheered wildly.

The next day the road show stopped in Milwaukee, Wisconsin. Hamlin had scheduled a visit to a union hall to thank representatives from across the state for their assistance in the fall campaign. "As the son of a union pipe coverer, I understand the needs of working men and women. I won't lie to you. I don't have too many calluses on my hands. I haven't welded together any pipes, attached any girders, leveled any cement or assembled anything in my life. However, I visited many times the working men and women of the Fourth Congressional District of Illinois on their jobsites. I have toured several assembly plants. Most importantly, I saw firsthand the effects from closing manufacturing plants in Matteson, Chicago Heights, Joliet, Aurora, and Chicago, Illinois. A few weeks ago I toured a neighborhood on the west side here in Milwaukee where a former brewery stood. What I saw, it was horrible. I wanted to drink a beer, although the place had been shut down," Hamlin says as the crowd chuckles.

"Anyone else making that statement would be heckled right out of here. At least when Hamlin says it, people feel a genuine sense of concern for the suffering they have," one leader from Racine whispered to an official from Chippewa Falls, both cities located in Wisconsin.

"For the benefit of some media representatives present who have never witnessed a manufacturing plant closing, or spoke to the people most impacted when it occurs, it's horrible. The workers' families let me try to help fill in the gaps," Hamlin stated. "What results is a monument to neglect. When the gates are locked and after the weeds poke up in the parking lot, the suffering really begins. People who did not go on to college, who went to work at the mill or the plant and learned one skill, are now out of work. The plant is gone and isn't reopening. They may have worked there for 20-30 years, never called in sick, did their jobs and cared about the product they made."

"When the plant shuts down, a lot of hope is lost too. Not only do we witness the loss of jobs, but there are other intangible costs too. The aspirations of the workers' kids of working there are gone forever. The city loses tax dollars to fund vital services, including maintaining roads and funding schools. Other services, such as police and fire protection, suffer also. Crime increases because people do not have the same disposable income as before. There are, also, social costs of drug and alcohol abuse, more divorces, and greater tension and violence in the home. There is no defense of people hurting other persons, but to sit here and believe the plant's closing doesn't impact the quality of life of the community is naïve," Hamlin declares as the workers' just sit there. Perhaps many of them are suffering from the same issues that Hamlin just discussed.

"I'm not going to stand here and say I can stop every plant from closing. I won't lie to you and wave a wand in performing some magic trick and declare the plant down the street will re-open. Life isn't quite that simple and you're all smarter than that. We have a *lot* of work ahead of us. I can't make a lot of promises in life. We all know that most promises are broken. However, I am going to say right now that things are going to change. Senator Touter and I, let me correct that, Vice-President Touter and I" Hamlin says as the crowd stands to show their approval.

"We are convening a summit which starts tomorrow in Des Moines, Iowa. I am very proud to say that Iowa is another state that voted for change last week. Tomorrow Senator Touter is leading a discussion of manufacturing plant closures. This problem has devastated communities from Kankakee, Illinois to Marquette, Michigan from Cedar Rapids, Iowa to Detroit, Michigan. In essence, it has impacted most of the Midwest. Well, tomorrow Senator Touter will gather a congregation of union reps, business CEO's, and other elected officials, including several members of the U.S. Congress. We're not just talking about manufacturing industries. We are going to discuss what happens to communities when the plant closes. More importantly, we're going to commence talks on what we can do to stop this madness which is ending jobs and killing the family structure in the communities where these events happen."

"The bottom line is we're going to stop pretending the problem isn't happening and we're going to work together in a new partnership between business and labor to create jobs and get in back in the world marketplace and beating the competition," Hamlin shouts. The people present clap and shout enthusiastically.

"Now, here's the bad news. There will be a price to pay to solve the problem. Fixing the problem won't happen overnight because it didn't begin yesterday. It may mean in the short term that more people will lose their jobs. It may mean we have to take pay cuts to keep the plant open," Hamlin says as the crowd boos loudly.

"How do we know we won't be lied to again?" one union leader yelled in anger.

"Now, here's the difference from past talk and promises. When we determine the best approach to move forward to developing a comprehensive plan to create a better tomorrow, we're going to move full speed ahead. It'll include money to retrain people for the jobs that will be here five years from now. We're going to work to extend unemployment benefits and create a tax system that rewards manufacturing for toughing it out. We'll provide tax credits and even *tax breaks* to reward those companies that choose to keep the plant open. Part of being an American means keeping jobs in America," Hamlin says as the crowd cheers again.

"It may mean there will be more layoffs. Yet, it also means that companies moved their operations offshore and received some financial tax credit in the past will now have those benefits ended, period," Hamlin says. Nobody said anything because they didn't know if he was telling the truth or making a promise he had no commitment to keeping. "Let me assure those of you who have reservations about the content of our speech today. Senator Al Howard of Louisiana made many statements in his life. People came to know his word was better than a signed contract. He was my mentor, advisor and good friend. You can learn a lot, as I have, from people who are genuinely sincere and more honest than we, ourselves are. You can take our words today to the bank," Hamlin says. He then resumes his discussion after a brief pause.

"I'm not running for re-election in four years. I'm here to work with people to solve the problem not sling some future fertilizer that a dairy farmer has to pick up in his field deposited by a cow. There won't be any B.S. in the Hamlin administration," Robert Hamlin speaks with a smile. Many in the audience smile and nearly all rise to show their approval.

"May God bless you all. We have a lot of work to do, but *together* I know we can make a positive difference for a better economic future for men and women across the nation, and here in the Midwest," Hamlin declares as the crowd rises in sustained applause.

After this event, they drove southwest to Rockford, Illinois. Previously the state's second largest city, its population had declined as numerous manufacturing plants had closed. He greeted local union leaders to extend his appreciation for their support and gave a similar speech as the one given in Milwaukee that day. Early the next morning, the entourage headed to northwest Illinois for stops in Freeport, Illinois, home of one of seven cities that hosted the famous debates in 1858 between Stephen Douglas and Abraham Lincoln (of the Lincoln-Douglas Debates). The other six cities were Ottawa, Jonesboro, Charleston, Galesburg, Quincy, and Alton. "Hamlin wanted to re-enact the debate format particularly since he was the challenger in the last campaign in seven different geographic regions of the nation, but President Crowe would not agree. After watching Hamlin clearly defeat him in the two debates held, I believe the president was trying to minimize his drop in the polls," one presidential debate historian said. In fact, many political pundits attributed the president's defeat to his poor performance in both debates.

After leaving Freeport, the *Encourage Road Tour* headed for a brief stop in Galena, Illinois. The town is complete with quaint little shops on Main Street that encompass all types of gift items and it is located ten miles east of the Mississippi River. It is a town full of history dating back to the Civil War. Today it is a frequent place for residents of the Midwest to go to relax, shop, and play golf. Hamlin wanted to stop at the winery located downtown for a small glass of wine and show his support for the part of the state for their support in the presidential election. "You know, Hamlin is the first Democrat to win these counties in NW Illinois in a long time. He won, I believe, because he always spoke fondly of the area in the campaign and made a stop here in early October - telling the people he needed their help," the editor of a local newspaper said. In one 48 hour period during the campaign, he made stops in Green Bay, Milwaukee, and Chippewa Falls, Wisconsin, Galena and Galesburg, Illinois, and then to Dubuque, Newton and Des Moines, Iowa.

On this tour he next headed west for a return visit to Dubuque, Iowa, and made a similar visit to meet with local union offices. "Today begins the first day in the rebuilding of a new America. Senator Touter, Mrs. Howard and I greatly appreciate the time and money you contributed to this effort. We apologize for not being able to stay long. We are due in Des Moines later this afternoon where Senator Touter is convening a panel on the manufacturing industry in our nation. We promised we would work with both labor and business in addressing this issue on behalf of the American workers, consumers, businesses, and taxpayers. Thank you again for your help and support. Let move forward to create a better future," Hamlin shouts to a cheering crowd.

They continued on their trip west to the state's capital, Des Moines. After arriving an hour late, Hamlin approached the podium to address the gathering of union and business leaders from across the nation. "On behalf of Senator Touter, Mrs. Howard, and I, we wanted to apologize for our late arrival. One bad feature of political campaign is the candidate always arrives late. Sadly, there is never anything that can be done about it. It's not an attempt to cover up for our late arrival, but we did want to apologize. Also, we wanted to thank the great people of Iowa for their support in the election this past week," Hamlin declares as the crowd slowly rises in sustained applause.

"Most importantly, we're here to begin a process of restoring a vital sector of the American economy on manufacturing sector. However, before we begin today, we want to make something very clear. We're not magicians and we're not miracle workers. What we're going to begin addressing today will not be easy, will not be painless and will not come about without further job losses," Hamlin states. The citizens present are very quiet. The looks on some of their faces even appear angry. "You see, it took a long time to create this mess. When I first ran for the U.S. Congress four years ago, I spoke outside a closed steel mill in Joliet, Illinois. I described the facility, which had been rundown and shut for three years at that time, as a *monument to neglect*. It was a place where proud people used to work and provide for their families. It was the focus of their lives. The place where friendships and relatives began....and ended."

"The signs of decline were evident from the dilapidated buildings, to weeds coming up through the parking lot to the numerous for sale signs in the surrounding neighborhood. The problems persisted with greater financial pressures on local governments for police and fire protection to the schools not being able to buy the supplies and equipment they needed. What's worse, as I said yesterday in Green Bay, these plant closings the nation tear at the heart of the family structure. The divorce rate goes up... There's nothing good about it.

"Here's something I don't discuss enough. You may see a white collar employee, perhaps a Republican who was a supervisor at the plant. Across the way in the grocery store from him is a blue collar assembly worker, male or female, maybe a lifelong Democratic voter. The only thing these two people had in common was they both used to work at the plant - or the mill depending on what town you're from. They don't attend the same church, don't buy the same types of clothes, and don't own the same type of car. The only thing they share and this is too common across our nation, is that they both used to work at the plant."

"Or even worse, take the next scenario. Generations of children have known through our history in the U.S. that if they could not attend college, for whatever reason, they knew that they could work at the plant or the mill. They believed their company and the town would always have a future. That's why we're here ladies and gentlemen. We're here to give back hope to the young people and their communities that we can stop the bleeding in an economy and turn this around. We're here to restore a belief in our young people and, in essence, in ourselves. We have an incredible challenge ahead of us."

"We may not leave in the few days without a solution. However, we begin now and we go forward in the future. Regardless of where you're from, whether it's Des Moines to Detroit, Michigan, from Chicago to Cleveland, from Moline to Milwaukee, from Paducah (Kentucky) to Pittsburgh (Pennsylvania) or from St. Paul (Minnesota) to St. Louis (Missouri), we can make this happen. At a minimum, we'll leave going back to the corporate settings or the union hall with a greater understanding of the other side's views and opinion and a greater commitment to work with people who, from our various life experiences, think differently than we do. It's not an accident why you're seated in a square shaped table. You'll be working as partners here. Hopefully, that will continue as you return home."

"I, however, will not be staying here. I will be heading south to Kansas City, Missouri. There, we are convening a summit on agriculture. We're going to discuss similar events in that sector of our economy. I have a great deal of respect for Agriculture Secretary Thomas Depew, previously the U.S. Senator from Missouri. I have asked him to lead a similar panel regarding agriculture, from everything from cows to corn," Hamlin says with a smile. We have a lot of work ahead of us. If the solutions were easy and painless, somebody else would have implemented them a long time ago and we wouldn't be here today starting this dialogue. However, that's why we're here, beginning today, for an even better tomorrow. Open your hearts, ladies and gentlemen; we have a lot of work ahead of us. However, some time in the future, whether its two days or two years from now, somebody from somewhere will be helped from our doing something to create a better future. What's required? You have to *believe* it can happen."

"Part of our effort here includes corporate executives and union members from other sectors of the economy," Hamlin says as he stands up to walk around the room. "They are not here to tell you how to run your business or your union local. We wanted them because Senator Touter and I believe they can offer some insight on what it is they do that is working. I feel it would be a huge loss of an opportunity not to permit them to express what is and what is not working in their business. This way, we all benefit. Look, I know this sounds too simple. However, I'm willing to take a chance that we can all learn from each other. Let's be honest; this path is not going to be easy. We have some difficult times ahead of us. Over the next two days, give your best effort to listen and contribute. We have two ears and one mouth," Hamlin says with a smile. "Anyone who knows me understands I don't use those (body) parts in that proportion. Even I know and believe I learn by listening and not talking so much. Just this morning I was reminded by my wife that I had won the election and that it was time to stop talking," Hamlin offers. The guests present all begin to laugh. "Give your best effort to learn and listen. The communities and children of our nation need your help. A few days ago we stopped campaigning. Today, starting now, we demonstrate our commitment to helping the taxpayers, workers, and businesses towards a better future. Thank you again and may God bless you all," Hamlin states.

He subsequently continues to 'work' the room for twenty minutes and saying hi to as many people as possible - much to the chagrin of the U.S. Secret Service agents present. One business owner present who voted against him whispered" Hamlin still feels the campaign is ongoing. Look at him greeting everyone in the room." A fellow corporate executive stated in response," Yes, but look who he is talking to. It's not his supporters from the unions. He is greeting prominent business leaders and very wealthy corporate officials. Hamlin is smart enough to know he needs their help to make this happen. You see, *that's* why he won the election and he asked people like us to come today. He's smarter than we are," he said.

After a short period of time, Hamlin said good-bye to his running mate. They walked down a private hallway which exited the building, yet would allow Touter to return and begin the event. "Thanks for permitting me to lead this panel, Mr. President. It's an issue I care deeply about. The textile industry in the South is getting devastated. I'll see you in Shreveport, Louisiana," Senator Touter offered.

"Mr. President, please. My name is Bob," Hamlin replied. "We ran as a partnership with Senator Howard guiding us. I'm honored to ask you to lead the discussion. Your experience on the commerce committee dealing with trade issues will be critical. This event is not just some token display. I'm hoping what is discussed here can be crafted into substantive legislation. At that time, I'll be asking you to draft such a bill that can both address the problems of our manufacturing industry and pass the U.S. Senate. From there, we'll apply public pressure to have the (U.S.) House (of Representatives) get it done."

"I'll be going soon to meet with Secretary DePew in St. Louis. If things go well, I'm thinking about asking him to remain in his cabinet post in our administration," Hamlin offered.

"But Bob, he's a Republican. Wouldn't you want someone from our party in that position?" Touter asks in response.

"Normally, yes that would be the case. You and I, Sam, are not going to do what's expected. In our administration we're not going to do things like everyone normally does. The first sign of that is our tour. No other person winning the office began the transition period with a road show before. We're doing this because we have a lot of work ahead of us and we…only have four years on this job assignment. If you wish to run for the presidency in four years, I'll support you. But in four years, I'm not running for reelection. There's a reason why I keep repeating this fact over the past few days. In four years, I'm leaving this game we call politics. Hence, since I'm not running for reelection, we can take actions that will not follow the normal rules in governing. You see in American politics, the whole premise revolves around winning elections. We won a few days ago. Everything we do, from this point forward, is geared toward addressing problems facing our nation and our people - for a better future. I'm leaving now for Little Rock, Arkansas. See you in a few days in Shreveport, Louisiana, the birthplace of Senator Al Howard. Smile Sam, we're in for a great ride the next four years," Hamlin said as he shook Senator Touter's hand.

Senator Touter just stood there in disbelief for a few minutes. "I thought for sure he was joking during the campaign of not running for reelection. All the time we spent alone together, I didn't believe him. Sounds like I was naïve in thinking he was just like all other politicians. You know Bob really is a great guy, a far better person than me," Touter sadly says. He is quickly brought back to reality as someone calls him. "Senator Touter, there are 200 people waiting. Your presence is requested."

Meanwhile Robert Hamlin was outside the building. His departure was delayed an additional hour as hundreds of people outside wanted to greet him. After giving a brief speech, one he had given at numerous impromptu stops the past few months, he stayed to greet a few hundred people.

One worker approached Bob to express his feelings. "Hello, President Hamlin; Mr. Hamlin...My name is Fred Tucker," he said as he extends his hand toward Bob.

"Hello Mr. Tucker, I'm Robert Hamlin. I'm not the president yet, but it's a pleasure to meet you" Bob replies.

"Mr. Hamlin; Congressman Hamlin. Yes, that's it. I wanted to say thank you. I had not voted in a long time. You see, I lost my job in the popcorn plant in Cedar Rapids (Iowa) two years ago. Everything you brought up during the campaign was correct. My wife left me after I lost my job. I had to declare bankruptcy and my kids won't talk to me. I feel like such a failure," Mr. Tucker says. His voice was breaking up as he began to cry.

Robert Hamlin turned toward the media and waved in a manner asking them not to take pictures. "Please, not now. Give him some respect," Bob sternly asks. Surprisingly the cameras stopped flashing. "Mr. Tucker, you're a good man. I have personally met hundreds of people the past few years with the same events after losing their jobs. You're not a failure. It's not your fault you went to work everyday for, where everyone failed to plan. A number of people are to blame here, including your elected officials and I. Well, it ends today. Mr. Tucker, my speeches the past few months, preceded by my efforts over four years now was not talk," Hamlin says as he places his hand on Mr. Tucker's shoulder. I, myself, saw the same issues when different plants closed in Matteson, Chicago Heights, Aurora, Kankakee, Calumet City, and Chicago, Illinois. I saw it my first two campaigns for the U.S. Congress. Worse, I saw it on the faces of the workers when I met with them at various union halls and I couldn't tell them, 'Yes I will save their job' when asked. I've grown tired of inaction on this issue. *That's* why we're here today and that includes everyone here. This affects us all and our quality of life in the U.S. Mr. Tucker, today begins a better future for us all, including you," Hamlin strongly declares. Many nearby begin to clap and hug Mr. Tucker.

Subsequently, as additional staff members got on the bus, word filtered to everyone what Bob had just done and said. Mrs. Howard was notified about what just happened. "I am incredibly proud of that young man. A lot of what he does could be labeled as selfish by some. His critics are relentless. However, in traveling with him I know he is genuinely concerned, wants to help people, and is sincere. Al (Howard) would be so proud of him," Mrs. Howard whispers.

A short time later in another section of the bus, Bob Hamlin was speaking with a group of reporters. "You know, everyone, I was asked during the campaign about policies, issues, and other personalities," Bob says with a smile. "Political campaigns are long and stressful. However, it's part of the game. Ladies and gentlemen, if you don't mind, I'd rather just sit here and talk. A lot of people believe I'm this 'issue maniac' who doesn't think like everyone else or that I don't have a sense of humor. Let's just talk the next couple of hours until we arrive in Kansas City, Missouri. After all, it's a long two weeks. Let's just...talk. Everything's off the record, ok?" Bob Hamlin inquires of the reporters present who were assigned to cover his campaign.

Deep down, they all probably wanted an exclusive interview with the president-elect. At first, the reporters were very hesitant to participate. Most were assigned to this trip after other reporters had declined. The idea of the tour was not announced beforehand, so the news organizations were caught off surprise. After all, the polls had always shown he was losing in the key battleground states until the last four days of the election. Thus, the idea of Hamlin winning was difficult to believe. "Ok, I'll go first. I'm Tom Trimble of *America Today*. What do you like to read?" he asks.

"Thanks for getting us started. As you know I've spent a lot of time reading policy briefs and campaign tidbits the past few months; Never been a shortage of those" Bob replies with a smile. "You know, when people don't even think you should be on the ballot, you have to work harder than the other guy. I like political, non-fiction books. I like reading about elected officials from the past and what they were really like as normal people. You learn how serious some people are, yet are surprised to learn of someone else's hobbies. We're all very different people. Some of us like to jump out of airplanes. Others chase tornadoes, which is something I've always wanted to do; some like listening to classical music," Bob answers.

"What kind of music do you like," Amy Snowe of the *Chicago Post* inquires.

"You know, I'm not a fan of country music and now we're heading to the south. Don't get me wrong, there are millions of country music fans across the nation including the people of Wisconsin, Iowa and my home state of Illinois. Imagine if the poll about music perceptions was taken before the election?" Hamlin jokingly asks the group. "Yep; there goes my chance in Kentucky, Georgia, and Louisiana, the states that enabled us to win. To answer your question, I like most kinds of music from rock to contemporary music in our church. I generally like music that is loud and uplifting. In particular I like a show that's in Boston (Massachusetts), Chicago, Las Vegas (Nevada), and New York. The guys paint their faces blue and wear brown outfits. They play drums and other improvised percussion instruments. The name of the show escapes me…

"The truth is we clearly would have lost the election if one of those three states hadn't gone our way. Worse, imagine the voters not knowing about the choice of music having a lot to do with the outcome of an election. So many problems and issues facing us all, as Americans. So many things we do together and we're divided by petty things such as what music we like. What kind of music do you all like?" Bob inquires. The responses varied from rap to rock and from country music to contemporary Christian music.

"Mr. President, do you have any hobbies?" Steve Samuels from the *Atlanta Daily News* asks.

"Yea, you know this may make you laugh but I love playing Par 3 golf," Bob says in response. A few of the reporters who actually golf are laughing very hard.

"With all due respect, Congressman Hamlin, why Par 3 golf?" Robert Thompson from *WBTE*, a radio station inquires.

"Well, it's good exercise and it forces me to improve my short game. I see you're laughing, I'm sure you play golf?" Bob jokingly asks.

"Yes sir. As often as I can. In fact, as we head to the southern states I'm hoping to play in the warmer climate," Thompson strongly declares. "I *live* to play golf."

"That's great. It allows me to practice my putting. Also, it reduces my score on a regular course because my score on the shorter hole is lower. By the way, my name is Bob, not sir. If you want to be official, please call me Congressman. Out of respect, we still have one president and until January 20th, he is our leader, not me."

"Back to golf," Bob says as everyone laughs. Bob was notorious for shifting topics back and forth. "One key item about golf is as follows. Many people mistakenly believe it's just 'hitting a stupid little white ball across some field'. Few things could be further from the truth. You see, countless business deals are complete on the golf course each day. Most people feel comfortable doing business or working with people with whom they share a common interest. For many people, golf is their main hobby and / or activity outside of work. It's the one selfish activity they may have. Look no further than many prominent athletes for evidence of that."

"Is there anything you'd like to do in life?" Roberta Pechar from the *Des Moines Daily* asked.

"Besides being elected president?" Bob jokingly inquires in response. "As I was growing up, believe me when I say this, I had no interest in politics. After winning the state lottery, I eventually turned toward using the money to help with some great charities and to place myself in the position of helping others. I came to learn politics was a means to the end goal of helping others less fortunate than I."

"That said I would really like to write a book, perhaps some fictional story about a young man from the suburbs of Chicago who is elected president," Bob offers to the laughter of those present. Did you know that until this week nobody was ever born and raised and elected to the office as a resident from the state of Illinois who is elected as president. After all, Abe Lincoln was born in Kentucky and lived in Indiana until he was 8 or 10. Ronald Reagan was born and raised here, but moved to California, became a movie star, was elected as governor…and the rest is history."

"I'm very proud of calling Illinois my home. Don't get me wrong, the weather is bad in the winter and it's hot and humid in the summer. The economy, as I have discussed throughout my entire political career, has its troubles. We have a school funding problem that our elected officials refuse to solve. In fact, countless people have beaten their heads against the wall wondering when will the General Assembly address the problem? However, I love the people here, their work ethic and their desire to help other people in need, as endorsed by the millions of people who generously give of their time to an assortment of charities," Bob proudly says.

"Anything else come to mind?" Samantha Powers of the *Springfield Monitor* requests.

You know, this may sound goofy, but I enjoy watching *The Weather Channel*," Bob offers. The reporters laugh from his honesty and candor or perhaps from the fact he was just different. "I have always wanted to go storm chasing. Yea, I would *love* to look for tornadoes. The drawback is the effort you spend driving around in your car and there's a lot of down time waiting for the storms to form. However, from what I've read the technology allows you to see the severe weather on a laptop computer in your car. I've always been fascinated with severe weather. I live in a state where tornadoes do occur, but luckily they are very rare. Perhaps it started when I was nearly one year old and a strong tornado hit Oak Lawn, Illinois. It was very close to our home. Thank goodness it missed us or I wouldn't be here to discuss it. Sadly, about 25 people were killed in that storm. Most of the people died when the tornado went through a busy intersection on a Friday afternoon during rush hour traffic and hit the roller rink. That said I don't think the Secret Service would be too happy with me in wanting to take up the hobby now" Hamlin offers with a smile.

"To be honest, my wife really wants to have a child. You know, we came back from our honeymoon and immediately began a campaign to run for a seat in the U.S. Congress. The incumbent was very sick and announced his intention to resign. Therefore, we've been going non-stop ever since. My wife is an incredibly generous and loving person. As I've said since the day we met, she's the better half of our relationship," Bob offers to the people present with a big smile. "God knows it's the truth. She has an incredible amount of patience. Look at what she has gone through being married to me."

"Hear me out on this. We get off the plane after our wedding and jump into a congressional race. One, in fact, the pundits said we couldn't win. Even I would include myself in that group. It was an incredible race with a fantastic and dedicated group of volunteers. My best friend, Kevin, performed a miracle in putting together a campaign message and the residents of the Fourth Congressional District placed their trust in me. If it wasn't for their support, we wouldn't be having this discussion today."

"Have you read any good books lately," Bob Thomas of the *Milwaukee Meteor* asks.

"Why yes, I just finished this excellent book. It offers multiple examples for Americans to demonstrate what I call true patriotism. It's titled *50 Ways to Stand Up For America*. It describes various activities Americans can do, regardless of where they live, to honor and show respect for and celebrate being here. Some include respecting the flag, donating blood, volunteering at a charity event, respecting the elderly, visiting Washington D.C., saying please and thank you. The last one reminds me of that purple dinosaur," Bob says while laughing. "Other items included fighting hate groups, attend a place of worship, etc," Bob says.

"Sounds like your political career and this recent campaign," one reporter of the *New Orleans Gazette* says in an unpleasant tone. All the other media representatives stare at him.

"Well, thanks for the compliment. No, I didn't write the book, contrary to private belief. I have, however, tried to pursue such ideas because I firmly believe they're important. I've been really blessed in my life from my parents, the schools I've attended, my spouse, winning the Lottery, and the friends I made. It's so easy and tempting for us as human beings to get stuck in our routines with our various responsibilities."

"That said, Americans are the most generous people in the world. We have been truly blessed with our economic wealth and success. Whenever a financial need in the world arises, we're there to lend a hand and provide generous resources," Bob declares. We don't need to be asked twice. Millions of Americans step up *each* time a need arises, from natural disasters to blood drives to serving food to the homeless."

"Are there any regrets you have?" Steven Trimble of the *Nashville News* questions. His paper was relentless in its negative coverage of Bob Hamlin's campaign. Trimble himself, was accused of lobbying other reporters to write critical news stories about Hamlin as an individual and his staff. The newspaper's editorials were incredibly mean-spirited. Not only did the paper help swing the state of Tennessee to President Crowe, the staff also lobbied papers in other Southern states in their attempt to defeat Robert Hamlin with negative editorials.

"Steve, it's good to see you today," Bob replies. Trimble was the only reporter addressed by name. In doing so Hamlin wished to convey a clear message about Bob's knowledge of the paper's efforts to defeat him. "You know, Steve, I can give as well as I get. Politics is like football; it's a tough sport" Bob says. "After all the work your bosses and some people allege, you made to assist the reelection effort of President Crowe, it's a minor surprise to see you here this week on the *Encourage Bus Tour*," Bob says with a coy smile.

"With all due respect, Mr. Hamlin, I cannot comprehend how you won. Luckily your term is only four years in length. Then, we'll beat you," Trimble angrily replies.

"First of all my dad is Mr. Hamlin, not me. Secondly, if the election results and the well-documented decline in your newspaper's subscriptions are any reflection, the shareholders of your paper can't be too happy right now. Third, if you and the paper were paying attention you'd know I'm not running for reelection in four years" Bob responds. "The editorials I read didn't even endorse President Crowe, who is a good man. Your newspaper went to great lengths to tell people what a miserable human being I am. Luckily our readers are intelligent enough to sort out fact from fiction. Feel free to tell your bosses this: their compassion reminded me of a bumper sticker I once saw displayed in the Chicago Area. It has a rebel from the South with a sad look on his face. The caption reads 'Deal with it, you lost," Bob says. He has a partial grin on his face.

"And your point is?" Trimble asks. Everyone in the room is quiet.

"The point is you and the newspaper lost. Now, it's time to deal with it. The next four years are going to be tough on everyone. We, as Americans, have a lot of work to do. I'm willing to look past the issues of the campaign because it's over. I'm hoping the *Nashville News* will also. Once again, I'm not running in four years. It's time to move forward and work together," Bob calmly says. He puts his hand out to Steven Trimble, as if he was extending an olive branch.

Sadly, Trimble gets up and walks away without acknowledging him.

"Wow. Despite all you went through in the election, you took the first step to reconcile your differences and he still turned you down," Mike Jones of the *Little Rock Gazette* states. "Are you okay, Congressman Hamlin?"

"Me, I'm ok," Bob answers in response. In this business, you learn that you had better have thick skin or you move on. As you saw, Steve just moved on," Bob says smiling. "Believe me other people face much greater difficulties everyday. When a tornado destroys a town or a subdivision and people, particularly those in upscale communities, are suddenly homeless that is suffering. You can't fix that overnight. Other people live in crime ridden neighborhoods or in poverty across our great nation. However, I never answered Steve's question. Remember he initially asked if I had any regrets? Well, I do. That said, as you know, it's been very tempting for me to convert. My wife and I attend a contemporary worship service at a Lutheran Church. God knows there were opportunities for me change my religious stripes and how it was in my best interest, politically, to do so," Hamlin says.

"By the way, I hate to interrupt, but why didn't you convert then? If you attend a Lutheran church, what's the big deal in making the switch?" Penny Senn from the *Modern Day* magazine from Madison, Wisconsin says.

"Well, it's not that simple. Politically, if I converted, I would have been accused of being soft. People would have stated that I switched for the clear reason of self-interest with the benefit being easier for me not having to campaign as a Catholic in Southern states. Political expediency, as it would be called. As you know I faced enough criticism across the South, in particular, the newspaper in Tennessee," Hamlin said as people in the room laughed. Therefore I decided to hold off on the announcement of my conversion until after the election."

"Is that on the record? Are we permitted to have that released?" Sherry Pierce of the *Pittsburgh Post* asks.

"No. When I joined you I stated my intent to have an open discussion...no holds barred. I suggested you feel comfortable asking me whatever you wanted. Any discussion about conversions will occur in the future after we return home. After all, I would like the opportunity to run the idea by my extended family. Don't think everyone will be very pleased.

"The truth is this: It's doesn't matter what membership card you carry when it comes to your religious affiliation. God doesn't care what building you worship in and what the name appears on the sign. He's more concerned with how you live your life, how you treat other people, do you recognize that His son gave his life for you and what do you do with the time, talents, and treasures He has provided" Hamlin shares.

"That said, there are far greater moral dilemmas to deal with. For example, say it's 4 (am) and you are awakened to learn the North Korean government has launched an invasion of South Korea. What do you do? Do you decide to turn the entire country into a parking lot or do you turn the other cheek? Or here's another scenario. You've just been told the North Koreans have launched a missile toward the United States. What would you consider a justifiable response?"

"Religious faith is a very complex issue. It's not as simple as cheering for your favorite football team on Sunday. We all are raised differently. Some of us go to church on the weekend. Some of us pray to St. Mattress," Hamlin says. The reporters all laugh. "Each time I make that statement it always brings a few laughs. Here's the sad, part: someone of faith may not laugh. They would wonder why you're not at church. Life is so complicated. Our time is constantly challenged. From work to little league games; from charity events to attending meetings for our kids. As parents, we have errands each day from getting oil changes to running to the bank. You name it; we're all very busy. However, a person of faith would ask 'you had time to go to the bar for a few hours, or time for a sporting event, but you didn't make time to go to church.'

"I was advised by Democratic strategists not to talk about religion throughout my political career. Some people would say we just don't do that. Over time I've seen how what they truly wanted to say was 'we white ethnic Democrats from the north don't do that!' Here's a news flash. I don't spend much time worrying about how the issues I pursue or the positions I care about are going to help or hurt me in a political campaign. It doesn't mean what people tell me isn't important or that I don't value their opinions. Or get this. It doesn't mean that they're not right."

"What I have learned in my spiritual growth and development is that faith does matter. We are pulled in every conceivable direction. We also all, including myself, face numerous temptations every day. In the First Amendment of the U.S. Constitution what's named as the *Free Exercise Clause*. In the U.S., we are free to pray to and for whomever we wish. We also have the right to do nothing. There are some people who believe that they're going to channel their religious beliefs into legislation. Sadly, there are some people whose actions are also associated with religious intolerance. For example, we have people who identify themselves as Strict Constructionists, meaning they believe in a strict and literal interpretation of the U.S. Constitution. They declare proudly how we are a Christian nation. Nowhere in the Constitution or *The Federalist Papers*, the only written record of what we discussed at our Constitutional Convention in 1787, does the name Christ appear."

"Don't get me wrong: You all know and have witnessed firsthand my beliefs in the Holy Trinity. I pray each day for my family, our nation, the less-privileged, and economy and a variety of other issues. I thank God each day for my wife, how we live in the greatest nation in the history of the world, and the trust the people of the state of Illinois place in my hands each day. Now as difficult as my and your days are, I am reminded each day of two things: there are millions of people in our nation and billions across the planet who face greater challenges than me each day. More importantly, there is a living God who guides and protects us all, whether we are Christians, Muslims, Jews, and also non-believers, each and every day."

"The bottom line is this: what we do, say, hope, feel, imply or pray about in our daily activities is not mandated by some laws. You know, I once heard a leader of my small group say for us it's not about being in control or using our positions of authority to control others or devising acronyms to address items. It's about being reminded of the need to love others through our thoughts, actions and statements toward Christ," Bob says.

"As a said earlier, it's really pretty simple: It's all about giving our time, talents, and treasures to serve Him. It's not about us. It's about reaching out through our prayers and activities to improve the quality of life for people less fortunate than ourselves. After all, he gave up his life for us. It's not too much to ask and challenge ourselves to use our talents, at least a little, for other people's benefit. If you're not a person of faith, then use the opportunity to donate money as a tax deductible contribution" Hamlin offers to those present.

"You know, Congressman Hamlin, many of us have spent substantive time with you the past few weeks and months. However, I don't think any of us have *ever* heard you speak in that way about religion," Rod Spears of the *St. Louis Flyer Gazette* declares. As he spoke several members present looked at each other with varying levels of surprise, even shock, on their faces.

"Aren't you a Democrat from Illinois?" another asked.

"I sure am. I was born in raised in a suburb south of Chicago. I began today by discussing how we could have an earnest, open talk. Maybe these issues weren't discussed the past few months because we spend too much time thinking about how we can torpedo our opponent in politics or even sporting events. Maybe it's also about finding news stories to sell new subscriptions. Don't ever be afraid to ask the tough questions in life. However, remember this, if your heart is not open to hearing the answer, don't ask the question" Hamlin whispers.

"However, when out of town I would lay in bed at night, unable to sleep, and ponder about things that happened during the day. One day after Senator Howard died, I was in Cleveland, Ohio, and had a 22 hour day. It hit me that I was running to be the president and that he had passed away. Some 29-year-old guy who never had any serious issues arise in his life, excluding an acne problem in high school, was now running to be the Leader of the Free World and have to decide what to do if Iran were to invade Iraq or if the North Koreans launched a nuclear missile at us."

"I decided to turn to praying more often. Believe me, I don't have any esteem issues," Bob offers with a smile. I guess I began to question if I, or anyone else, really was qualified to be the president. Praying, campaign donations, the energy of volunteers, the thrill of the race, my family, all together, is what got some through the past few months after Senator Howard passed away."

"You know, prayers aside, I really miss Senator Howard," Bob says. There was a great deal of grace and calm in his voice. "He was not only a great human being, as is his wife, Lillian. He was a good person who held elective office. We're all at a loss without him, particularly me. You know, he selected me as his running mate when a lot of people, himself included, vocally questioned his decision-making process."

"Shortly after the convention, we were on a campaign swing though Georgia, Ohio, Kentucky and Southern Illinois. Around 11 (pm), I asked him why he picked me and he replied 'because I trust you, I believe in you, and I know you'll pursue my policies if something ever happens to me," Bob said. His voice was cracking with emotion. "I'll never forget that," Bob whispers as a tear is rolling down his eye.

After pausing momentarily to gain his composure, "Each day I turn in prayer. I seek his input and advice on the complex issues is our campaign and political battleground. However, I defer to God for guidance and support in prayer. I seek counsel for the decisions I make and for the strength to be firm in my decisions. Believe me, it's not easy because my family, my political party, and my God don't always agree on the issues," Bob declares. Several of the reporters laughed at the comment, others perhaps not knowing Bob's sense of humor, did not join in the humorous exercise.

"Being in compliance with your request to be called your first name, where do we go from here?" George Roberts, senior political editor of the *Philadelphia News*.

"We're taking a tour of a number of states. Is that what your question pertained to?" Bob inquires in response.

"No. We should be just outside of Kansas City. I'll be on board until Baton Rouge," George says.

"I'm glad you're here. As you know our campaign won the state of Louisiana. However, as I have stated countless times, our team would not have won without the assistance of Senator and Mrs. Howard. I am so blessed to have had the opportunity to work with them," Bob replies.

"Congressman Hamlin, I have a great deal of respect for you. Don't get me wrong. I don't agree with you on every issue. In fact, I truly questioned whether you were qualified to be president. You, yourself, have acknowledged this fact. In fact, I will patiently await the future and see how you respond to a serious foreign policy crisis."

"However, I did vote for you. In watching you the past few years, I will credit you with being the hardest working member of the U.S. Congress. You have stepped back and given other people the opportunity to lead at the appropriate times. You helped Senator Howard years before other Democratic officeholders chose to bother with him. You have made an effort to assist key members of the Congress, including Senator Howard, who did put in their time - following the norms and traditions of the U.S. Senate. Deep down, in watching your progression, I feel you're a good person."

"I voted for you because you're an honest person, a refreshing change in the political realm. I believe you'll stick to your guns, particularly if you keep your campaign promise of not seeking a second term," George offers.

"Thanks. That last point will be the easiest campaign vow I made. In fact, my wife is right on that point. Believe you me, she already has the date marked on the calendar," Bob says as the media representatives laugh. "She reminds me daily it's one term and we're out" Bob declares with a smile."

"Anyone who is married understands your point," George replies to the laughter of the group.

"My original question pertains to doing what's next on faith. As you know many people in Louisiana, well throughout the South, have a great deal of faith. In fact, their lives revolve around their religious faith. Many people want to know probably because it is their hope for you to pursue moral values. They want you to appoint judges to the federal courts that will overturn *Roe VS. Wade*. They want you to lead by example in the White House because we are a Christian nation as you noted earlier. The bottom line is this Congressman Hamlin: where you gonna be on this vital issue?"

Many of the reporters were taken aback by his candor.

"Pardon me, Congressman Hamlin, we have arrived in Kansas City," Joseph Roach, a staff member states. I hate to interrupt you all but it's been a few hours since you began talking. We're here."

"Saved by the bell," Bob exclaims to the amusement of the reporters.

"Please, Mr. Hamlin, can you please be as so kind as to answer the question. It's important" George says.

"Every question is important. I'll be glad to answer your question after we address the crowd," Bob says. "There are hundreds of people here to see Congressman Hamlin," Joseph replies.

"There's time to talk to them later. I want an answer now!!" George shouts. The reporters are now in shock and complete surprise. They know, from firsthand experience, there is a way to obtain an answer from an elected officeholder, let alone the President-elect of the U.S. Bob walks up to George and leans forward to whisper in his ear. He extends his hand as if to say hello. He speaks in a low, but clear voice. "You'll get your answer later. It will come in a time and place, not decided by you. Bob says.

The look on George Robert's face is comparable to if he has seen a ghost. "Until next time, George," Bob says to George in front of the other reporters. George picks up his items and storms out of the room.

"In a democracy, you can't get everyone's vote and you can't make everybody happy. I have a funny feeling we didn't receive George's vote in the election," Bob says to the smiles and laughter of those present in the room.

Chapter 4:
New Challenges from the Past

Ten minutes after Bob Hamlin had departed from his meeting with the reporters, he was introduced to the crowd. As he stepped forward, the crowd roared their approval.

"Hello Kansas City," Bob yells as the crowd cheers again. "Notice I did not say hello Missouri. That's because as you know, Kansas City is located in both Kansas and Missouri. I wanted to make a personal visit and thank you. However, the residents and taxpayers of the great state of Missouri helped put me over the top. You helped vote for positive change this week. Senator Touter, Mrs. Howard, and I thank you," Bob offers as the crowd roars its approval.

"Now, for those of you from Kansas, we're not here to be negative. After all, we did much better there than most Democrats do in presidential elections. However, we're hoping that four years from now when another Democrat is nominated, you'll continue that positive movement and vote for him or her, even if we fell a little short this week. Is that fair to ask?" Bob asks with a smile. The crowd cheers again.

"Sorry to disappoint you, but I am going to speak very briefly today" Bob conveys as the crowd boos. "I know. What type of campaign event would I be attending if Hamlin does not speak for two to three without notes? Today, I just wanted to say thanks. We did very well in St. Louis County. Yes, I promised the mayor there I would stop by and visit St. Louis next week. Today, I wanted to stop by and visit the great people in the western part of Missouri and I wanted to proudly deliver my appreciation," Bob provides as the crowd applauds. They even started cheering his last name. "HAM-LIN, HAM-LIN, HAM-LIN."

"Come on folks you're making this tough," Bob states as the crowd continued yelling his last name. "This week, we begin a new order. In my final two minutes I will promise you this. Last week I stopped by and visited an auto plant in Kansas City, you know which one I am talking about. I promised you the plant would not close. There is legislation pending on Capital Hill to provide a huge tax break to the company. It is supposed to enable them to retool their equipment in older plants across the nation, including the one I promised to save.

"Today I am meeting with the CEO of the company in Detroit. I will clearly convey the following: unless there is a written and signed provision to keep the plant open the next 15 years, I will veto the bill," Bob promises as the crowd cheers. "I assure you, the plant will remain open if the company wants the multi-billion dollar tax break in the Hamlin administration. After all, if they're not going to modernize the plant, they don't need the tax break. If the CEO of the company didn't know it beforehand, he'll learn next week: *The Buck Stops Here*," Hamlin says as the crowd cheers wildly at the news.

"Once again, I wanted to thank you for your trust and support in voting for us. We have to get going, but I'll be back. Remember this, we're not leaving; we're going. I didn't make a lot of promises during the (presidential) campaign, but I'll make one now: Things won't be the same in Washington D.C. after our victory by Hamlin in memory of Senator Al Howard. We're on to Little Rock. Thank you and may God bless you all."

After Robert Hamlin and other staff members from the campaign boarded the bus, they departed and began to head to the Deep South. Their next stop was Little Rock, Arkansas. Congressman Hamlin lost the state. The incumbent president made a last minute campaign appearance in a state that was rated as a toss-up on the eve of the election. "We could have stopped here too. However, we decided to make our last minute appearances in Detroit, Michigan, Louisville, Kentucky and Atlanta, Georgia. We needed those three states to win and we pulled the trifecta," says Thomas Jones, a senior campaign aide. "The three states we needed to get to 270 (the number of electoral votes needed to win on election night) all supported, with their votes and not just their hearts, the Hamlin-Touter-Howard Team," Jones offered. His answer that included a reference to Senator Howard was mandatory, a direct statement by Congressman Robert Hamlin himself.

Back on the bus, Hamlin returned to the same section designated for campaign staff. Never being able to relax, he sought to read a policy briefing from the National Security Council. During the presidential campaign, both he and President Crowe were provided a manual each day, which pertained to issues of national security. Across the globe, there were potential hot spots where civil wars and regional conflicts that could pose threats to the national security of the U.S.

"Aside from all the problems of the world, the two that pose the greatest risk to our nation are Iran and North Korea. Not only because they are described each day in my policy briefing book. Ten years ago, when I was in college, I wrote a paper regarding the threat Iran posed to peace in the Middle East, but also to the West (the U.S. and Western Europe). The more things change, the more they stay the same."

Hamlin reaches for the interoffice pager to contact his most trusted advisor, Kevin Chapin. "Hello this is Bob. Yes, it's Robert Hamlin. It's good to talk to you too. Do you know where Kevin is? He's asleep," Bob replies with a laugh. Ok, but I need a favor. Get me Pete Thomas, a national security expert from Hamlin's campaign and congressional staff) and have him join me us too. There are some issues I want to talk about. Also, when Kevin wakes up, please have him join the two of us. Ok?" Bob requests. He didn't mean to be rude, but he was no longer an insignificant Congressman from the state of Illinois anymore.

A few minutes later Pete Thomas joined Bob on the train. "Pete, I need a favor from you. We are due to arrive in Little Rock in eight hours and we won't be stopping in any other towns for two to three." Bob had been notified there were towns where 500 to 1000 people at a time would meet. Normally the bus would stop and he would address the crowd for a few minutes. In all, the bus tour would be slowed for a time period of approximately fifteen minutes, including security checks.

"I want to ask you one question: What issue poses the greatest threat to the national security of the U.S.?" Bob asks.

"That's simple. Nuclear Proliferation, Mr. President," Pete states.

"Come on, please. Last week I was Bob or Congressman Hamlin. It's late and it's just you and I. Kevin is joining us in a few minutes. For now, Bob is fine. Mr. Hamlin is my Dad," Bob replies.

"Ok, ah yes Sir," Pete says.

"That's fine. You're incredibly smart. Kevin and I could use your help. This is incredibly important."

"Alright, here are the facts. You may very well be faced with a national defense crisis in the near future. The clerics in Iran (the religious leaders who determine the President in the country and who have the power to remove him) have been painstakingly pursuing the development of a nuclear weapon. Previously, it was thought they were still about six years away. However, I have sources that tell me they may be able to construct one within twelve months, maybe sooner," Pete clearly says in response.

"Come on Pete...We both know the CIA is good, but there have countless examples where their information was not accurate," Bob declares. At this point, Kevin Chapin enters the room to join them.

"I hope I wasn't interrupting something important" Kevin inquires.

"No, in fact, I'm glad you're here. I wanted to speak, off the record with you and Pete regarding national security matters. By the way, where have you been?" Bob says with a smile.

"I was sleeping. After all, it's nearly 10 (pm) and we've all been going for 20 hours now, not including the past month of sleep deprivation," Kevin replies.

"Man, it's alright. I just wanted you to be aware of Pete's opinion on this issue. If you can, please repeat what you last said before Kevin joined us," Bob says, requesting clarification on the issue from Pete's prior comment.

"As you know, the Iranian government has been actively pursuing the development of nuclear materials. They have a very aggressive program of uranium enrichment. Well, from what my sources tell me, they appear to be farther along from what our intelligence sources have been aware of," Pete explains.

"The CIA has been stated they're still about five years away. Who are your sources?" Kevin inquires.

"I'm not at the liberty to divulge who my sources are, but thanks for asking," Pete replies. The lack of a smile on his face clearly indicated he was not joking. "My sources are good and from my personal experiences, more accurate than the CIA. Remember the incident with the WMD's (Weapons of Mass Destruction) in Iraq," Pete states.

"With all respect, there were WMD's there. They were moved by the Russians before the war. It's alleged and documented the Russians moved them to protect themselves and hide the extent of their involvement. I think you would refer to it as CYA (covering your ass)," Kevin responds.

"My sources told me they weren't there before the war. Saddam had WMD's, but he abandoned those years before. Regardless if you think they're right or wrong (his sources), no WMD's have been found to date," Pete declares. He is normally very calm and collected, but Kevin's questioning of him is now clearly proving to be aggravating.

"Ok guys. Thanks for your spirited effort to revisit the Gulf Conflict. I found it to be a great effort to defend your positions on a controversial war. However, that was some time ago. I'm not asking about some national security issues from the past. I'm referring to today. I don't think that's too much to ask, ok?" Bob asks.

"I know and trust you both. You're both very good at what you do. Let's please stick to the topic at hand, alright? Pete, since you began the discussion, can you be more specific for us, please?" Bob asserts.

"Not a problem, sir. It is the conclusion of several contacts I have developed over the years, from their analysis of the data available that the Iranian government is much closer to the development of a nuclear bomb than previously thought. Part of the problem is compounded by the fact we don't have a) a large number of agents there to verify or refute the information received and b) its a very closed society. Reporters are jailed or imprisoned for criticizing the government and c) even the international weapons inspectors are now prohibited from doing their jobs. The Iranian government has banned the inspectors from these facilities," Pete declares with a strong degree of commitment.

"Why have the Iranians stopped the inspections?" Kevin inquires.

"For the fear that the inspectors will prove what has been alleged. The same reason that Saddam threw out the (weapons) inspectors in 1998" Pete says while looking toward Kevin. "They found some information at specific sites which upset the Iraqi government. It's amazing what you can find on a Q-Tip," Pete says.

"See, evidence of wrongdoing in Iraq," Kevin declares.

"Kevin, as Bob stated earlier, we're pursuing what's occurring in Iran today. We toppled and removed from office Saddam Hussein and his henchmen in 2002. Believe me, Saddam was no altar boy. However, the Iranian government poses a greater threat to the security of the Middle East than Saddam did when he was removed," Pete offers.

"How can you say that?" Kevin says.

"Within five years the Iranian government will have what al-Qaida does not: a nuclear weapon. Also with expanded arms trading and economic development efforts with China the past ten years, they have made incredible progress toward obtaining long distance missile technology. Not only will they have a bomb, they'll have the ability to deliver a nuclear warhead up to 500 to 1200 miles away, which includes the state of Israel," Pete calmly says.

"You know that timetable is farther ahead than what our CIA describes in written reports. Are you sure?" Kevin asks in disbelief. Bob Hamlin is intentionally remaining quiet. He trusts both people a great deal.

"Yes, it is. We cannot precisely determine how far they are in the development of the weapon or the delivery system for a variety of factors. The main problem, of course, is the fact the Iranian government has chosen not to honor our agreements pertaining to the Nuclear Non-Proliferation Treaty. On this issue, their signature means nothing and their word means even less," Pete sternly declares.

"Pete, let's say for a moment that the CIA is not right in their assessment. Say hypothetically they can create enough uranium to produce a nuclear weapon in two years...or even one," Bob inquires.

"Come on, Bob, that's ridiculous," Kevin asserts. "Are you saying he's correct?"

"No, I'm only inquiring about the possibilities. In about two month's time (following the Inauguration on January 20th) it's going to become my responsibility to know. Remember, since we won the election we'll be making foreign policy decisions to protect the American people " Bob assets.

"I commend you for asking Bob, I mean, Mr. President," Kevin offers with a smile.

"Please, it's Bob... Before the cameras or in the presence of other people, it's the other title, ok?" Bob replies.

"Yes Sir! I'm very glad we're taking the time to discuss this. The Crowe administration has been living in the '*World of Make Believe*' and King Friday (a character from a famous TV program on public television) has been the ruler," Pete offers. Bob and Kevin break out in laughter from the comment.

"Actually, it's worse. King Friday is a puppet in a fictional world. President Crowe has been the leader of the Free World for the past four years. At least you gave me the opportunity to discuss the issue and share my opinion." His staff members were so focused on winning an election for the past year they forgot what their primary responsibility was," Pete says.

"And what was that?" Kevin asks.

"Protecting our nation. For the employees at the National Security Council it was decided the effort to re-elect the president was more important than keeping the President informed to enable him to make decisions to keep us safe and secure," Pete asserts.

"How can you say that? What evidence of that statement do you have?" Bob inquires.

"I dropped off reports and sent emails to them. There was nothing labeled as classified. In fact, they were policy position papers, comparable to college term papers. I've never heard from them, not once. My contacts there never replied. No e-mails, no voicemail messages, no return phone calls."

"Bob, hear me when I say this. It wasn't just your campaign that won: the American people did as well. I don't care why they didn't respond, whether it was by choice or if they were given strict orders by their superiors not to any share info. We had written agreements, as you know, between both (presidential) campaigns to exchange info on matters of vital importance. They didn't," Pete states.

"Why wasn't this made clear to me? Never mind, the election is over. Hear me now. If the leadership or members of the Intelligence Committee of the Congress asks for such information in the future, we're sharing it with them. Hear me now, Pete, I'm not running for re-election in four years. Whoever wins the next election will not have to endure the *'reindeer games'* you just described. Do I have your word on those two items I just referred to?" Bob questions. The determination for the request was not only clear, but they could sense anger in his voice.

"Yes sir. Clear as the blue sky on a sunny afternoon. You can count on me," Pete replies with hesitation.

"I know I can. That's why I said it to you. Kevin, you heard both what I said and did not say, right?" Bob inquires.

"Absolutely! I've known you a long time and know when a point is both made, implied, shouted, and whispered. I'm on board," Kevin asserts.

"Good. I know in hearing your answers it'll be done. Now, Pete, back to the issue at hand," Bob says. He is interrupted by a staff member who helps the scheduler.

"Congressman... I know Bob. My apologies for walking in unannounced. However, we are due to arrive in ten minutes," Sally Pearson says.

"Arrive where?" Bob responds.

"Little Rock, Arkansas, sir," she answers.

"Already?" Bob questions her in disbelief.

"Yes, you three have been here for hours. The press was wondering where you had gone. I tried to contact you an hour ago, but there was no response," she answers.

"Ok, it's not a problem. Tell you what; you guys get some sleep. I'm going to address the audience. When I return, I'll resume my previous open discussion with the press team. I'll talk with them until we arrive in Shreveport, Louisiana. After that, the three of us will continue this discussion, cool?" Bob inquires as they both nod in the affirmative.

Bob departs the other two gentlemen and walks to the bathroom. Regardless of how he's been now going for nearly thirty (30) hours, Bob still has a strong sense of energy. "All I need to do is throw some water in my face, take a deep breath or two, and I'm in business. The truth is I'm tired. The bus tour is important. It's nearly 6 (am). Maybe I should address the crowd and then take a brief nap. After all, nearly everyone else has slept the past few hours. I'm entitled to a break, also," Bob maintains. The cool water thrown on his face now appears as beads, almost a mist, on his face.

Hamlin departs the bathroom and is greeted by two Secret Service agents. "Congressman I have just been contacted by my supervisor. He's at the City Hall in Shreveport (Louisiana) and was just notified a threat has been received, against you. We've been asked to cancel this stop," Special Agent Al Warren declares.

"Not a chance. We won this election because Senator Howard's home state voted for us last week. In honor of Mrs. Howard, and the memory of Senator Howard, we're not stopping. This appearance isn't for me, it's for them (the citizens)," Bob responds.

"Congressman, once again, I must repeat what my supervisor has told me. Our job is to protect you. We can't do our jobs if you refuse to help us," Special Agent Warren says.

"Do me a favor. Contact Mrs. Howard in the other bus. Tell me what she says," Bob calmly answers.

Five minutes later the agents return to speak with Bob Hamlin. The press corps is now getting anxious about why they have not left the bus. "Congressman, we have Mrs. Howard on the line. She is ordering you to cancel the event. You can speak to her now," Agent Warren offers.

"Bob, this is Lillian," Mrs. Howard calmly says.

"Mrs. Howard, good to speak with you. How is your bus ride?" Bob replies.

"Bob, listen to me. I want you to cancel the stop," Mrs. Howard declares. She is being very stern. "I've been notified by the Secret Service has been called in. It's serious; Everyone didn't like my husband and he was born and raised here. Please listen to me and cancel the event," Mrs. Howard states.

"What do you mean?" Bob asks. His heart rate is increasing by the second.

"There were murder threats called in frequently against Al (Howard). Mostly they were from white supremacists who didn't like the idea of the (federal) government helping minorities. As you know, Al cared a great deal about everyone. Please, cancel the event," she replies.

"It's 6 (am). There are, I've been told, 3-5 thousand people here. I have an idea. Let's delay the event. Surely there is a high school gym around here. If someone calls someone who has the keys, we can move it. That way the Secret Service can check the people for security purposes. We can delay it for a few hours."

"However, the people of this state, your state, voted for change a few days ago. We would not have won without the support of the citizens of Louisiana. This will not be cancelled. I'll order the buses to be moved to a separate location where the Secret Service feels it's safe. How does that idea sound?" Bob says. Hamlin is very scared despite not showing it.

After some delay, Mrs. Howard responds. "Why are you so damn stubborn? You're just like Al. If the heart attack from the blood clot didn't kill him, some assassin would have," she says while choking back tears.

"What do you mean by a blood clot killed him? I know what a blood clot is, a distant family member died from one a few years ago. The autopsy showed your husband had a heart attack, right?" Bob inquires. He is very puzzled because he was very close to the

Howard family. However, his death from a blood clot was not announced to anyone, including Bob Hamlin.

"Yes, he died from a heart attack, but it was not from heart disease. A blood clot in his leg broke free and went to his heart. We didn't tell you because the focus of the past two months was the events of the funeral and the election. In fact, I personally requested not to be given the results of the autopsy until after the election," she answers.

"Mrs. Howard, you told me you were provided the autopsy report. That is correct, right?" Bob asks. He is genuinely concerned about what he has just been told.

"Bob, I lost the one and only man I ever loved. Part of my grieving process was continuing his legacy. He died, but he truly lived what he preached. You were chosen to continue the message by Al. You are the messenger to continue his political and legislative agenda. You were picked by Al to fight for justice and fairness," she replies.

"A blood clot? That's not a heart attack, Mrs. Hamlin," Bob responds with a sense of urgency in his voice.

"A blood clot formed in the lower part of his leg. He tripped and fell on a sidewalk three months beforehand and hurt his ankle. The clot must have formed at that time. It traveled in his veins to his heart. So, he died of a massive heart attack. However, the autopsy showed it was caused by the blood clot. Can you please cancel the event?" she states after answering his question.

"No. We will delay it until someone can open a local school so the event can be held in a gym. That will allow the Secret Service to effectively do their job and screen the guests," Bob replies.

"You're just like him. Sometimes you're too stubborn to see the danger," Mrs. Howard says. She offers a big sigh of frustration afterwards.

After a delay Bob replies "Mrs. Howard, I assure you if the need to greet people was about me, I wouldn't go. We won because the people of Louisiana voted for us. I just want to go speak briefly to say thanks," Bob says with a sincere voice. "We'll go in together, and greet the audience in three hours," Bob declares and then turns to the Secret Service agent.

"Three hours. You'll need to get with Tom Snyder, one of our logistics and advance guys. You know who he is?" Bob asks.

"Yes, Congressman Hamlin, I do. We've prepared for a number of events together," Special Agent Al Warren responds.

"Fantastic. Although we don't have a lot of time, we can pull this off. Set up security around the perimeter. Set up metal detectors for people to pass when leaving and entering. If someone has a gun, you'll find it," he answers.

"Do you have any idea how long that will take?" the agent angrily answers.

"We've got time. Besides, there's hundreds of police here now. Just have them park their cars so no one can leave without going through a designated location. If anyone attempts to leave without following the procedures....well, you know what to do," Bob says.

Bob Hamlin and the buses of *The Encourage Tour* were moved about one mile away. This would allow the crowd to disperse and be searched while leaving and entering the schools. One hour later a commotion broke out in an area where people were not allowed to leave. After about ten minutes Special Agent Warren contacted Robert Hamlin.

"Sir, it appears the security concern was correct. Three individuals were identified with firearms on their person. There was a struggle and one officer was hurt, but all three were taken into custody," he declares.

"Did they say anything? What was their response?" Bob asks.

"Yes it appears they may be part of the Klan or some supremacist group. Apparently, they have tattoos, shaved heads, and used some pretty ambitious language. The good news, all three are in custody and headed to being in protection of the U.S. Government. I'm sure they'll have a lot of questions to answer," the agent answers.

"Great job. Let's go visit the trash," Bob says.

"What? Congressman Hamlin, we're not allowed to bring you to them, sir," the agent answers in complete disbelief. "The consequences...."

"Let me worry about that. I've always seen these losers on TV and wondered if they could write complete sentences, talk or, spell a full sentence using the English language. You know the same language they defend and criticize immigrants for speaking with difficulty. Come back here and pick me up. You and I will be introduced to the geniuses shortly," Bob says.

"We can't do that. What are you going to say?" the agent asks.

"Don't worry about that. I want to see the look on their faces when they walk in. The price of trash being introduced to the man they agreed to kill: priceless," Bob answers while hanging up the phone.

"You know you'll have to call Mrs. Howard and let her know," Kevin says…"Now, let me make sure I heard you right, you're going to meet with the people who were arrested. The same people who were going to kill you?"

"Yes. Hey, think about this: Where do you put trash Kevin?" Bob asks.

"I don't know," he answers.

"You pick up trash and put it in the garbage can. That's how you deal with the problem of excessive garbage," Bob says.

A few minutes later, they were successful in reaching Mrs. Howard, located on another bus, via telephone. "Yes Mrs. Hamlin great news. The police and the Secret Service arrested three individuals in the crowd. They were all possessing firearms. They tried to leave the gathering in an unauthorized manner. After a scuffle, all three were taken into custody and transported to a safe location. I'm going to meet with them," Bob asserts.

"What? Are you crazy? What if they try to harm you?" Mrs. Howard replies. Her tone shows she is in complete surprise and anger with Robert Hamlin.

"You know, I've heard about these loser morons, pure white trash, for years. It's time someone stood up and told these idiots the truth about life and the human beings we interact with. That's aid I can defend myself." Bob responds.

"You'll do what? You could get hurt!" she answers. She doesn't know what to say.

An hour later after various arguments between his staff and the Secret Service, Robert Hamlin arrives at the police station. Since his last conversation, the subjects had been moved to the county jail. Robert Hamlin arrived at the building accompanied by twenty police cars. After going through various security checks, Hamlin enters the room with one of the subjects. Upon his "subtle" request the other two are transferred to the same room. "Hello gentlemen, my name is Robert A. Hamlin, Congressman from the state of Illinois. And get this, I am no longer running for President," Bob calmly says. The three subjects sit there in complete shock. They have no idea why he came to the jail to visit them.

"Let me kindly repeat what I just stated, my name is Robert Hamlin," Bob says as he extends his hand. The subject closest to him responds with an offhand remark and a smirk on his face. "You know there must be something on my hand because most people shake my hand when it's extended. Your mother would be embarrassed to see your damn face and behavior today. But don't worry, you can be sure you'll be on the news tonight," Bob states.

"You can go screw yourself asshole. Go back to Illinois; that's 'Integrated Illinois' you (expletive term to describe people of color) lover," the first subject answers.

Bob smiles and leans forward to whisper to the individual. "I know you're trying to impress everyone present in this room, including your intelligence-deprived friends. If you so much as look at me one more time, I'll hit you so hard you'll pass into next week. You and your friends, pure losers, are going to sit here and listen," Bob answers, as he stands to walk away.

"Gentlemen, I've spent a lot of time the past five years giving speeches, smiling for cameras, shaking hands, and trying to impress people, much of it to try and win votes. I can assure you, my last political race was the previous week. Much of what I say and do the next hour will have nothing to do with winning a future election. Also, years ago there was an assassination attempt on Pope John Paul II in Rome. A few years later, out of the kindness of his heart, he went to visit him in prison and accepted his apology for the assassination. He forgave him for shooting him. Gentlemen, I'm not the Pope and you're not going to be that lucky today."

"First, when someone extends their hand, you reply with a handshake. I was born and raised as a Catholic in the suburbs of the great state of Illinois. Earlier you described it as 'Integrated

Illinois'. Can you spell both words? That may not mean much to you," Bob declares as he turns his head toward the first subject. Bob leans forward to him and whispers, "I thought I told you not to look at me, sir. If you don't wipe that smirk off your face, I'll do it for you," Bob sternly offers to the first subject.

"Second, the fact you're white trash doesn't impress or scare anyone. Forty years ago you would have run around with your white sheets and burned crosses on people's front yards. Someday I would love to hear one of you PhD candidates explain how Christian men burn crosses… can't see how that helps the cause, Mr. Wizard, " Bob declares (he was poking fun of the title of being the Grand Wizard in the Ku Klux Klan).

"Third, what's with shaving your heads?" Bob inquires.

"We wear our hair short as a sign of togetherness. That we're in this together," a second subject yells out.

Hamlin pauses before responding, "You're in what (organization) together? I doubt you're referring to the chamber of commerce. If you want to become closer as friends or a group, you can join a church, help some worthwhile charitable cause, and assist others in need less fortunate than you. It doesn't matter what cause you help as long as you're giving from your heart. I assure you joining the white trash union doesn't build any level of community. Sir, you will not speak today until I tell you so. So, sit your uneducated and intolerant ass down and shut up," Bob says in a very low key and calm demeanor.

"You shut up you (offensive term to African Americans) lover. You have no idea of the political and economic power we have. Millions are coming to our cause," the third subject yells in response.

Bob calmly looks at him. He turns toward his lead security officer and tells him to remove the handcuffs from the third subject who just spoke.

"Mr. Hamlin, with all due respect, he probably does not fear you. You could be placing yourself in harm's way," Special Agent Al Warren replies.

"Oh, I doubt it. Big mistake insecure and weak people have is underestimating their opponent. Go ahead and take the handcuffs off," Bob answers. He is looking directly at the third subject directly in his eyes. Bob knew that looking directly at violent people tends to anger them. He was trying to create an expected response.

"Are you sure?" the agent questions.

"Yes sir. Have no reason to be fearful with God and you all protecting me. You can remove his handcuffs," Bob provides.

The agent directs the officer who owned the handcuffs to remove them. Seconds afterwards, the third subject jumps up and sprints toward Robert Hamlin. Just before making contact, Bob jumps in the air using a defensive technique and kicks the subject. His foot lands a direct hit in the subject's groin area. He falls over, laying on the ground curled up like a ball. From the sounds he's making and holding his groin, he is in extreme pain.

"Hey, what the hell are you doing?" the first subject yells. "You had no right to do that. We're gonna sue you," he yells.

"No right to do what, defend myself? If you look right there, you'll see a video camera. The tape will clearly show the handcuffs were removed and that he charged at me. Under the law, sir, you have a right to self-defense. By the time the trial ends, and after some 40 witnesses testify against you and your friend, you'll be paying me money," Hamlin declares. The law enforcement officers begin to laugh at the defendant's statement.

"I can see it now. News flash: Member of Congress kicks member of white supremacist group and scores victory for decent, law abiding Americans. Tonight at 10 (pm)," shouts a sheriff's deputy from a local parish. Most of the officers present begin laughing. Even the Secret Service agents broke a smile or two, impressed with Bob's defensive maneuver. In Louisiana, counties are referred to as parishes.

Bob gets on one knee and whispers in the ear of the first subject, "If I have to repeat one more time, the importance of keeping your mouth shut, you'll be next. I'm not same person you people target when they're by themselves. For you and your friends, today begins a new order," Bob Hamlin offers to the first subject.

"As you can see, I didn't come down here to apologize. I want to hear firsthand what prompted you idiots to think you'd settle some score with me? I want to hear some reasonable explanation of how killing anyone, let alone the President-elect of our nation, would help your cause?"

"Don't you idiots get it? Laws have been written and the courts have issued various rulings to protect all Americans. It's called equal opportunity under the law. Everyone who is a citizen in our country is entitled to the guarantees of the *Equal Protection Clause* of the 14th Amendment. If you don't know what that is, read the U.S. Constitution. That is, if you're literate and you can read," Hamlin declares to those present in the jail. A few of the officers laugh at the comment.

"When are you going to move forward? God knows, it is so easy to hate people, particularly those who are different than ourselves. Hear me on this one: you guys lost the Civil War in 1865," Hamlin shouts. To no one's surprise, none of the officers laughed or smiled. "We don't have to love each other. We are, however, going to grant everyone a minimal level of respect because we are all human beings, precious in the eyes of God."

"Everywhere I go I am criticized by someone who is Pro-life, Pro-choice, Pro this or Pro that. Don't worry, I'm a big boy and can take the criticism. What really alarms me is we spend all this time trying to protect ourselves or others who are not even born, when we don't give a rat's (rear end) about many people who are born, live here in our nation, go to church, pay their taxes, and just want a chance to prove their self-worth in life, regardless of their skin color and religious beliefs" Hamlin says with his voice elevated. After a brief pause, he resumes.

"You know I didn't come down to Louisiana during this political campaign to criticize the people, your culture, or the core beliefs of people from this region of the country. In fact, the truth is the people of the South have been incredibly gracious, and caring. I have seen, firsthand, their hospitality and warmth. I love my home state of Illinois and its people but many of my peers could learn a lot about how to treat other people by spending a few days down here."

In the same way, the people of the South have traveled a long way in race relations, economic opportunities for all, and coming together despite our differences. I bet you guys wouldn't know much about that, however," Bob asserts to the three subjects in front of him. "You spend your life on activities that can include burning crosses, distributing hate materials, feeling sorry for yourselves because you're uneducated and can't get hired for a better job. In that scenario it's real easy to ignore the positive contributions of society by people who are different than you."

"I'm going to ask you individuals one last time why you're here today? What prompted you to think that shooting me or threatening to harm me was going to improve the standing of you and your group? Do you have any idea how many years you're about to spend in jail now?" Bob inquires. "Any of you geniuses want to answer?" The first two subjects sat there with smirks on their faces. The third subject continued to lie on the floor holding his private parts in pain. Every few seconds he would groan or generate sounds to reveal he was truly hurt.

"Well I apologize for wasting your time. I should have known I would not hear intelligent thoughts or any inspiring ideas. I mean, why should I have believed for one minute there would be a plausible explanation for why you some people can improve your position or standing in society, particularly from you three PhD candidates. Man, I was really facetious in thinking anything good would come from being here. Hey, contestant #1: you can look at me now because I'm talking to you. I'm getting really impatient with that 'deer in the headlight' look on your face... That's ok. You don't realize it yet but you're about to spend the next twenty years in a jail cell to think it over. You may not realize it, but you'll probably have a new girlfriend within a week. Hope you enjoy your stay at the resort called *Club Fed*," Hamlin declares. The law enforcement officers present in the jail laugh at Bob's statement.

"Last, I regret to notify you that your movement of millions last week failed. We won in the Electoral College because Louisiana, Kentucky, and Georgia voted to move forward for change. Some things in life you can't buy at the grocery store, like class. Say hello to the Grand Wizard (of the Ku Klux Klan) when you see him," Bob asserts.

Bob wanted to thank each of the law enforcement officers for their help. "I greatly appreciate the professionalism you showed today in protecting the people of Louisiana and I. Many times we do our jobs, day in and day out, without recognition. Just wanted to let you know I appreciate what you did today," Bob declares. Afterwards he spent about thirty minutes personally thanking each officer and person present.

"Congressman, I think we should return to the bus. That way we'll have a better sense of control of the situation," Special Agent Al Warren states. His sense of urgency was extremely clear.

"We have one more stop to make. We're going to visit the officer who was injured today. Can you determine where he was taken so I can personally say thanks," Bob replies.

"I think we should return to the bus. I'm not sure the officers appreciated your comments about people from the South, sir," Warren says.

"Is that what you're worried about or were you thinking about the fallout of my kick in the 'gentle-talia' of subject #3?" Bob questions as the other agents begin to laugh. After all, they were very impressed with his maneuver of 'treating' the suspect.

"Well, I am worried about the questions we'll have to answer regarding how the handcuffs were removed. We clearly did not follow all established procedures today," Warren answers.

"Don't you go worrying about that issue. I knew all the cameras would be working in the jail. If I thought for one minute we would be in jeopardy, I would not have asked for the handcuffs to be removed. I can assure you this: your security detail saved my life today and kept a lot of people safe from danger. If anyone gives you any smack (trouble) today about the events of today, you let me know ASAP. I will call them at 3 (am) to offer my praise and thanks for your work…plus, how often does a law abiding citizen get to 'offer' some Southern hospitality to a loser Bob offers.

"You used a very effective crane kick to the subject, sir. Wonder how it will look on the videotape?" Warren asks.

"It will be even better because you can rewind the tape and watch it to your heart's content. You know I saw that kick performed at the end of the movie '*The Karate Kid*'. It worked in the movie and it worked today in the jail. Take a bite out of crime," Bob declares.

Thirty minutes later Robert Hamlin and his security detail arrive at the hospital. Hamlin insisted on visiting Tim Jones, a Task Force Officer from Shreveport, Louisiana, who had been injured earlier in the day. He was an eleven year veteran of the county's sheriff department. He received a cut on his face when punched by subject #3. This was the same person who Bob had "greeted" at the jail. Despite numerous awards in his brief career, he was unable to be hired as a federal agent. Detective Jones was incredibly surprised to meet Robert Hamlin even saluting him as he approached him in his hospital room.

"Sergeant Jones, I presume. Good morning I'm Robert Hamlin," Bob says while extending a handshake to the impressed officer. "I wanted to stop by and say thanks for your help today. You know you prevented a lot of people from being injured this morning, namely me. Wanted to make sure you're ok and extend my appreciation for a job well done. More importantly, how are you?"

"I'm ok. Just have a cut on my face. They're checking to make sure my wrist is ok. I guess I'm more embarrassed that some clowns injured me," Sergeant Jones replies in a deep Southern accent.

"What do you mean?" Bob asks.

"Congressman, I was born and raised in Louisiana. I love the people, our culture, the pace, the food…everything. We get teased a lot by outsiders, but I have a great deal of love for the quality of life here. However, I just have no respect for trash like that. They are the reason others look down on us. They still think it's (the year) 1950 and they can deny anybody who is different from them their rights under the law. What they say and do is not what most people believe down here."

"Don't get me wrong: There are good reasons why certain laws were passed. We shortchanged ourselves in educating all of our children, not just African-Americans. Our actions turned off businesses for a long time that wanted to move here. These people's actions from the lynchings lots of and churches being burned down were just wrong. You know, they burned a lot of white churches too…wanted to make it look like the African-

Americans did it," Sergeant Jones says. A tear forms from his left eye as it slowly rolls down his cheek.

Hamlin pauses to give him time to compose himself before continuing. "That's a very moving portrayal of what happened. It's obvious that you care about your state and its people. I do too, as did former Senator Al Howard" Bob replies as he motions for others to leave the room. I think it's really a strong character trait when you're thinking about the suffering of others while you're in the hospital. Is there anything we can do to help you?" Bob calmly inquires.

"Well, there is one issue, but I don't think it's the right time," Jones whispers.

"There's really no better time than the present. After all, how often do you get to make a request of the next president. Hell, I don't even get to do that," Bob says with a smile.

"Ok. I've tried to apply to be a federal agent. I believe one of the greatest problems we have in our country is drug abuse. I want to work for the federal agency that pursues these cases. I just think it's wrong that people can make a lot of money selling that useless crap, pardon my French," Jones declares.

"Well, I don't see a problem with your application. I think with a few phone calls that issue can be resolved for your benefit. After all, you weren't bashful in protecting me" Hamlin declares.

"Yes sir, I've been accused of being aggressive at times," he replies.

"And don't ever be afraid to ask for something. You're a good man. We met because you were doing your job, as a professional. You kept a lot of people safe today, including me. I will always remember that. One more thing, Special Agent Warren can you do me a favor?" Bob says.

"Yes sir," he responds.

"Please contact the Special Agent in charge of recruiting. Let them know I spoke with a Detective Tim Jones from Shreveport, Louisiana this morning. Kindly inform him that President-elect Robert Hamlin was very appreciative of Jones' efforts on the security detail. Also, please extend my belief that he would make an excellent Special Agent. Now, Detective Jones, you don't have any issues, such as drug arrests, that would hurt your application do you?" Hamlin inquires.

"No sir. What you see is what you get," Detective Jones answers.

"Good. That's what I thought. Special Agent Warren can you make that phone call later this morning?" Hamlin asks.

"Yes sir. No promises on the application status, but I'll make the call," he responds.

"Gentlemen, need I remind you that the President of the U.S. selects the Administrator for all federal agencies. Detective Jones, thank you again. You should be receiving a phone call in the near future. They, like every government agency, have a lot of paperwork to complete. Good luck to you sir," Hamlin declares. He extends a firm handshake to the Task Force Officer. Then Hamlin and the Agent Warren join the other members of the security detail outside the room. Ten minutes later, after the building was secure, they exit the hospital.

"We have to call Mrs. Howard. I'm sure she wants to know what has happened. After searching for ten minutes, the phone connection between the two was established. "Yes, Mrs. Howard, its Robert Hamlin," Bob says.

"Hey, I heard the commotion about the potential assassins. Is everything ok?" Mrs. Lillian Howard inquires. The fear in her voice is clearly evident.

"Yes, Mrs. Howard everything is alright. There were three armed white males in the crowd. As you probably heard, there was a fight. All three men were taken into custody. Luckily no one in the audience was hurt. An officer was taken to the hospital. He should be ok. In fact, we just visited him. I waited to thank him personally for his efforts today," Bob asserts to answer her question.

"Now Bob, I want you to tell me the truth. I heard a rumor that you wanted to visit with the bad people after they were arrested. Is this true?" she inquires.

"Yes we did meet with all three of the subjects in the jail. We had a little chat…," Bob replies as he is interrupted.

"A talk? These people were dangerous. You could have been injured. I know I was correct in urging you to cancel the campaign appearance. I want you to promise me you will not speak here today. Three people hated Al and everything he stood for. They are mean people and mean nothing but harm to everyone who disagrees with them. They could hurt someone!" she yells.

"Mrs. Howard, we are here in town to show our appreciation to everyone who voted for us. I was just told the event will occur one hour from now. We are proceeding as planned and we'd be honored to have you join us," Bob answers with a smile.

"I don't know. You are so stubborn. Also, I heard a rumor that you kicked one of these people today. Is that true?" she angrily asks.

"You have some very good sources, Mrs. Howard. When I was in the jail, I was giving the subjects a speech about tolerance. I told the officers to take off the handcuffs of one of the subjects who didn't like what I had to say. He charged at me and I exercised my right to defend myself. The entire episode is on video," Bob asserts.

"You did what? Please tell me you didn't hurt him. Wait, you said the whole episode is on a video? Oh, please tell me you didn't. Al had no sympathy for violence. He believed it didn't solve anything," she answers in a clear but firm response.

"Mrs. Howard, I can assure you this individual won't be bothering anyone today. When his friends watch him get 'dropped like a bad habit' on the tape, he'll be the laughing stock of the Klan," he replies.

"What are you going to say when asked by the media about what happened? Don't even think they'll have some questions?" she asks.

"I'll tell them to watch the tape," Bob proudly replies.

"I also heard you said some bad things about people from the South. Is this true?" she politely inquires.

"I told the subjects and anyone else who listens to the tape that they lost the Civil War. I stated they would never appeal to most Americans when they pursue activities like burning a cross. I declared how we were no longer in the 1950's and that it was time to move on. However, I praised, again, *praised*, the people of the South for their hospitality to me and your family during this campaign. More importantly, I commended the good people of the South for their diligent efforts of overwhelming perceptions held by 'trash' and people like them who sat in the room with me in the jail who engage in negative, criminal, and intolerant acts in this country."

"Senator Howard spoke countless times about his state and the people of the South. He stated, courageously, that the negative times of Segregation and the perceptions it created in the Northern states. He declared, without fear of retribution, about the pride he saw in the 'Silent Majority' of the people of Louisiana and the region forming a New South. In the presence of the law enforcement community, three criminal defendants, and now anyone who watches the tape, I stood up for Senator Howard: The good people have 'turned the other cheek and will protect the vulnerable members of clearly defined racial and religious minority groups. It includes people who were not born and raised in the South and who, tirelessly, pursue the legislative agenda of decent human beings, like you and Senator Howard," Bob asserts.

"Bob, I only fear that it will cause conflict with those types of individuals. They're not the most sympathetic people to outsiders," she answers.

"Have no empathy with people who threaten harm and suffering to my family, myself, or the general public. Those three clowns, as you warned, were intent on shooting me today. If we lived in Iran they would have been executed by now. They should give thanks to how they live here, in the greatest country in the history of the world."

"The only reason they have a voice is because they are permitted to hold parades and recruit other uneducated people due to the freedoms guaranteed to them under the U.S. Constitution, the same government structure they criticize. The rights to Freedom of Speech and Assembly, as is written in the First Amendment, don't protect them when they violate the precedent of the '*Clear and Present Danger Test*'. If some of them are mad, too bad. Here's a news item: they and their intolerant belief structure lost the election last week. The voices of doom and gloom were defeated," Bob calmly says.

After a brief pause Mrs. Howard responds "You're just like Al. You'll never understand and they'll never accept you because you weren't born and raised here (in the South). Let's go to the rally," she answers with a sigh as she terminates the call.

Thirty minutes later Hamlin's entourage enters the gym. The rally, previously scheduled for 7:30 (am) has been delayed for a few hours. This was done to permit for the events of the past few hours. Around 9:40 (am) Bob is introduced by Mrs. Lillian Howard to the thunderous applause of the audience. Bob graciously hugs Mrs. Howard at the podium.

"I want to begin by giving thanks today. A few hours ago three subjects were taken into custody when we were previously in the town square at city hall. Due to the professionalism of the law enforcement officers and Secret Service Agents present, nobody in the crowd was injured. One officer was himself wounded. I went to visit him at the hospital and he was in good spirits. He's a good man and deserves your support," Bob says as the crowd wildly cheers.

"I want to thank you all for your patience today. I'm sorry about the delay. My advisers were going to cancel our appearance here until Mrs. Howard intervened," Bob declares. She is not pleased with how he is bending the truth. "No, she told me in no uncertain terms that the people of Louisiana voted for change last week. She said 'we're stopping this bus to show our appreciation to the people of Shreveport and throughout Louisiana," Bob offers. Mrs. Howard shakes her head the entire time because she insisted on canceling the event and grins at Bob's comments.

"There are a lot of things I want to say this morning. However, if we can be serious for just a few minutes… I want for us to pause and offer some words of thanksgiving today for Senator Al Howard," Bob says. It is so quiet in the room you can hear a pin drop. "A few months ago when Senator Howard asked me to be his running mate, there was a lot of hesitation. It also came from me. I felt there was no way that I had the right to be in the same room as Senator Howard, let alone run with him.

"After he passed away, I sat there in shock, just like millions of you did then, wondering what had happened. There isn't a day that passes that I don't pray for him and seek his guidance.In fact, I do a lot of things that really concerns and at times, upsets Mrs. Howard. One thing I will never do, however, is embarrass you regarding the policies we pursue for the benefit of the nation, in his name," Bob says. He walks over and gives Mrs. Howard a hug.

"You really get me frustrated at times. Do you know that?" Mrs. Howard whispers to him.

"Yes, I know. It's never meant to hurt or demean anyone when it's done," he says in response. The audience is cheering loudly, but cannot hear their private discussion.

"I wanted to share some information with you. Earlier today some individuals were arrested that allegedly were planning to commit violence toward us. There is a videotape that you may see in the near future. I asked that one of the subjects be released from his handcuffs. Subsequently, I said something he didn't like and he ran toward me. Rest assured, as you'll see in the video, I allegedly took the proper steps to defend myself," Bob offers.

"More importantly, I made some comments about certain individuals that many people from the South may not receive well. I want to be very clear. I love the people who live in the Southern states. The progress you've made pertaining to tax revenues, race relations, and economic development has been remarkable over the past sixty years."

"However, what will not be tolerated is when bad persons wish to harm other people, using words of hate directed at people who look different than them. You know who they are. Forty years ago they hid behind the white sheets and pretended they were 'protecting us' Now, they hide behind the First Amendment and declaring their need to protect us again."

"They look different now, of course. But it doesn't matter if the costume is white or if the head is shaved and the body contains tattoos in defense of a master race. Luckily, good people across the nation and throughout the South know that Halloween is a one day event so the costumes won't fly. They also know that the circus may come to town, just like when a politician visits for Election Day. The election cycle always ends and the circus packs up and leaves town, until the next show."

"When I declared on the video that you lost the war, it wasn't about opening old wounds. It's about the need for all of us, me included, to grow as individuals. It does not mean we'll all join hands and sing a song, then never talk to people in the choir again. It's about facing up to our responsibilities, learning from our mistakes from the past, and deciding to take a chance in life. I know it's hard to make an effort know people who are different from ourselves."

"You know it's so easy to cast aside people who aren't just like us. We've all done it, even me. Missing opportunities to expand our businesses, increase our circle of friends, meet new people and grow in our faith lives. I know what you're thinking: Hamlin has left the North again and is getting too much oxygen by breathing our cleaner air. Or try this, you're wondering if I took another blow to the head or inhaled some funny or illegal substances," Bob offers to the crowd.

"You go Hamlin," someone yells out to the laughter of the crowd. His comment brought a smile to Bob's face.

"Believe me I understand. It was normal when I was a child to urge children to follow the social norms of the day. Hang around people who looked like you, spoke like you, and went to the same church as you. In fact, you went along to get along, much like it was here in Louisiana."

"You see, we in the Chicago area are a lot like you all from the South. We have many of the same habits too. Today we would refer to it as cloning," Bob says to the audience. Nobody was laughing. "I was politely told when growing up, 'this is how things have always worked'. It's been successful in the past, it'll work in the future."

"Traditions are great. They make for nice holidays and give us something to share in common. They also pose roadblocks toward solving problems. Traditionally, we've encouraged businesses to do what they want and let them buy other unrelated industries. Then we wake up one day and we discover the mill or the plant has closed. We stand at the closed facility and people like me refer to them as *monuments to neglect*. On the other side of the table, my union counterparts fight pay cuts or job losses when the corporation needs the capital to recruit new capital to invest in the facility. Then we're notified the plant's closing and moving to Mexico. Either way we stand there, point fingers and delay making changes to create a better future for everyone. Why? Because someone reminds us, it's always been done this way."

"In the recent election I was labeled a liberal by the incumbent, particularly his spin doctors and hired guns (political consultants and other elected officials recruited or paid to put the best 'spin' intended to benefit a candidate). I stand here as a liberal in the proud legacy of Senator Al Howard. He never accepted traditional behaviors politically, particularly if it meant hurting one's position. He called for investments in education, for all our children, before it was acceptable for a white U.S. Senator from the South. He was urging labor and management teams to heed the other's warnings, long before the Midwest became the 'Rust Belt' in the early 1980's (parts of Illinois, Ohio, Michigan, Wisconsin, Pennsylvania and Indiana negatively impacted from plant closings of the steel and auto business).

"You see, I get very concerned when people defend various traditions without understanding the basis for why the tradition occurs. For example, we celebrate Thanksgiving the end of November. Yet many historians will tell you the fabled banquet between the pilgrims and the Indians probably happened one to two months earlier in the calendar. Thanksgiving Day is celebrated on the 4th Thursday in November due to an executive order by former President Abraham Lincoln. It's completely unrelated to the settlers and Native Americans.." Bob declares.

"Here's what I am calling for. It's time to change what we do. We need to adjust our spending priorities based upon needs, not wants. We need to fashion our economic priorities and modify the tax system to help the economy of tomorrow, not the one we used to have. We need to challenge ourselves to educate our children so they can compete in the world's marketplace, not to defeat the kids in the adjacent town. After all, we're not competing against cities or parishes next door or to recruit manufacturers. We're pursuing employment opportunities against foreign countries located across the ocean.

"As parents we need to be engaged in our children's upbringing. There was a news report recently about a young man beaten in a high school in the City of Chicago. One of the four individuals who inflicted the beating was disciplined just the week before for taking a separate student's train tickets. At his disciplinary hearing, his mother addressed the panel by saying, 'why did you arrest my angel?' She then proceeded to object to his suspension when more than 20 witnesses identified him with the three other subjects. Since I didn't name the person, I can't be sued for defamation of character. However, I can assume this angel is a punk and his Mom's in denial," Bob conveys to the audience. Many people nod their heads or clap to reveal they agree with Bob's analysis.

"Luckily, the good people, us, can see through the emotional fog. After all, if you want to catch trout, you don't go to a catfish pond," Bob says. The crowd laughs and loudly applauds to demonstrate their approval. In fact we continue to pretend that problems will go away or that they don't even occur. Quite simply, we are all creatures of habit, sometimes creatures of bad ones. We can all help to make the world a better place and it begins with each of us, including me."

"I wanted to thank you for caring and for your patience today. In particular, I wanted to close by praising someone who is not with us today," Bob declares. The gym is dead silent. "I know many of you have heard this before, but I'll be saying it for the next four years. As you know I wasn't chosen by our party last summer at the convention to be the nominee. I was asked to join the team, which was to be led by Senator Howard. Well, the same status holds true today. I'm still on the team and I will continue to seek his input. I still refer to both written and video speeches by Senator Al Howard. We will, as Mrs. Howard and you are my witnesses, pursue the legislative policies that Senator Howard fought for while representing the great state of Louisiana. The same state that voted for us last week in the election."

"We can be successful. We can renew the American spirit. We can revive our economy. We can educate our children. We can provide for the national defense and we can uphold the remaining principles of '*The Preamble*'. Thank you. May God bless you all," Bob clearly states to the crowd. U.S. Congressman Rod Andrews, recently elected as the new U.S. Senator to replace Al Howard and heir to another political dynasty in the state of Louisiana, begins leading the crowd in a cheer. He alternates back and forth as the audience repeats his statements. "We are…Together; We are… Together; We are…Together; We are…Together." The crowd continues to repeat Congressman Andrews' statement for the next twenty minutes continuing even as Hamlin was departing the school.

"This is simply remarkable!! How is anyone supposed to make heads or tails over this? Why were these problems never addressed?" Bob shouts as he tosses the report down on the floor. He leans forward to push the intercom.

"Yes Sharon. How are you?" After a brief delay Sharon answers.

"What are you still doing up at this hour?" she asks while yawning.

"It's 24/7 on the Hamlin presidential campaign, you know that," he replies. A loud, clear, audible yawn is heard by Sharon on the other end of the phone.

"Sure. Bob, I have a news flash for you, the campaign ended last week. In fact, you won the election. Now, will you please get some sleep?"

"I'm not really that tired. In fact, in a lot of ways I'm like (former U.S. President) Bill Clinton. The race never ends," Bob replies.

"That's ridiculous," Sharon answers back immediately. "You're not at all like Bill Clinton. I've known you now for five years…Yes, you have a lot of energy, where it comes from I don't know! But stop kidding yourself with the Clinton stuff. I won't name anyone, but he made a lot of people look bad, often. Since I met you you've been nothing but a complete gentleman to me and everyone else I've met in this business. Wait, let me correct that. You've never taken a pass at anyone, but there are times you drive people crazy," she answers.

"What do you mean?" he asks.

"You can stop it. I heard about your stunt with the people who wanted to hurt you. Do you have any idea how mad Mrs. Howard is? Many times she pretends to ignore your actions, until after you have left the room. Then the staff has to calm her down all the time. Please, stop playing dumb. You drive her and the (Secret Service) agents crazy," she declares.

There is a pause in the conversation. "Yea, I know. I make mistakes all the time. Yes, I'm fully aware of what threat the geniuses posed this morning. Learning that I'm the subject of a death threat is never a positive event. Why do you think I floored the PhD candidate at the police station? I don't care how upset he and his minions are. After learning they wanted to kill me I wasn't much interested in hearing their feeble views or justifications. That said, I hear you; Aside from my respect for her husband, I always praise Mrs. Howard everywhere I go for a lot of reasons," Bob says in response.

"You know she really does like you. She's already lost one man she deeply cared about. Maybe she's cautious for fear she'll lose you too. After all, her husband trusted you, as does she. I remember the first time I met Senator Howard. I was off to the side, watching his actions and body language. I've learned politics is a tough sport and it's hard to believe in a lot of people in this business… But he trusted you. *That's* why she cares Bob," Sharon answers. In speaking, her voice was calm, sincere and believable.

"Thanks. You know, I'm going to follow your advice and take a nap. If you can, please tell Peter and Kevin I want to talk to them again, say 10 or 11 (am)" Bob states.

"Can I give them a heads up about the topic?" she inquires.

"Tell them I want to resume our conversation from this morning about the world at large. They'll know what the agenda is about. However, tell them to bring me some stats, quotes, hell, evidence of their respective positions. If you can, please invite Garrett Johnson. He's assigned as a staff member to the campaign from the National Security Council. Please ask him to secure a copy of the daily briefing, tell him to read it and ask him to join us. It's very important," Bob declares.

"Wow; Seems like you have an important item to talk about. Can you provide any more details?" she asks. The tone in her voice reveals a strong sense of curiosity but she has no idea about the topic for Kevin and Peter.

"I'm sorry, but I can't. I always try to encourage the participation of those attending knowing that what they say there stays with the other people present in the room. I hope you understand," Bob delivers.

"No, I never do. However, I've also learned that when Robert Hamlin avoids answering a question, it's important," she answers.

"Everything we do is important to the rest of the nation now. A few months ago, what we did was only important to the people from Illinois and ourselves. Now, the level of importance is a little higher," Bob responds. A strong degree of sadness can be detected in his voice. Bob trusts Sharon but also knows he is not at the liberty to tell her. "Understand?"

"No, but that's ok. I know you well enough to believe that when you don't want to answer the question, it must be important," she responds.

"Ok. I'm going to get some sleep. If you don't hear from me by 11 (am) can you have someone wake me up? Thanks. Oh, one last thing. As you know, I have been very busy the past few months. Despite that, I didn't want you and our staff to think I didn't appreciate all your help during the campaign. We couldn't have won without good people, like you," Bob declares with a yawn. "I just wanted to say thanks." The tone in his voice indicated that he was tired but sincere.

"Thanks. It's always great to hear a compliment. You're one of the few people, especially in the political business, who understands the importance of saying thanks. I spent a lot of time speaking with candidates for various offices the past few months. You wouldn't believe how insensitive, selfish, and damn mean some of these people are. I have countless examples of rude some jerks. As for the women, they're even meaner. Some of them border on being the Queen of Narnia. I mean, being in the business, I understand that most men have esteem or control issues, but the women: amazing!" Sharon shouts.

"Well, I'd prefer not to reply to the last comment. I'll just say this: there are a lot of people who have bad days. There are less people who are mean. There are fewer who are just jerks. I once had a boss who said there are three types of people in this world. They are: those who make it happen; those who watch it happen; and those who ask 'what happened'?" Bob offers. Sharon begins laughing very loudly. "The people who ask what happened, you don't want running the government or having authority to make any decisions," Bob shares.

"That makes a lot of sense. I loved the comment from your prior boss," she says with a laugh.

"It helps explain the nature of the decision-making process," Bob says while laughing. "Hey, I'll talk to you later" Bob asserts

"Ok, I'll make sure Kevin and Peter are ready before 11 (am)," Sharon replies. Ironically there is no reply from Bob. As a safety measure, she paged a Secret Service agent to make a courtesy check on him to make sure he was ok. Two minutes later the agent returned.

"He's fine. Congressman Hamlin is sleeping," he responds.

"Are you sure?" How can you tell?" she asks.

"He's snoring," he replies.

"So let me get this straight: You win the presidential election in the future?" Emily asks. Bob nods his head to show his approval. She is seated next to Bob on the bus. They are returning home after their weekend. Not knowing each other beforehand, they are discussing the merits of Bob's dream. "Ok. Give me one good reason why I shouldn't get up and leave you?" she asks.

He immediately responds, "I'll give you four of 'em. First, there are no other seats available. Second, you could have gotten up some time ago. In fact, when you sat down next to me, there were many seats left. Third, I think you stayed because you've enjoyed the conversation. If you didn't have a good weekend, it's not my fault. It is indeed rare to learn about other people's futures," Bob answers in response.

In amazement Emily sits there, in near shock. "Oh…I thought you said there were four reasons?" she asks. Her tone revealed she was condescending and really thought Bob was strange.

"I did say four; Just wanted to see if you were paying attention" Bob replies. He stares right at her while saying it and then turns away from her.

"How did I do?" she asks.

"You passed" Bob answers.

"What?" she asks in a seductive manner with a smile.

Chapter 5
Issues When We Avoid Solving Them

At exactly 10:55 (am) Bob walks to the back of the bus. He engages in a number of short conversations with various people. At 11:10 (am) he sees Peter Thomas, who immediately terminates his conversation with another staff member.

"Mr. Hamlin, I heard you wanted to resume our discussion from earlier yesterday," Pete says.

"Just seemed like a few hours ago when we spoke. It's been an interesting 24 hours" Bob replies.

"Yes sir, it has been. I was very concerned when I heard the news about the assassination attempt. It made me think about how we can leave this world at any time," Peter sadly says.

"Hey, it's alright. Nobody was seriously hurt. No shots were fired... You referenced how we never know the future. We never know when it's our time. It reminded me how precious life is and how important it is to keep open lines of communication. Life is too short to waste time holding grudges and about being upset what someone said. What we all do in life is important, but not more valuable than the needs and actions of others. You have a few minutes?" Bob inquires.

"Sure. Want me to find Kevin?" he asks.

"Won't be necessary, I'm right here," Kevin declares. His voice lowered as he completed his sentence.

"Are you alright?" Bob asks.

"I guess so...You mind if we talk later on?" Kevin asks. His voice conveyed he has something else on his mind.

"Absolutely. How 'bout you, Peter, and I finish our conversation from yesterday. When we're done, I'll be honored to talk about whatever's on your mind. We won't be in Baton Rouge (Louisiana) for 4-5 hours anyway. Got lots of time to listen to you both," he states.

"Thanks," Kevin responds. The delay in his answer clearly demonstrates something else is on his mind.

They proceed to Bob's private room in the back of the bus. "Good news guys, I requested food be brought in. I figured we'd be here through lunch. I ordered cantaloupe, apples, sandwiches, fries, Twinkies, sodas and some chocolate snack cakes. All the basic food groups are represented," Bob declares with a smile.

"Both guys smile, but they're both fighting some other emotion. They are standing in the room and for whatever reason have decided not to sit down.

"Ok, gentlemen. What's on your minds? I doubt it's the Iranian government" Bob responds.

"Perhaps we're both concerned about what happened earlier today," Peter says.

"Ok, but why delay the conversation? In fact, I heard you were advised not to go to the event. Is that true?" Kevin angrily asks.

"Hell, you could have been killed!" Peter asserts.

"Guys, I want you to sit down," Bob replies after a brief pause. "Here's the scoop. Yes, I was advised there could be danger beforehand. I am told, on a daily basis, of a potential security threat on my life. Presidential campaigns bring out the best losers in our society. Yes, there are a bunch of idiots in this world who have nothing better to do than try to make others fearful of them. Today, as we saw, the danger became reality. I can assure you at the jail I addressed the issue of reality to those three clowns. One felt reality, firsthand, when I kicked him in the groin," Bob answers.

"You did what?" Peter asks in a surprised manner.

"What did you say?" Kevin asks with a smile.

"You both heard me. The video will clearly show what happened and that I kicked him in self-defense when he came after me. When he did not have handcuffs on," Bob declares.

"This will help the poll numbers. Great way to begin the term in office buddy," Kevin replies. He is shaking his head in disbelief from Bob's statement. Deep down he's smiling, but knows this won't help win legislative votes in the months ahead.

"Don't feel bad. The (Ku Klux) Klan took one today, right in the gentletalia," Bob offers. Peter begins laughing. Kevin is just standing there, not showing any emotion at all. Peter suddenly stops laughing.

"Well, Jedi master; Do you have any regrets?" Kevin inquires.

"Yes, I only hit one of 'em. Three clowns is a good start toward forming a circus. However, only one of them lunged at me. I believe the other two subjects were enlightened from seeing their friend fall to the ground and didn't do anything," Bob responds.

"Nice job...Real nice," Kevin says with sarcasm.

"If you want me to express regret for kicking someone who had planned to kill me, then you're wrong. The line to apologize is over there and I'm not in it," Bob angrily replies. At this point Kevin and Peter remain very silent.

"I've known you for some time. You never let your anger get the better of you," Kevin says.

"Believe me, I wasn't out of line. I was educating the young men about how it's time to let go of our hatred for people who are different than us. Being in jail, I assumed the security tapes were recording. I didn't just kick Clown #1. I struck a blow to let the simpletons of the world know that violent actions toward other people in our society are not going to be tolerated. Previously, lynchings, murder, and discriminatory practices occurred in the South for a long time. Any such *Romper-Room-like* behavior will be proactively addressed in a Hamlin administration. We won't all love each other, join hands and sing songs of praise. Don't get me wrong. It's ok if we don't all love each other. Family members don't all love each other and they're related by birth. However, examples of evil, violence and hatred will not stand today or five years from now. Is that understood?" Bob asks.

"Yes... Yes sir," they intermittingly respond.

"Wait, what do you mean five years from now?" Kevin inquires.

"Five years from now I won't be the President. Each term is only four years long. I'm not running for reelection. Got that?" Bob declares in a clear, firm voice. "More importantly, 'reindeer games' will not be permitted by the Iranian government in the next administration either. Pete, I'd like you to substantiate, as best you can, your position on the threat they pose. I don't need names or sources. If I want them, I'll request you provide them when I review reports by the CIA and the State Department.

Talk from the heart. What's your gut feeling? What did the other sources tell you?" Bob asks.

"I believe the regime poses the greatest threat, bar none, to the national security of the U.S. for a number of reasons. They have invested a great deal of monies the past ten years to develop the technology to allow them to enrich uranium. They recently announced they can now do so. They do lack the number of centrifuges that are operational. If they can get more of the machines up and running, they could produce three to four nuclear bombs a year. Their explanation in enriching uranium is that it is for civilian, peaceful energy purposes. However, they apparently contain the largest reserves of oil, after Russia and Saudi Arabia. Therefore, I believe, as do several of my sources, that any such justification is pure B.S., pardon my language," Peter declares.

"Oh, come on," Kevin immediately responds.

"Carry on," Bob clearly replies in a firm voice.

"Second, they have recently made threats to threaten the existence of the State of Israel. Now, such comments from that part of the world have been heard before, particularly during some of the previous wars. However, this would represent the first time that a nation, who is developing the technology to carry it out, may be able to do so in a few years," Peter says.

"Who is giving you this info?" Kevin yells.

"Continue please," Bob calmly interjects.

"Third, Iran is located at a prime geographic place of importance to the national security of the U.S. They are located adjacent to the Persian Gulf where more than forty percent of the world's available oil passes through each day. Every time the Iranian president makes threats against the existence of Israel, the price of crude oil increases by a few dollars a barrel. If he launches a missile across the Gulf, just to prove his nation could do it, the price of crude oil would increase by $10 a barrel. The Iranian Government has the capacity, now, to threaten the safety of oil tankers that pass through the Gulf. For example, only thirteen percent of our oil needs to come from the Gulf. However, more than eighty percent of the oil needed by Japan passes through there. Losing thirteen percent of our nation's oil would be catastrophic to the economies of both the U.S. and the free world," Peter offers.

"I'm interested to hear what we should do if the Iranian Government chose to take that course of action," Bob clearly says.

"We can discuss that in the near future," Peter responds.

"We can talk about it now" Bob says.

"Give me a break. We just won the election. You have not even been sworn in as president," Kevin declares.

"These issues could occur some as late as January 21st, or even sooner. The three of us are beginning a dialogue on these issues. They do not represent an executive order. As you were," Bob politely asserts.

"Fourth, we are susceptible to world opinion not being favorable to us. Many nations around the world do not like us. If we were to practically destroy the military capacity of the Iranians to threaten its neighbors, world opinion would rally against us," Peter says.

"Then why attempt it? Why should we bother to destroy their ability to produce a nuclear bomb if the consequence is us getting pounded in public opinion polls across the world?" Bob asks.

"Quite simply; we have to. The Iranians would know they will have the ability to do it. The issue sir is not if, but when they will have access to a nuclear weapon. They have publicly stated their clear desire to use it against us or Israel. Also, we haven't won the *'Most Respected Nation in the Middle East Award* for a few decades anyway. During the Carter administration, when Egypt gave up their objective to destroy Israel (in *The Camp David Accords*), other nations stepped up to fill the void," Peter offers.

"Are you guys alright? I cannot comprehend that we're even having this conversation. This is never even going to be reviewed by other reasonable people," Kevin shouts.

"Sadly, I regret having to be the one to tell you this. We received word today, from noted intelligence experts in the Crowe administration, that the Iranians are negotiating military deals with other Third World nations. Normally, they deal with Russia or China to pursue various weapons projects. However, intelligence from multiple sources has confirmed that the Iranians will be ready to sell and deliver a nuclear weapon within twelve months. Get this; they already have buyers," Bob replies in a firm manner.

"Are you sure? My sources tell me they were five, maybe ten, years away? In fact, I just spoke with two of them in the past 24 hours. This can't be true!" Kevin declares.

"Apparently, it is true. They have played games with the Europeans for the past three years. We know they pretended to be in serious negotiations to not build a weapon. The documents were provided to our intelligence experts by our allies and confirmed by additional sources. Apparently one of the Iranian representatives inadvertently or intentionally distributed it at their discussions with the negotiators from France and Germany. Our allies are even angrier than us with the Iranians because they are the ones who were misled in the 'games' (discussions) with the Iranians. Maybe they even thought the Iranians were serious about negotiating. I know we (the U.S.) didn't believe the B.S. for the past year or so," Bob replies. His voice is somber and lowered.

"So much for developing the technology for civilian (non-military) purposes," Kevin asserts. There is a tone of sarcasm in his voice. His voice was incredibly sad but clear, probably never more so in answering an opinion or viewpoint. "That said, how does this affect us? What scenario is altered by this?" Kevin asks. He was rather taken aback by Hamlin's prior response.

"The facts are as they were just presented Kevin. I've seen the documents. They were graciously provided by the Crowe administration. It has a direct effect on us. Since we just won the election, the problem is about to be passed to us in about ten weeks. We're about to inherit an issue that presidential administrations over the past forty years have avoided," Bob states. The sincerity in his voice is genuine.

"That can't be what's happening! These geniuses in the Crowe administration have been planning this since Day One. It's the war they've always wanted. Now that they're walking out the door... Hell, shoved by us because we won the election, they're pulling this stunt. It's all lies, I tell you," Kevin yells while pounding the desk.

"No, it's not a lie. The Iranian Government has been actively pursuing the development of a nuclear bomb. For whatever reason, they either got caught today or the material was intentionally released," Peter says in response.

"Yea right…Tell me one good reason why negotiators from Iran would intentionally give us the paperwork to show they've been guilty the entire time," Kevin rudely declares.

"Here's a great reason. There are elements within the Iranian Government that don't agree with what the Mullahs (religious leaders) are doing there. Many people of their regime, just like employees who work for the U.S. Government, don't agree with the internal and foreign policy actions of their leaders. The paperwork may have been left there with the intended hope that they would be found and turned over to some country, perhaps us, to expose the actions of the Mullahs," Peter answers.

"That's ridiculous and you know it," Kevin says.

"Okay, how they were able to have more than ten U.S. Operatives and intelligence figures able to verify the content of the papers obtained by our negotiators yesterday in addition to six allied nations, most of us who usually don't agree what our nation does, concur unanimously,?" Bob replies in a firm voice.

"Whose side are you on?" Kevin rudely asks. The red-colored secure phone begins ringing but no one answers it.

"I'm on the side of the American taxpayers and citizens. We've been friends for a long time. However, you can't question facts. The documents don't lie. They were handed to us by their negotiators. Our duty is protecting the American people and our way of life," Bob calmly replies.

"I'm telling you, (President) Crowe has set this all up. He's wanted to go to war in Iran for a long time!" Peter shouts. His level of disbelief was clear.

"I can assure you of this; President Crowe did not plant the documents or drop them on the negotiation table. Since most of the locations where the Iranians have been testing and enriching uranium are underground, he couldn't have used the satellites to give us their 'pictures'," Bob says. He tosses the intelligence photos on the desk next to Kevin. At the moment the red-colored secure phone rings again. Everyone now remembers what they were instructed on beforehand: it would only ring if there was a matter of an emergency or world crisis.

After thirty seconds or so, Bob picks up the phone. "Hello, this is Congressman Robert Hamlin. How may I help you?" he asks.

"Yes, Congressman, this is Vice President James Marron. I am calling to speak with you on the secure line. Do you understand how this system works?" he inquires. The tone in his voice is very sad.

"Not well. Since my familiarity with the system is limited all I understand is that this phone call is not good news, Mr. Vice-President," Bob replies as he sits down.

"You are correct, Congressman...Bob I'm calling to let you know that President (William) Crowe collapsed this afternoon in the White House. Efforts were immediately undertaken to revive him but they were not successful. He passed away," Vice President Marron says. In speaking, he was fighting back crying.

"Oh, my God. That's horrible. Man, I'm terribly sorry. That's just not right," Bob replies. In saying it, a tear begins to slowly roll down his cheek.

"You're right. I've known President Crowe for about thirty years. We were elected to the U.S. Congress the same year. He's a great man," Marron declares.

"Yes sir...That's absolutely horrible news. Man this is really tough. Do they have any idea what prompted this?" Hamlin says.

"What happened?" Peter asks.

"Bob, what's going on?," Kevin inquires.

"Not yet. An autopsy will be performed tomorrow. However, the physician on call here believes it was a fatal heart attack. One minute he was standing up talking. I walked into the room from another meeting. He then collapsed and fell to the ground. Every effort was made to save him, both on the spot here, in the ambulance and at the hospital. He was pronounced dead about one hour ago. The doctor suspects President Crowe was dead before he hit the ground," he says in a soft voice.

"That's terrible. I'm....really sorry," Bob says, fighting back tears.

"Are you okay?" Kevin asks. He notices Bob's face is turning white and he's beginning to cry. Bob hears his friend, but is oblivious to his question.

"Bob, I want to assure you of something. You ran a tough, but fair campaign. I'm personally calling you to assure you this isn't your fault... Politics is a tough business and it's not for everyone. President Crowe *loved* politics. He loved running for public office. Yes, he was surprised and disappointed he lost last week. But, he was genuinely in a good mood the past few days. I don't want you to blame yourself for this.

"I'm making this phone call, myself, so you can hear my voice. You're a good person. Politics isn't for everyone. However, I truly admired the speech you gave at (Senator Howard's) the funeral a few months ago. The fact you won, fair and square, demonstrates that people trust you. You can rest assured you will continue to receive the support in the transition period (the time after the election preceding Inauguration Day) from me and our staff. You have my word on that. In this business, you know what that means," Vice-President Marron declares.

"Yes sir, I do. Thanks," Bob responds.

"One last thing before I let you go and before the press gets hold of this; Don't be surprised if you are asked to deliver the eulogy. As I said earlier, you did a great job speaking on behalf of the Howard Family."

"Wait, won't you be giving the eulogy?" Bob says in disbelief.

"No, I won't be for a couple of reasons. First, I am too close to President Crowe and his family. I've known him for thirty years. He was not just my boss and running-mate, but he's my closest friend. I'll be in no condition to give the speech," Vice-President Marron whispers. His voice is breaking up. It's evident he's trying not to cry. Second, he really wanted to have a bipartisan government regardless of who won. I'm asking you to make that happen. Therefore, if you're asked by his family, please do it...for the country's sake. I'll call you tomorrow and I'll walk you through what I would say, if I could. I'm going to let you go now. The phone lines are lighting up, as you can imagine," he whispers.

"I'll do as you ask. Call anytime tomorrow night," Bob replies.

"I know you will. That's why I called.....Bye" Vice-President Marron responds as he hangs up the phone.

"What's wrong?" Peter asks.

"What the hell happened?" Kevin strongly asks.

After a pause to gather his thoughts and to blow his nose Bob replies, "You won't be able to blame President Crowe anymore... He died today. That was Vice-President Marron calling to tell me he was pronounced dead about one hour ago. He....." Bob offers in a somber tone.

"How? What from?" Peter excitedly says.

"Was he shot? Don't tell me there was a conspiracy after what almost happened to you today?" Kevin yells.

"No, he died from what they believe was a massive heart attack. He was at the White House. After a meeting ended, he was talking to people and then suddenly collapsed and died. The doctor thinks he may have been dead before he hit the ground," Bob says.

"That's horrible. No one expected this," Peter declares.

"How do you think his family and staff feel? First he loses the election and now this" Bob says as he briefly pauses. "Many of those people have been with him for a long time. He brought a lot of them with him when he went to Washington after he was Governor of Ohio...If you don't mind, I want to be left alone," Bob says. A tear is rolling down his cheek.

"What about the rest of the bus tour? What do we do?" Peter asks.

"I think the tour is over. The election was last week and we won. As of now, there are more important things going on," Bob sadly responds.

"I'll notify the team. Come on Peter, let's get going. We have things to do," Kevin declares. He knew Bob really wanted to be left alone. After they left, they resume talking outside Bob's office.

"We have our disagreements at times, but he (Hamlin) really trusts you. I know you're his closest friend. You have policy differences, but he really respects your opinion. What's going through his mind right now?" Peter asks.

"It's pretty simple. He blames himself for the president's death...It was a really rough campaign," Kevin says.

"That's not true. We ran on the issues. People came to trust Bob. Hell, I came to trust him too. It's not his fault," Peter says. "We should make sure he's ok."

"Let me put it this way: Say you just defeated the incumbent President in his re-election bid. One week later he dies of a heart attack. What would you be thinking?" Kevin inquires.

"Maybe we should leave him alone. Let's check on him in an hour," Peter replies. In the background they can hear Robert Hamlin crying in the next room.

Chapter 6:
Talking to the Nation

"This is Congressman Robert Hamlin. How can I help you?" Bob says in response.

"Bob, this is Vice President Marron again. Calling, as we discussed yesterday, pertaining to the funeral," he declares.

"Hey, more importantly, how are you doing? How are you holding up?" Hamlin asks.

"It's tough. You know the American people expect strength in these situations. But when it's your best friend that you've known forever....it's hard," Marron sadly answers.

"I believe you. Hey, before we begin, do you mind if we pray?" Bob inquires.

"What?" Marron questions. "You were breaking up on the phone."

"I suggested we pray together. You know when times are tough I always turn to The Lord. You don't know how many times I prayed during the past few months. Also, I frequently would ask for Senator Howard's advice the past few months. I felt like I lost a close friend. The one person I respected most in politics was gone. Much like your situation... I've learned I can always turn to God and ask for his help. He never fails and He always knows the outcome. We don't that's why we get nervous or scared," Bob offers.

"Why didn't this come out during the campaign? Why wasn't anyone told?" Marron asks.

"Why would they need to know? Besides, if I announced it to the world it may not have seemed sincere. You know what the critics would have said 'Hamlin seeks votes by declaring his love of God to Christian voters!' You know how politics works. It's no one's business who I pray to, when, what for, and why. I was asking if you wished to pray thinking it would make you feel better. I was just offering to help," Bob says.

"That's alright. I am ok for now. Bob, I wanted to inquire if you wanted to deliver the eulogy at the funeral. I was asked to do so by the family today, but declined. If you say no, I'll completely understand," Marron offers.

"It's okay, I'll do it. When someone passes away the best thing is to provide comfort and solace to the family. However, in our situation, we also have to demonstrate to the nation that we're available...That we're ready to lead and confront the challenges that lie ahead. We, also, have to notify our enemies that we're awake and not playing dead. I'm here to help you and President Crowe's family," Bob asserts.

"I figured that. You're a good person Bob. You're wiser than your 29 years would indicate. Obviously, the American People saw what I know to be true. You're a leader. You're honest and can be trusted. With more experience, I'm sure you can do this job (being the U.S. President). Since you won the election, you'll have the opportunity to lead and the responsibility of demonstrating your ability," Marron asserts.

"Thanks. Always nice to hear good news or a compliment, especially considering the events of the past 24 hours," Bob says.

"You're welcome. Now, I wanted to discuss some ideas of what I'd like you to say at the funeral," Marron replies.

"Wait a minute. I'd really wish you'd reconsider your decision on giving the eulogy. You've known the President a long time. You're his friend. The country needs you," Bob calmly says.

"His family needs me. Yes, we were best friends. That's why I can't give the speech. However, you can. Be strong Bob. As we discussed yesterday, the President was considering a bipartisan administration had he been re-elected. Luckily, he didn't or I'd be leading the nation the next four years," Marron declares.

"You make it sound as if that's horrible. That it would be bad for the nation if you had won. You've been there everyday the past four years. Who's more ready, Mr. President, to perform the job now than you?" Bob inquires.

"Anyone but me...In a way, I'm happy we lost. Don't misunderstand me. We tried our best. President Crowe wanted to win. As for me, it's been a great ride. I'll get to end my political career as President. How many people can say that?" Marron asks.

"Not too many people, Mr. President," Bob responds.

"Please, it's Vice-President Marron. In the short-term, at least, that's how I preferred to be called. Anyway, I've decided I'm not talking at the funeral. More importantly, the Crowe Family asked me to convey their request that you speak on Friday. They feel it's important that you describe, in a clear voice, his legacy as a person. Also, they specifically demanded that you speak as the President. Reporters should stop complaining about how you are in any way responsible for his death. You had nothing to do with this, Bob. The autopsy results will be announced tomorrow. He died of a massive coronary induced by a blood clot," Marron whispers.

"What? That's amazing…Did you know Senator Howard died of the same cause?" Bob asks. "He had a heart attack that resulted from a blood clot?"

"No, I didn't know that. You know it's hard to keep a secret in this town (Washington, DC), but that one passed me by. Senator Howard was a good man. We had our political differences, but he always kept his word. You are always correct in your praise of him," Marron says.

"Yea, thanks. I miss him a lot. His death gave hope to a lot of people. As I mentioned I still seek his guidance. I'm sorry about your loss," Bob sadly says.

"I believe you. I came to respect your behavior during his funeral and the grace you've shown toward his family afterwards. Some people, the experts, viewed it as grand-standing. I never did. I always felt you were sincere…President Crowe's wife (Kathy) would be honored if you could show the nation the same dignity in giving the eulogy," Marron offers. In saying it, he spoke in a sincere, but firm manner.

"Yes sir, I'll be glad to help," he answers.

"That's great. I'll even ask the pastor to state how you, at the behest of the Crowe Family, are speaking today in honor of our fallen President. Here is what I want you to say…

The following day, three days before the funeral, (now) President Marron and President-elect Hamlin meet at the White House. In a surprise discussion, they agreed to talk and briefly meet with the press afterwards. Marron approached the podium accompanied by Hamlin and a few staff members, to talk to the press and a national TV audience.

"We have a brief joint statement we would like to make. Due to the events this week and of the content you about to hear, we will not be taking any questions today," President Marron declares. A series of sighs and groans are heard from the media members present.

"President-elect Hamlin and I wanted to reassure the American people, our allies abroad, and other interested parties, that our nation's defense posture is firm and ready. We just spent the past few hours participating in a series of individual conversations and conference calls with various world leaders. We jointly are here to affirm that despite the loss of President Crowe this week, all defense postures, agreements, and positions remain the same as they did seven days ago.

"We are both attending the funeral in a dew days in Cincinnati, Ohio. We will be in communication, with you all again, next week. On behalf of the family of President Crowe, we wanted to extend their appreciation for the phone calls, prayers, and letters over the past few days from millions of Americans.

"Thank you and God bless our nation," Marron states in a clear voice. They begin to depart the room as the media all shout out a number of questions. They varied to what was happening to who is giving the eulogy at the funeral.

Marron returns to the podium and replies in a clear voice, "It really doesn't matter who will be giving the eulogy. It's more important what is stated, rather than by whom. Thank you all, again, for your patience. We'll talk more in the days ahead."

Three days later the funeral was held in Cincinnati, Ohio. It was the birthplace and hometown of President William Crowe. He had never lost an election in the state of Ohio including the presidential election the week before. Ohio and Missouri are the two states that have selected the presidential winner with the greatest frequency the past eighty years. In fact, it was only the third time the candidate who had won Ohio had lost the presidential election. Quite simply, the people of Ohio loved

President Crowe. They, like the rest of the nation, felt a great deal of sadness over his passing. "I remember the President well. When he was Mayor of our city, he personally made sure my sidewalk was fixed. To most people, it was only a sidewalk, but to me it was a safety issue after I broke my leg. We'll miss him in Ohio because we knew him best," an older gentleman of 75 years old said. After speaking, he sat down and began to cry.

The news began to leak out the day before that Hamlin had agreed to give the eulogy at the funeral. When confronted at the Cincinnati Airport, located in Northern Kentucky, Hamlin replied, "My wife and I are here to pay tribute to a great American. Like other guests, we're here at the invitation of the Crowe Family. There will be more information available in the days ahead," Bob replied.

At the funeral service, President-elect Hamlin and 700 plus guests are gathering at the First Presbyterian Church of Cincinnati. It was not the church that the Crowe Family attended. It was, however, the largest church available, of that faith, in the city that was not being utilized for other funerals at the same time. President-Elect Hamlin was joined by the Family of President Crowe, Vice-President Marron, all the members of the Cabinet (minus one) and several members of the leadership of the U.S. Congress, and other invited guests. For security reasons, one member of the Cabinet is always in a different location when the remaining members are at the same spot at the same time. The remaining members of the U.S. Congress, who made the trip, were convened in the gym of a public school located across the street. They were able to view the funeral via closed circuit TV.

At the designated time in the funeral, Pastor Mark Peterson and Congressman Robert Hamlin, at the invitation of the Crowe and Marron Families, will be offering a few words today. Hamlin stands up to approach the podium. "Good morning," Hamlin says in a firm voice. It was said, almost in an encouraging tone.

"Good morning," many people offer in response. Hamlin quickly notices that most of the people present do not reply. The tone is somber.

"You know, it's not easy to say good-bye to people we like. It's even much harder to lose a loved one, such as a family member, a close friend, a co-worker who has passed away," Hamlin offers in a polite manner.

Immediately, one guest in the church wants nothing to do with Hamlin. "You killed him! It's your fault he's dead! You did it," he shouts.

"Hey, that's enough. That's uncalled for. We're in a funeral and nobody, let alone our families, are going to tolerate that! President-elect Hamlin is here because I asked him on behalf of the Crowe Family, to talk today," President Marron shouts in response.

The man who was shouting sits down, somewhat embarrassed. "No, it's okay," Hamlin says. He stands up and walks down to the twentieth row where the man is seated. He encourages the man to join him in the aisle. When leaving the podium, Bob gestures to President Marron that it's alright. The male individual is very scared, not knowing what to expect. After some hesitation and repeated encouragement he joins Hamlin in the aisle.

"Thanks for coming today. What's your first name?" Bob asks.

"Ah, Tom," he replies nervously.

"No need to be scared today. Tom, it's nice to meet you. My name is Robert Hamlin," Bob declares. When speaking, he offers Tom a firm handshake. Tom, by contrast, is hesitant and barely makes eye contact. He's more focused on looking around.

"You're not going to tell us again, how wonderful you think you are and what government programs you'll promise us, but have no intention to deliver are you?" Tom inquires in a rather condescending manner.

"No, not today. The election and the campaign ended last week," Bob replies. The speed of Bob's response prompted some people to smile.

"You just don't get it, do you? We *loved* President Crowe. He was a good man and deserved to be elected. You have no business being here today," he says. A tear begins to roll down his cheek.

"You know, it's okay to express your emotions. It's obvious you respected and miss President Crowe. Countless people do as evidenced by the millions of e-mails, sympathy cards and phone calls sent to the White House. The secret is I miss him too. Everyone here today and millions of other citizens across the nation miss our friend and President," Bob says in response.

"How can you say that? You ran against him. He lost the election because of the stress you put on him," Tom says.

"That's enough, again!" President Marron declares to the mourners present.

After a ten second pause, which seemed like an hour, Bob began talking. "I said it, sir, and I'll say it again. You see, I didn't create his heart attack. I didn't make other medical conditions (the blood clot) that caused his heart attack. I'm only a human being. I spoke with President Marron earlier in the week. I didn't invite myself here today. I was asked, on behalf of President Crowe's family, to talk. You see, President Crowe wanted to have a unity government if he had been re-elected to a second term. He wanted, to his character, to address the problems that confront us as a nation, together.

"That said, I understand your pain. My political hero passed away three months ago. I didn't believe in myself, on a lot of issues, either. However, after accepting to run with him as his running mate, I was reminded how much of a good man he was. For reasons of integrity, honesty, and just simple decency, Senator Al Howard and his wife, Lillian, are genuine and sincere people.

"I didn't talk about this much during the campaign, but I sought his advice everyday. More importantly, I prayed to God each day. I've prayed in the last three months more than I had in the last three years. I prayed not for myself, but for the strength to ask God to keep watch over my family, our campaign staff and our nation. I also sought strength to make decisions that would be in all of our interest, not just my own. God knows I still make mistakes and screw up every day. My wife and Mrs. Howard are witnesses to that. Believe me, I hear every day from Mrs. Howard how I didn't do this, that, or something else right," Bob says. Some of the audience members begin to laugh. "At first, I really started to wonder if she liked me. Then one day she confessed she was concerned because she liked me as a person, but also because Senator Howard respected me as a partner in this business.

"That's enough about me. I want to make sure you're okay. Before Senator Howard died, I had never lost anyone close to me. It's at these times when we learn adversity doesn't build character; it reveals character. President Crowe was a good man, as are you in respecting him," Bob says. He extends his arm to shake Tom's hand. After receiving Bob's hand, Tom breaks down and begins to cry. Bob holds his hand tighter to allow him to weep. "It's going to be okay man. Hang in there…You alright?" Bob whispers to ask. In fact, he stayed there the whole time until Tom looked him in the eye and said, "I'm okay, thanks." They continued to shake hands as Tom even gave Bob an embrace. "It's okay, sir," Bob replied while hugging him back. The Secret Service agents are briefly caught off guard. However, Hamlin signals to everyone that all is okay.

Bob begins to walk back to the podium. While walking, everyone begins to applaud. A few, in fact, begin to stand. When asked by his wife what he was doing, one man replied, "I'm standing because Bob Hamlin just showed me he's sincere. It would have been easy to tell him to sit down. We all saw that happen a few minutes ago. However, Hamlin chose to listen and extend his compassion. I've never seen anyone in politics do that. I wish I had voted for him!" he offers in response.

"Good morning to all. Thank you for the courtesy of your time and patience today (over the past few minutes). Together, we can be better than if we acted by ourselves. Please, let us pray…Dear God, thank you for bringing us together today. Please keep watch over President Crowe, his family, and our nation. Please be with us, the living, today and beyond. Amen.

"On behalf of the Crowe and Marron Families, particularly Mrs. Lisa Crowe and, now, President Marron, I wanted to thank the American people for their thoughts, cards, e-mails, phone calls and prayers the past few days. Under the suggestion of President Marron, we're going to do things very differently today. As you know, there are a number of speakers today, many who are better qualified and eloquent than I. They also, knew President Crowe a lot better than I did. In that regard alone, they'll be better messengers when talking about a great human being's life.

"I briefly want to acknowledge the individual laying before us today. President Crowe, our leader and Christian brother was a good man. Yes, he made mistakes. Yes, he did things we may have disagreed with. But there is no one in this room who is without fault, error or blame. I once attended a funeral where the pastor described our lives as a two act play. Act I is our time here on Earth. Today we gather and mourn the loss of our friend. The pastor referred to this period the past few days as intermission. Act II is the time afterwards in eternity. Where we go in Act II has a lot to do with how our time was spent in Act I. My pastor described our service in how we use our time, talents and treasures that have been given to us by God. He wants us to use these gifts for the benefit of helping others. We are all selfish at times, including me. God expects us to make mistakes. God understands we can't approach the passion of perfection he alone has. My pastor mentioned our desire to strive toward using our time, talents and treasures to help others less fortunate than ourselves.

"He refers to God's ultimate gift of GRACE. It stands for Growing, Rescuing, Adoring, Connected, and Enslaved. I'll be very honest with you, when you are an elected official; it's very difficult to give all your free time toward a GRACE-filled life. In fact, any effort to give your time, talents and treasures to the general public is viewed with cynicism. 'Oh, he's just trying to get votes, is a response you'll generally hear.

"I wanted to convey to you all how President Crowe was a good man. There are things during a political campaign that are offensive and mean-spirited. Many times negative comments are just downright mean. Regardless of what you do as President, ½ of the people won't agree with you. 1/3 of the people may even hate you," Bob offers. A few people laugh from his comments.

"On election night and again the following evening, President Crowe called me. He not only wanted to offer his congratulations, but genuinely showed an interest in me. He said, "Call me anytime of the day. He stated, 'Hamlin, I'll give you two reasons: One, you'll be up anyway so calling will give you someone else to talk to at 3 (am) beside yourself,' Bob conveys as the crowd laughs. He said we're fully aware of your tendency to be available 24/7 to everyone.

Anyone who you're lobbying at 3 (am) wasn't going to vote for you anyway," Bob says. The crowd begins laughing very loud, followed by a few seconds of applause. He pointed out, "Two, this is a tough job. You need to laugh, every day, when doing it. You never have a day off being President of this country. Don't get me wrong... It's the greatest job in the world. I loved it so much I ran for a second term," he stated. In hearing this, no one was laughing. You could hear a pin drop in the church.

"Then he continued," Bob offers.

"That said, Congressman, you won this job fair and square. We ran a great campaign. Vice-President Marron and I worked 15-20 hours a day, every day, for the past two months. As the race tightened up, we worked even harder. You know how this business works. Not everything is fair in politics. God knows our consultants tried to find something, anything, to use against you. The more we looked the more positive things we heard and learned about you.

He said "Congressman Hamlin, you're a good man. I wish you were less liberal," Bob conveys. The crowd begins to smile and clap again. "However, I'm proud to say you'll be succeeding me. You can call me anytime. I'm signing an Executive Order tomorrow commanding my staff to fully comply with the needs of the transition team. More importantly, the order includes the Vice-President and I. We are going to help you during this time period and afterwards, become fully acclimated to being ready to be the President of the U.S. on day one.

"You know I had a lot of respect for Senator Al Howard. His word was like a written contract. That was the absolute truth," Bob offers. The crowd rises to its feet and starts applauding. He said I knew Senator Howard a long time. We came to Washington D.C. in the same year; He from Louisiana and I from Ohio. We lived very different lives and fought for different issues. However, we both have one thing in common: our word. I like to think I can keep a promise too, just like President Crowe and Senator Howard did," Bob says in an upbeat manner.

"I wish to give you all two last things today. President Crowe did indicate there are some problems we, as a nation, will be confronting very soon. There are some countries in the world who don't like us. In fact, their distrust and anger is becoming more common each day and their hatred is gaining supporters across the globe. Together, he said, we can protect our American way of life and standard of living. We can't be consumed by our petty differences anymore," Bob declares. The attendees slowly stand, one by one, to reveal their support for Bob's statement.

"In closing, I wanted to convey how President Crowe genuinely impressed me most over the years: with his religious faith. Yes, we had our political and policy differences. You know it's difficult to discuss our religious beliefs when running for public office. It's even harder if you win and hold elective office to talk about our faith. I wanted to share my belief that President Crowe's religious convictions were genuine and sincere. I recently shared some of my beliefs with President Marron the other day. You'll be hearing more in the days and months ahead on this topic. President Crowe's life here was Act I and our time this week is Intermission. His time in eternity, with our Father, is Act II. In a famous book that was a nationwide bestseller, the author declared our goal in life is to determine our purpose for why we're here. What is it we can do to share our time, talents and treasures with others? Once that is discovered, that's what we would do with God and others in eternity.

"I think President Marron will be a consultant on world affairs or be a Political Science instructor. When we join him, we'll know we're being taught by the best. Please bow your head and pray...Oh Heavenly Father; please keep watch over the Crowe and Marron families in their time of loss. My fellow Americans, may God go before you to show you the way, above you to protect you, below you to support you, behind you to encourage you and may He go within you...Amen," Bob says in praying with the attendees in the church. When concluding, he departs the podium. After saying a few words to both Mrs. Kathy Crowe and President Marron, he walks across the church and joins his wife, Tracy, in the front row. She grabs his hand to offer a sign of support. They exchange looks at each other of acknowledgment. Bob leans toward her and say, "You know, it doesn't get easier to do this as you gain more experience and years."

"You did a great job up there. You helped provide a shoulder to their family to lean on," Tracy offers.

"Thanks. He's a good man. I'm glad to help: Bob replies.

"I know you enjoy campaigning and meeting the public. I missed you when you were on the bus tour," Tracy whispers.

"I missed you too," Bob replies as he grips her hand tighter. I'm sorry it took the President's death to end it (the bus tour). It was nice to visit cities in our nation by meeting people in their small towns. It's a lot better than flying from city to city and holding press conferences or staged events," Bob declares.

"I'm very proud of you Bob. I love you," Tracy says with a smile.

"Thanks. I love you too," Bob answers with a smile as a tear rolls down his cheek.

Chapter 7:
Inauguration Day

"...I do solemnly swear (or affirm) that I will faithfully execute the office of President of the United States, and will to the best of my ability, preserve, protect, and defend the Constitution of the United States. So help me God," Bob Hamlin proclaims to the crowd. Hundreds of thousands of people are gathered in Washington, D.C. as Robert A. Hamlin, the newest President of the U.S., is sworn into office. After a series of long ovations he begins and quickly stops his speech a number of times before the honored guests begin to sit down.

"Thank you once again. Thank you for coming and for your time. Thank you for your support and for your trust. A special note of thanks to both President Marron and Mrs. Kathy Crowe. They have been very helpful, gracious, and kind the past 2 ½ months. They have demonstrated, by both their thoughts and actions, a remarkable level of dignity. Feel free to stand and recognize them in our presence today," Bob proclaims. Once again the crowd rose to applaud for a few minutes. Afterwards, they sat back down and Bob resumed his speech.

"Okay, thank you for your thoughtfulness. In fact, there's a lot of work to be done after today. The election in November was a wakeup call for the entire nation. As you know I've had many recent discussions with President Marron. There were many common themes between the legislative and foreign policy decisions President Crowe would have pursued in a second term and what will be occurring in the Hamlin Administration. As stated earlier, President Marron was incredibly helpful to me. I've asked him and he has accepted, to serve in our administration as the Secretary of State," Bob declares. The crowd was so quiet, you could have heard a pin drop.

"Yes, I told you things were going to be done differently the next few years. Permit me to back up a little bit. When I first asked President Marron to stay on, he adamantly refused. I'm sure there were a number of reasons why. But after many hours of discussing the issue the past two months, I asked him one last time to accept the position. Why? We need him. While speaking with him, I portrayed our foreign policy relationships with a number of scenarios for the nation.

"My fellow Americans, we have some foreign policy issues that we are going to face in the years ahead. I asked President Marron to stay on as the Secretary of State, the leading foreign policy advisor in the country, because we need him. We're going to be asking our allies to do a lot with us. We needed to choose someone who our allies know and trust. We, as a nation, have to select someone that other nations respect and know that we're serious. Yes, it is a move that does not fit the norm. However, the presidential campaign and election over the previous four months certainly did not fit the norm either. We are not here to follow and react. During the next four years, we will continue the trend of leading. We'll also be challenging you, our nation's citizens, including me, to do things differently. We will think outside of the political and legislative box," Bob assures the audience. Some polite response was provided from what they heard. Perhaps they are shock form what here hearing.

"We're also going to address the competitive situation of our businesses in the world marketplace. I promise you this: we are going to rebuild our manufacturing sector in this nation," Bob declares. The crowd, consisting of thousands of union workers from the Midwest, wildly cheers the news. "However, everyone, it's not going to be easy. It took a long time to get into this mess: manufacturing plants deteriorating, the surrounding roads not being maintained and the tax base of countless communities disappearing. It's going to take time to fix the problem. There will be a lot more jobs lost before things get better.

"On a positive note, we've already started to begin the process to create a better future. Vice-President Touter led a meeting in November about our manufacturing sector in Des Moines, Iowa. A lot of inspired, forthright, and ambitious discussions were held on what to do. Some were heated and a few more hostile. However, that's good because each side, labor and management, had ample opportunities to express their ideas on the problem. However, I want you to understand that things are going to get worse before they get better," Bob announces. There was no positive response from the audience hearing the previous statement.

"We, also, have a lot to do with how we interact with each other. When writing this speech the other day, I was advised not to refer to certain topics, including this one. However, I'm not trying to win the award for Mr. Congeniality. In fact, the election was over two months ago," Bob says with a smile. We all know what I'm referring to. We, including me, have difficulty approaching people who are different than us. We may have different views, religious beliefs, skin color and orientations.

"You may be asking: why are we even having this discussion? Here is a simple answer to the problem: Focusing on our differences stops us from building common ground to solving problems. Here's an example: Consider the problem of illegal immigration. We have millions of people who are living here illegally in the U.S. Much of the hatred stems from the fact that many of those individuals are a different skin color and don't speak the English language. I am here, today, announcing the need to grant a general amnesty to anyone who can prove they are here today. That's paperwork with their name on it and being able to prove they are living in the U.S now," Bob says. Thousands of people applaud the statement.

"However, here is a view many of you don't want to hear. Let me repeat the fact that few people dispute: there are millions of people who are living here illegally. They are not supposed to be here. So here is a compromise that will be submitted in a bill and sent to Capitol Hill next week. I will be proposing that we offer amnesty to the millions of people who are here, illegally, today. They will have to obtain written documentation and get it notarized to prove they are here today. Proof of their residency here could be a paycheck, pay stub, letter, or an electric bill. After today, that's it. We're not going to allow anyone else to be here who is not here legally. After today, if you can't prove you were here today, we're sending you back," Bob says. His comment was met with both wild cheers and boos.

"Wait a minute. Why are you booing? Everyone wants compassion on this issue. I'm offering to send legislation to the

Congress to let millions of illegal immigrants stay here forever. We've had too many people abuse the process. For example, if you're being paid in cash and don't receive a pay stub: You're breaking the law, again. I know a news flash. The employer who is paying you without taxes being withheld is also breaking the law. Get this folks: millions of middle-class, American citizens, have to pay their fair share of taxes. Starting now, everyone will pay their share of income and Social Security taxes. The days of the free ride of not paying your taxes regardless if you are the employee or the company or business owner are over," Bob affirms. Thousands of people cheer and roar their approval.

"Rest assured, my fellow Americans, we are going to address tomorrow's issues today. How many of you like the job we're doing in educating our children in our schools?" Bob inquires. Thousands of people boo. Folks, I don't like what we're doing either. The system is bad. Our public school system has found a way to find opponents on both sides of the political spectrum. A sure sign of how poorly a governmental program is operating when no one likes what we're doing and neither side can agree on what to do."

"My fellow Americans, today we begin a new journey. We are going to improve our public school system. Statistics from major television networks support how poorly U.S. high school students each compare to counterparts from around the world. We have failed you. After a great deal of research, I have determined who's to blame. You want to know? Well, look around you. Or better yet, look in the mirror. We're all to blame. You see, it boils down to everyone is fighting for their specific special interest. From the school administrator to teachers to parents to other union members to principals, we all have our fears and are pursuing a defense of our positions in the system. My question is who, of all the people involved in the day to day operations of the system, is fighting for the school children?" Bob asks. The crowd is incredibly quiet.

"It appears, from your lack of response or anger that there aren't too many people fighting for the children. After all, they don't make political contributions, cannot provide endorsements and legally can't vote. Let's be honest, it's real easy to ignore their needs and interests. And God knows we certainly don't want to discipline the bad apples or upset '*Johnny*' because we're afraid of getting sued. Here's a challenge I'm issuing today: Let's stop fighting for ourselves and start considering fixing the problem. I'm going to begin incorporating the involved participants.

"Legislators: I'm beginning with you intentionally. Too many times we, the decision-makers, believe it's really about us. After all, we are most concerned about getting reelected. Oddly, many of us pretend to know the answers about public education even if we have not stepped foot in a school since the day we were a student there. Many of us believe we are experts and parents, yet we don't even have a student attending a public school. Many of us think we know what to do, but we've never been an instructor in the classroom for a day," Hamlin states. Thousands of teachers in the audience begin to applaud loudly. "We demand more accountability in our schools, yet we don't demand the same standards of excellence for the billions of dollars appropriated for road construction projects. Could it be because the contractors donate millions of dollars to our political campaigns when a school child doesn't or can't?" Hamlin challenges the people present to the support of those present.

"Let me give you an example. Back in my home state of Illinois, the members of the General Assembly can't agree on what ranking we are in terms of our tax contributions Critics of an inequitable system state we are ranked 45th or even last (among the states) regarding the amount of our investment and the wealth of our state's citizens. Opponents of budgeting more state tax dollars defend the effort we're making by saying, 'we're not really last; we're 22nd.' They combine the state and local tax dollars and declare how that's really the state's contribution because the legislature created or can take away the local units of government appropriating the monies. The amazing thing is that their proud of being ranked 22nd. Don't the children deserve to be ranked #1?" Hamlin shouts as the audience stands to applaud. "Let's make it simple and ask yourself this: What college football team would be happy to be ranked 22nd when they have the talent, resources, and capabilities to be the best or a national champion? If you can figure it out, please let me know" Hamlin offers. The seriousness in his desire to accomplish this is clearly evident.

"Students: we're going to provide the resources to make your schools safer, your textbooks more current, the buildings more appealing and your technology more meaningful. I promise you today and I guarantee to the Congress now; as a nation we will commit , my ourselves to obtain the necessary monies for the soul and spirit of our school children!" Bob shouts while raising his fist. The crowd erupts in approval providing a standing ovation for the deceased Senator. "Throughout his life former Senator Al Howard gave his time and energy toward many issues, including monies for our public schools. As he believed in me, students, I believe in you. That said, put down the stupid video games, take off the baseball cap, turn off the explicit rap songs and complete your homework. Make an effort to try harder and be a responsible participant in the school system," Bob declares to the audience. The teachers present stand and wildly cheer his position.

"Finally, an elected office holder has the spinal cord to tell our students to put away the negative influences that impede their ability to learn," a school administrator from Pittsburgh, Pennsylvania whispers to a school principal standing next to him.

"Teachers... Boy do you have a thankless job. Regardless of the hours you put in and the efforts you make, we never seem to get the help to our students in need. Too many people believe you work 9-3 and celebrate every conceivable holiday. They never see the endless supply of papers you have to grade. And God forbid sending a note home to '*Johnny*' to notify his parents that their son has a behavioral or learning problem," Bob says. The teachers loudly shout in hearing their pleas confirmed.

"That said, I want to tell you something. You're not going to want to hear this: we need to modify the tenure system," Bob declares. The teachers present become very quiet or hostile.

"Didn't we give President Hamlin our support? Haven't we endorsed him every election in his career?" one leader of a teacher's union from Illinois reluctantly asks.

"Yes, teachers, you have helped me. In turn, I have supported your legislative agenda. As I made clear to the students, we're going to create better schools and provide the necessary resources, including money, to make it work. But please listen to me. I can't do this alone. The Senate is controlled by the other political party. In return, for their agreement to allocate more money into our schools, I will propose the following: that we end or curtail tenure for elementary school teachers," Bob offers. The crowd becomes very animated. The teachers present in the crowd are booing loudly. Other attendees are applauding, but they are clearly the minority.

"My fellow Americans and in particular, my friends, please let me explain my rationale. In high school and in college, we discuss topics that are much more controversial. We need to permit academic freedom of thoughts and ideas. A democracy rests on the consent of the governed. It requires an open exchange of debate to encourage dialogue on issues that provide us with the greatest challenge. On the other hand, students in high school are young adults. In many states, they are old enough to be tried as criminals. College students are legally eligible to vote. We should not alter the process for these students.

"However, elementary school children are not adults. They cannot vote. Legally, they have few, if any, rights. It may not be fair, but that's how it is. More importantly, I read a series of statistics earlier of how high school students are performing. Please, let me repeat the numbers from earlier. Evidence from a variety of sources reveal how poorly U.S. high school students rank and compare with their counterparts from around the world. We have failed you. My goal is to address what we're doing in grammar school so we don't read about how poorly our high school students are doing when compared to other nations. These numbers demonstrate the system is broke and we need to fix it.

"Please allow me to offer a better example. Every employee at the school knows there is one, maybe more, teacher there who has overstayed their welcome. You know who they are. The classic example is the teacher who is 2-3 years away from retirement. They have countless years in the district and won't leave because they have tenure. In truthfulness, they are, also, victimized by an under funded pension system. They are frustrated and in a rut. Despite having the greatest level of job security, they are the teachers who are the least willing to try to do something new. They rationalize their opinion by saying 'well, we've always done things this way', Bob offers. He pauses to add emphasis to his last sentence. Many of the more vocal critics of Bob's position are very quiet at this time.

"You know who else can name the one (one more) teacher at their school I'm referring to? They are the parents, the students and the administration. Every participant in the system knows the problem this employee creates and no one can do a thing about it. Frequently, you'll see two effects on the students: One, they run this classroom. The teacher, since he or she gave up years ago, refuses to maintain the level of discipline needed in an elementary school classroom. Two, you'll hear the parents bring the up the lack of innovation into their child's classroom. They'll say something like, 'well, in the other second grade classroom, here is what they're doing. That sounds like fun.'

"Subsequently, you'll see the parents bring up the lack of innovation in their youngest child's room. They may even say, you know these exercises sound a lot like what my eldest son was doing, eight to ten years ago. Maybe these exercises worked then, but could we try something new? They may even suggest that all the second grade teachers meet to jointly plan activities for all the children of the same grade. Statistically, you'll see this teacher will refuse to participate, criticizing the importance of the concept. They'll decline to discuss the idea and fail to see the importance of working as a team to fulfill and dare I say exceed, the expectations of the school district.

"God knows we can do better than that. God knows there are a lot of reasons why our schools are failing. We need to finally find a pension system .... get this...so we can remove these types of teachers from the classroom," Bob shouts. Many people in the crowd now cheer enthusiastically on the idea.

"Parents: What a vital role you perform... You help out at lunchtime and on Hotdog Days. You attend Parent - Teacher

Nights. Also, you help provide a lot of monies of our local schools via the property taxes you pay. In fact, you pay anywhere from 50 to 95 percent of the costs of our local school districts with the fees and taxes you pay. You have every right to demand excellence in our elementary schools from each perspective.

"That said, you have to stop fighting with the teacher in that same second grade classroom," Bob declares. The teachers present are now cheering. One teacher from Merrillville, Indiana says, "He's right. It's about time an elected official stated this. We've known for years how these 'helicopters' hover over their children, failing to see any weakness in their prince or princess."

"It's time to not only be empowered but support the truth. Now, you understand how I just upset a lot of people with the proposal to end tenure for elementary school teachers. Fact: If your child brings home a note from Mrs. Smith about how *'Johnny'* was disruptive in the classroom today, again, it's time to catch on. Once is an incident. Two or more events are a trend," Bob says. Many in the crowd are laughing from his example. "Believe me; teachers have a lot of better things to do than write 'nasty grams' to the parents of the children who impeded the other children from learning in the classroom.

"All too often we hear 'the teacher was picking on my son, Johnny, again.' Too many parents continually believe their son is doing nothing wrong. Time after time, you hear them complain how their angel is being unfairly picked singled out, again. Come on; let's get real. If 30 notes are sent in a semester, how many of them can be false complaints? I've never met a teacher who was that bored! Parents…it's time to be the mature adult and discipline your child when their bad behavior is brought to your attention. Tell your kids to take off the baseball cap, turn off the music with offensive lyrics, turn off the video games and most importantly, do their homework. If you don't, the criminal justice system will," Bob asserts in a clear voice. Thousands of people stand to applaud and express their approval.

"We're now gong to change the subject. As stated earlier, President Marron has agreed to become Secretary of State. Our nation will be facing a number of foreign policy challenges in the years ahead. I'm sad to report that these issues will have to be addressed sooner than later. We hope and pray that a number of countries who have announced their desire to ignore policy agreements they previously signed, will respect the will of the world and comply with the agreements they signed," Bob mentions in a short, clear voice.

"We also have to find alternative ways to fulfill our needs for energy independence. We're all part of the problem and we all will be part of the solution. Yes, I will urge the Congress to drill in additional places. Yes, I will urge legislation to create tax incentives to fund research projects on solar, nuclear, renewable sources, wind, hot air, hell, whatever it takes," Bob says as the audience laughs at the last reference.

"However, we also have to find ways to save energy. We, including me, waste so many resources here. Ask yourselves 'how big does an SUV have to be? How much leg room do we really need? Do we really need pickup trucks that approach the 250 or 500 level series? Are we really serious about addressing the problem of imported oil or is it about trying to overcome our own individual sense of insecurity. We have American military personnel, men and women, placing themselves in harm's way to protect what, our right to drive some vehicle that can hold 50 gallons of gas?" Bob inquires. People begin to laugh at the last question. "For example, there was a movie a few years ago that described how the animals in the forest were discussing the SUV. One of the animals asked another (animal) how many people a SUV usually holds. The answer was one," Bob states. Nobody laughed at the last point.

"In concluding, I want to thank you for listening and for your support. You know, I don't do everything right either. I have made many of the same mistakes and done the same activities in the past t that I just referenced. I'll let you figure out which ones. The bottom line is this: We have an incredible number of challenges ahead of us. If we don't work together and each do our part to solve, not address, but to fix these problems, we'll just be circling the airport. The fact is your neighbors, people of faith, people of different ethnic backgrounds, and people of different ages and income levels and I need your help. Nobody can solve these problems by themselves. I don't mind taking the heat, but we need to turn down the temperature on a variety of problems.

"One last thing, I have stated this several times and I'll keep saying it: My fellow Americans, believe in you. Every time this great nation has faced challenges deemed as impossible, including putting a man on the moon, defeating our enemies in World War II, ending the Cold War, hell you name it, we were successful. We can create a better school system. We can reduce our dependence of imported oil. We can teach others to understand the importance of attending church and worship services because of the blessings God has given to our nation. We can encourage people to understand that are part of a larger community. We can prevent other nations that signed the Nuclear Non-Proliferation Treaty from developing a nuclear bomb. We can assist emerging democracies to succeed that formerly were authoritarian governments. We can teach our children the values of being honest, working hard, and reaching for the stars with their dreams.

"We know they can because numerous generations of people born in the U.S. have done it before. Listen to me please: Senator Al Howard believed in me despite several reasons not to. As he believed in me so I believe in you, the American people. Let us close today in prayer. Dear Lord, please help us to succeed in the various issues we as Americans heard today. May you go before us to show us the way; May you go above us to protect us; May you go below us to support us. May you go alongside us to accompany us and may you go within us. With your help, we've been the greatest country in the history of the world. Just because we're the best you know it doesn't mean we can't be better and address the serious problems that confront us. Through you, Father, all things are possible. With this God's people said Amen," Bob declared to the crowd before him.

"I'm glad he's not afraid to lift praise to God. Robert Hamlin may not be the most qualified person to be President of our nation. However, he will be the hardest working position to hold the office and he is a believer, as am I," Michelle Marie Landis from Wheaton, Illinois says.

After the speech, Bob Hamlin, his wife Tracy, Lillian Howard, Vice-President Sam Touter and his wife Rose traveled to the Inauguration Parade. In fact, all five individuals exited their vehicle at one point in the parade. This action was clearly against the orders of the Secret Service. They walked two blocks of the route to wave to the crowd. One couple from Louisville, Kentucky, one of the last three states on Election Night that gave Bob Hamlin his victory, held up a sign that said, '*We voted for Hamlin because he believes in US*'. The sign conveyed the message of the day. Hamlin pointed to the sign and waved to the couple. He then walked over to take his picture with them. The photo appeared on the front page of most newspapers across the nation the following day. In addition, many newspapers, even those that didn't endorse Bob Hamlin in his campaign for the U.S. Presidency, also ran the same picture on the front page of their newspapers too.

"They've got a lot of work ahead of them. Hamlin will learn that the campaign and the free ride are over," stated William T. Rhodes. He was the Speaker of the House of Representatives from Ann Arbor, Michigan.

Chapter 8:
Hail to the Chief

"Who rounded up three votes to deny this bill from passing? The Speaker did what? Are you sure? He promised us this bill would pass because he had received assurances last night of a minimum number of votes. That's it…No, thank you for the call…Yea, we'll talk later," states Kevin Chapin, the Deputy Chief of Staff in the Hamlin administration. "You won't believe this, he's done it again, that ******* (a 7 letter curse word) jerk."

"Who did what?" asks Roy Blanchard, Chief of Staff of the Hamlin administration. He was a former twelve-term congressman from Bowling Green, Kentucky. He was instrumental in providing thousands of votes in the Bluegrass State. He personally campaigned for Hamlin the last four weeks of the election. His effort helped to tip the balance in the state for Kentucky by only 32,000 votes, which helped to elect Hamlin as President. Plus, his knowledge of the legislative process as the chairman of the House Appropriation Committee was invaluable.

For political reasons, Hamlin also appointed Blanchard to assist with his relationships with other members of the U.S. House. "Congressman, I want you to be my Chief of Staff. I am forever indebted to you in assisting me to win the state of Kentucky. More importantly, your contacts will be invaluable in helping to get legislation passed. Welcome aboard" Hamlin declares after Blanchard had provided his acceptance of the appointment.

"As you know, Senator Howard was a good man, Mr. President. I worked hard to elect you because you're a good person. Your respect for the Senator from Louisiana was immeasurable, particularly to the people of the three states that helped you win: Georgia, Louisiana and Kentucky," Blanchard says.

"Speaker (William) Rhodes promised us he would have the votes to pass the President's education bill. Up to three hours ago, we had 'em (the votes). He screwed us, again, sir," Kevin clearly assets

"Hey, it's going to be okay. Tell you what, have the President be ready in three hours. I will have Speaker Rhodes here to speak with us at that time," Blanchard calmly says.

"What's going to prompt the Speaker to come here now. He proved today he has no incentive to help us" Kevin states.

"I'll personally tell him that the President wishes to speak with him. I can assure you, I'll be firm and direct with Speaker William Rhodes about what happened today and how it will not happen again. I've had issues with the guy for a long time. It's time he be notified that what he did was wrong and won't be tolerated!" Blanchard asserts.

"I don't understand how you're so calm, Mr. Blanchard. I mean, I'm really upset," Kevin says.

"In this town, Kevin, you can't take things personally. I've been here a long time, 24 years now. I've seen the good and bad qualities of elected officials in this town. Most are good people. Like every profession, there are bad apples. Most of the members of Congress are good, honest, and hard working people. It's the bad apples you hear about in the news," Blanchard replies.

"I've been here four years, sir. With all due respect, I've never liked Speaker Rhodes. The fact we lost control of the House (of Representatives) ten years ago was bad enough. Combine that with the fact that the House's leader, third in line of the Presidency, is someone who I don't like very much. It's troubling," Kevin complains. The tone in his voice demonstrates frustration.

"Well, he's done some things I didn't always agree with. However, I've never seen this type of behavior from him before. As you stated, he promised the votes would be there today on the education bill, but it didn't pass. We're not going to give him time to have a press conference to discuss or celebrate our defeat this morning. Do me a favor, get the President ready. I'll make some calls to have the Speaker here in three hours. Tell the President to let me run the meeting and handle the discussion. I think Speaker Rhodes needs to learn there's a right and wrong way to do things in this town. This was handled the wrong way... Can you do that Kevin?" Blanchard inquires.

"Yes sir. Consider it done. If the President wants the Speaker to hear his real thoughts, I'll tell him that he is to tell him that you're the Chief of Staff and that he should listen," Kevin answers. After leaving the room, a smile forms on Kevin's face. He jumps up and kicks his feet in mid-air just as President Robert Hamlin taught him to do when they were college roommates.

Exactly three hours later, a number of people are gathered in the West Wing of the White House. Gathered were four staff members, the sponsor of the bill, Congressman James Smith, Chief of Staff Blanchard, and Deputy Chief Kevin. At this time, Speaker Rhodes was escorted into the room. Nobody said anything to him as he took his seat. He had a smile on his face as he looked around the room. "Sorry about the bill today, Roy. We just couldn't deliver the votes," Rhodes said.

"I knew he was not to be trusted, but I never knew he was a snake," Kevin declares to himself. He didn't have the guts to say it out loud.

"Couldn't or wouldn't get the votes, Mr. Speaker?" Roy Blanchard politely asks.

"As you know Roy, it was a tough bill. Bills, as such, are tough to pass the first time. Lot of opposition by the unions to the tenure position," Rhodes replies.

"Lot of support by the teacher unions to have the bills passed. It had a great deal of new money for the schools. Strong promises for accountability. Lots of children across the nation, including Michigan, would have been helped by this bill, a good bill, Mr. Speaker," Rhodes says. His tone was polite, but clear.

"Tough bill, Roy, tough bill. You know how difficult it is to pass controversial legislation, even if it is intended to help people. Surely, this bill had some good ideas. However, some pretty powerful people opposed it," Rhodes affirms.

"We saw that firsthand, Mr. Speaker," Blanchard responds.

"Saw what Roy?" Rhodes says in a condescending manner.

"How some powerful people opposed the education bill, Mr. Speaker," Blanchard answers.

"What are you alleging Roy? Are you implying that I hurt this bill?" Rhodes asks. His attitude has changed to being very negative, even hostile, since arriving for the meeting. He stands to demonstrate his opposition to the last question presented to him.

"I stand by my statement, Mr. Speaker," Blanchard calmly replies. At this point, President Robert Hamlin enters the room. He is accompanied by two Secret Service agents and another member of Roy Blanchard's staff. Everyone stands upon the President's entry. Speaker Rhodes stands, but the speed at which he moved was very noticeable.

"Good afternoon everyone; Please be seated. I'm glad you could attend on such short notice. Mr. Speaker, I know you're very busy having previously been a former member of the House. I greatly appreciate you making time to join us here.

"With all due respect, Mr. President, I don't understand why I was called here. After all, I did all I would could do with the bill today. In fact, after a great deal of opposition one month ago, I got us within a few votes. I'm terribly sorry," Rhodes says.

"Well, Mr. Speaker, I truly value your help the past month on this bill. I know it took a number of revisions and countless hours lobbying undecided members of the House. Thank you again.

"...However, Mr. Blanchard, my Chief of Staff requested that we sit down and talk today. So, with your permission I'm yielding the balance of my time to Mr. Blanchard. You have the floor, sir," Hamlin states. He intentionally chose these words because they are frequently used within the U.S. House of Representatives itself.

"Thank you, Mr. President. I've been here a long time and I'm proud to help work for you sir," Blanchard says. He receives a nod of appreciation from President Hamlin. "In fact, Mr. Speaker, I'm well-educated with how the U.S. House works too, having served there a total of 24 years. I was, also, a committee chair for two years and the minority spokesman for the last two years. I know it's a difficult job with long hours. You are confronted by a variety of interests, everyday."

"However with all respect, Mr. President, having served in the House for a long time, I can tell when someone was railroaded," Blanchard politely states.

"Say what! Are you implying that I was to blame for what happened today Roy?" Rhodes angrily asks.

"Mr. Speaker, I'm not implying anything; I'm shouting it," Blanchard answers.

"Who the hell do you think you are?" Rhodes yells across the room. If there wasn't a lady present, I'd say something that would truly be mean and offensive," Rhodes declares.

"Ms. Newby (Karen Newby, the Secretary of Defense) is a tough cookie, Mr. Speaker. That's why the president hired her. That said, your language here can't be any worse than the offensive behavior you displayed today on the education bill," Blanchard asserts in a clear, but elevated voice.

"You can shut the hell up, Roy! Mr. President, I'm not going to sit here and be talked down to here by him or anyone else. I'm the Speaker of the U.S. House!" Rhodes shouts.

"How dare you come here and pretend you don't have a clue what happened. The bill lost, Mr. Speaker, because you made phone calls this morning to ten members of the House and convinced three of them to switch their votes from yeas to nays!" Blanchard yells.

"You're full of crap. I was lobbying to have the bill pass until last night," Rhodes angrily protests.

"Then you worked this morning to defeat the bill....I called and spoke with members Jones, Smith, and Powers. They verified what I had suspected: you contacted them and demanded that they switch their votes or their bills would be pigeon-holed in committee, forever," Blanchard states to those present in the room.

"That's a damn lie Roy! I view any such allegation as an attack on my character. I demand an apology before I leave this room in protest! Mr. President, aren't you going to intervene against this hypocrisy," Rhodes angrily shouts.

"I would intervene, Mr. Speaker, if there wasn't any evidence to back up the allegation. However, I was delayed to this meeting because I, too, spoke with Congressmen Jones, Smith and Powers. All three of them confirmed your discussions with each of them this morning. In addition, all three of them confirmed the threat you made against other legislation to benefit their districts if they did not vote to oppose this bill. Carry on, Mr. Blanchard," Hamlin asserts.

"Why you SOB! Who the hell do you think you are?" Rhodes shouts in the direction of President Hamlin. The individuals present in the room gasp in shock.

"Mr. Speaker, I've been in this town a long time. I've seen big egos come and go. However, I've never seen anyone berate and talk down to the President of the U.S., regardless of their political party. There's only one SOB in this room, Mr. Speaker, and it's you!!" Blanchard yells back in frustration.

"As long as I'm the Speaker of the House this bill will not be approved. In fact, any such legislation introduced by the Hamlin administration (stated in a condescending tone) will never pass!!" Blanchard yells. The staff members sit there in surprise as the Speaker just acknowledged that he lied about what happened with the education bill just a few hours earlier.

"...Mr. Speaker, let me tell you what's going to happen. Tomorrow, you are going to re-introduce the bill. Next week you will suspend the rules of the House to allow for a second vote in the House. This bill has the votes to pass. As you know, the Executive Branch has the authority to place a hold on the expenditure of monies from appropriation bills. If you don't have the bill voted on next week, all federal monies appropriated for the state of Michigan can be suspended, indefinitely," Blanchard calmly states.

"You a------(a seven letter curse word) Do you know you'll never win Michigan in your re-election bid if you do that?" Rhodes jokingly answers.

"Mr. Speaker, Robert Hamlin is not running for re-election to a second term. He has already made that announcement publicly, at least, on three to four occasions. I believe he keeps his promises" Blanchard declares.

"For the record, President Hamlin has made that statement, at least, ten times," Kevin affirms. All eyes turn to him as he says it.

"Unlike you, Mr. Speaker, I've come to learn and appreciate that President Hamlin is a man of his word. He may be a number of years younger than you. However, he's honest and is a man of strong character to perform the duties of being President of our nation. It's a level of character that you will never have," Blanchard answers. (During the last campaign numerous critics, including Speaker Rhodes, questioned Robert Hamlin's character to be the U.S. President).

"You wouldn't! You can't! Mr. President, say it isn't so," Rhodes yells.

"We spoke with our lawyer this morning Mr. Speaker. Turns out Mr. Blanchard is correct about the issue of impounding federal monies. Given the events of the past 24 hours, I believe the offer presented by Mr. Blanchard is incredibly fair. Congressmen Jones, Smith and Powers have a press conference scheduled outside the door of your office, at 9 (am) tomorrow. I doubt the taxpayers and voters of Michigan or this great country really want to learn the truth of how this bill lost. In fact, I believe you, Speaker Rhodes, will be a big supporter of various legislative proposals of the Hamlin administration for the years ahead," Hamlin replies.

"And if I don't?" Rhodes quietly asks.

"Then the three Congressmen will share with every political correspondent (reporter) tomorrow what happened this morning. All three are prepared to ask for your resignation tomorrow," Blanchard says in response.

"I see…Well, given the choices available, I will comply with your request," Rhodes says in a somber manner.

"Mr. Speaker, it wasn't a request or an idea. It's an order," Blanchard calmly says.

"Well, sounds like we have made some progress here this morning. I have to step out for a few hours. I have decided to take flying lessons. Today is my first flight with the instructor," President Hamlin declares in an upbeat mood.

"What are you learning to fly, a private jet?" Kevin angrily asks.

"No, it's a combat aircraft. We're going to fly with some officers of a F-16 squadron today. It's always good to take up a new hobby. Keeps the mind alert…Never know when such training would be needed," Bob replies.

"Oh, hell no. Tell me he's not going to go on a mission sometime" Kevin whispers to himself as Hamlin departs the staff meeting.

"Wait a minute… You were learning how to fly a plane?" Emily asks.

"Yea, lots of weird things occurred last night" Bob replies.

"Have you ever had this dream before?" she inquires

"Never; Not once. Things like this you don't easily forget. I'm sure of this; if it had happened before, I'd had remembered it" Bob responds.

"You're kidding me, right" she asks. Emily is not sure whether his story is believable or it Bob has other deeper issues to work through.

"No I'm serious. Look, I'm not crazy. I've never had a dream like this before, ever" Bob offers, sensing Emily's fear.

"What happened next?" she questions. She was torn between wanting to run, just have Bob end the conversation or have him share more information. "For some strange reason, I believe you…"

"You have reports that who is doing what? Are you sure?… Has this been confirmed by the usual sources?…I see….Well, we suspected this would happen…No, not a surprise at all…Yes, it appears the day we've feared may now be upon us…Thanks for your call…Yea, we'll talk later…," Peter Thomas says.

"Who was that?" Mike Harnett, a member of the National Security Council, asks. He worked for Pete Thomas and had known him for the previous six years. He was very concerned about Pete's body language. Are you alright?

"No, I don't think so. Just spoke with a contact I have at the CIA. He stated that he has two sources who just confirmed the Iranian Government has successfully launched a missile. It can fly 1500 miles, maybe more. It's the third successful test of the missile in the past year," Pete nervously offers.

"Wow, that's pretty far. Was it successful? Meaning?" Harnett replies.

"It hit the target. The fact the missile works is not the worst part. My contact indicated that a number of sources, multiple people, confirmed that the Iranian Government is moving materials from their underground testing facilities. He is fearful they may make threats to launch an attack against Israel," Pete declares.

"Come on. The Iranians make a lot of noise, but they wouldn't dare attack another country. Israel would retaliate and bomb them back to the Seventh Century," Harnett answers.

"You don't understand. He has contacts over in Israel. They apparently notified him that Israel won't wait to see if the missiles can be retro-fitted with a nuclear warhead and still work. He is very fearful that Israel will attack very soon...No later than 20 days," Pete replies.

"If Israel attacks, that will start World War III. The other nations of the region won't tolerate Israel attacking anyone. It does not matter that their actions could be in self-defense to deter a larger attack on their country. The region's countries would view an attack on a Muslim nation as an invasion on them all," Harnett responds.

"Exactly," Pete states.

"You'll have to notify President Hamlin what you've learned. We can't let them attack, even if it's in their best interest," Harnett states.

"You're right," Pete says. He pauses and makes a phone call. "Sharon, can you contact President Hamlin?" Sharon Perry was the receptionist at the White House. She personally worked at Robert Hamlin's Congressional Office back in Homewood, Illinois and later in Orland Park, Illinois when the office was relocated.

"Sure. He's in a meeting now. I'll have him call you as soon as it's over," she replies.

"Okay, but afterwards, we may need to gather the Vice-President and the National Security Council," Peter Thomas declares.

"Is everything alright Peter?" Sharon politely asks.

"Not really... I just received a phone call that requires immediate attention. It's not good news," Peter Thomas replies.

"I'll see what I can do regarding a later meeting. In fact, it may be easier to convene this than get the President. Let me make a few calls and get back to you," she answers.

"That's great. I understand how busy the President is. I'll wait to hear from you. Thanks for your help," Pete Thomas says.

"What happened?" Mike Harnett inquires.

"Get ready. I know it's late in the afternoon but we'll be attending a meeting tonight. Sharon Perry knows how to get things done," Pete offers.

At approximately 5:45 (pm) a meeting of key administration officials and the National Security Council (NSC) was convened. The attendees included President Hamlin, Vice-President Touter, Rob Lowenstein, the National Security Advisor, Pete Thomas, Mike Harnett, Karen Newby, Secretary of Defense, Roy Blanchard, Kevin Chapin, Bill Ashton, Director of the Central Intelligence Agency, Secretary of State Marron, Congressman James Turner (D - Merrillville, Indiana), former Chairman of the House Intelligence Committee and now the Minority Spokesperson on the Intelligence Committee. House Speaker William Rhodes was also invited to attend. He had not arrived yet, but was in route.

Those present began speaking amongst themselves with Lowenstein and Newby giving a historical presentation of Iran. Karen Newby was a former six- term congresswoman from Santa Monica, California. Privately, Robert Hamlin greatly respected her. She was a former Republican who had switched political parties five years before. She was a moderate on most issues, but was a very strong supporter of the Defense Department. She had immersed herself in studying defense-related issues after her husband, Gregg Newby, died in a car crash. He was a former State Treasurer in California, who previously was a Congressman himself. Many pundits believed he had quite a political future ahead too. After his death, she decided to immerse herself in work; partly due to grief, partly as a way to become more knowledgeable on a substantive policy issue.

It wasn't that she was a strong defender of American foreign policy. She did, however, have a large number of defense contractors headquartered there. She switched political parties over the party's position on abortion. "Some day, she will be elected President of our nation. Regardless of what viewed as gamesmanship over one issue, she will win (the presidency) some day. She's incredibly intelligent, even smarter than me," Hamlin would say to all audiences of Democratic activists each time he was asked about her.

"At 5:58 (pm) President Hamlin enters the room. He is accompanied by House Speaker William Rhodes. Beforehand, Blanchard had asked, point blank, why Speaker Rhodes would be invited. President Hamlin replied by saying, "One, we may need his help on obtaining support on this issue and other legislative items. Also, since you addressed him two months ago, he's been very helpful to us on Capital Hill getting our bills passed. He's become, through your efforts, a very helpful member on the team."

"Well, if this issue escalates, it will be a real test regarding his spot in the team photo, Mr. President," Blanchard says.

"It may be a severe test for us all. Let's ask for God's help that we don't need the Speaker's assistance. If we do, things have really gone down hill, sadly," Hamlin answers.

Everyone invited was now present. President Hamlin describes the reason for the meeting. He introduces Pete Thomas and asks him to repeat what he had been told earlier in the afternoon. Pete begins by describing key information and specific examples about how his sources have been correct in the past. The examples surprise some experienced and hardened participants in American foreign policy the past ten years. Some of the people in the room had been part of previous administrations that had sent American troops in various missions across the planet. On some instances, American soldiers were killed as a result of their decisions.

"That's amazing how accurate your sources were," Secretary of State Marron declares.

"Well, I'm sad to report Mr. Secretary that I spoke with several of them today. As you can assume, they don't have great news for us," Pete Thomas says in response.

"In fact, it's been a long time, nearly three decades, since we've heard good news from Iran. I'm very fearful what Peter is about to say is bad," Secretary of Defense Newby adds.

"It is with great sadness your fears appear to be justified, Ms. Secretary," Pete Thomas answers.

"Pete, please explain for everyone what you and I briefly discussed today," Robert Hamlin offers.

"Yes sir, Mr. President. Everyone, today I contacted, spoke with four sources from various federal agencies. They each have their own contacts in the Middle East. Before I begin, please understand that these four people were directly involved with having knowledge of some of the foreign policy incidents listed earlier. They are, bar none, the best intelligence officers I know and have worked with each of them on numerous occasions. They have incredible success rates," Pete Thomas says.

"Well, it only begs me to ask, but have they ever been wrong," inquires Rob Lowenstein, National Security Director and Pete's boss.

"Never on intelligence issues sir. I'm sure they have picked the wrong professional football team on Sundays but never on national security matters. Never," Pete reiterates. Not one person present laughs at the football comment.

"Where do they fall on the political spectrum (liberal, moderate, or conservative)?" Speaker Rhodes asks.

"I'm not sure where they fall on political issues. However, on foreign policy matters, they lean toward being conservatives," Pete Thomas answers.

"I like what I'm hearing already. Accurate and intelligent," Speaker Rhodes says.

"Mr. Speaker, with all due respect, the issue pertains to the credibility of Pete's sources, not whose candidate to vote for," Don Blanchard replies.

"Nor does it pertain to being too sensitive, Don. Sometimes, serious issues require taking a step back and introducing some humor. I apologize to everyone here, who took offense at my last comment," Rhodes states.

"Gentlemen, there are important problems that face us in the world today. I wanted to share what I learned afterwards. In addition, I placed a call to a different source. He alleges the Iranians are ready to retrofit a missile with a nuclear warhead. To do that, they'll need more processed uranium from their production facilities," Pete Thomas offers.

"Do we know where these facilities are?" Speaker Rhodes asks.

"Yes, we do. The locations are underground. The problem is there are several of them and facilities are hundreds of yards in length and width. It would take a number of precision bombs from an aircraft squadron or more to destroy them. It may even require some follow-up with additional cruise missiles after some 'bunker buster' bombs were dropped there," Secretary Newby answers.

"Would it be easier to attack them when they're moving the uranium when it was being moved?" President Hamlin inquires.

"Yes, but that comes with difficulties also. We would have little to no warning when the trucks would be departing the facility. We would have no way to verify if all the uranium was being transported or if some was intentionally left behind. I assure you we can and will eradicate whatever moves from these locations. All we would need is the order to be given by the President," Secretary Newby replies.

"We have the ability to move our satellites to watch any activity at those locations," Bill Ashton, Director of the CIA provides.

"Make a phone call, please, and have one to two satellites view what's moving there," President Hamlin states.

"Yes, Mr. President. Consider it done," Bill Ashton says.

"How accurate is it? What can it see?" Mike Harnett asks.

"We'll know what's being moved and when it starts happening," Ashton answers.

"Bill, please go make the phone call and report back here when it has been completed. Thank you," Hamlin declares. As soon as Hamlin completed his sentence, Ashton was on the phone commanding the order.

"You know, I appreciate your sources' accuracy and service to our country, Mr. Thomas." However, please allow me to play the devil's advocate. How do we know your sources are right? Let's say, hypothetically, that they're incorrect. Don't get me wrong: The Iranians are no friends of ours and have financed a number of terrorist organizations the past twenty years. Are you prepared to begin a Third World War if your sources are not right?" Vice President Sam Touter inquires. His tone is polite, but very clear.

"Mr. Vice President I am seeking verification of this information from a number of additional sources. The people who contacted me are very good. However, to this date, they have never been wrong on national security matters," Pete Thomas responds as his phone rings. He steps out to answer the call.

Bill Ashton returns to the room. "Mr. President, I have been notified the satellites have been redirected over the nuclear facilities where we believe the uranium is being reprocessed. If anything departs from or arrives at these locations, we'll know right away," Ashton declares.

"Thanks… Now Karen I have a question on preparedness. If we were to learn the trucks were arriving at or leaving these facilities, right now, how long would it take our fighter planes and cruise missiles to reach their destination?" President Hamlin inquires.

"It's hard to say," Karen Newby answers as she is cut off.

"Since we have satellites pointed directly at the site, we'd be able to track and follow the trucks, correct Bill?" Hamlin questions.

"Yes, Mr. President," Bill Ashton replies.

"Let's try another approach. Say we had our planes in the air near the Iranian border, 24 hours a day, how long would it take us to hit 'em?" Hamlin asks.

"It would take us about an hour to take out the trucks," Secretary Newby responds.

"…We would probably follow the truck's demise with B-52's terminating the facilities. They would never be able to be used again," President Hamlin affirms.

"That's not bad. However, the problem is we don't know where the trucks would be going," Vice-President Touter asks.

Bill Ashton walks away from the door and runs toward Vice-President Sam Touter. He leans forward so only he can hear and whispers, "Actually, Mr. Vice-President, we do, have a strong idea where they might be going," Bill Ashton whispers.

"Any estimates available if we were to launch a pre-emptive strike, how many casualties there would be at the manufacturing facilities? Do we know how many people work there on each shift?" President Hamlin inquires.

"Why does it matter?" Rob Lowenstein answers.

"It matters because I'm the Commander-in-Chief. If we're going to bomb these facilities, I want to know how many people work there and how many people would be terminated," Hamlin declares.

"Mr. President, are you hesitating on attacking the locations?" Lowenstein inquires.

"I am committed to defending the national security interests of the U.S., but thanks for asking. In fact, I've been training the past few weeks at the Air Force base. If the day comes where we have to attack, I'm going with our servicemen and women to participate, personally," Hamlin says.

"What?" Lowenstein replies.

"I'm not going to deploy our military personnel unless I'm willing to go myself. I don't want anyone here to forget that I'm of draft age. Yes, I won the Presidential election despite not having a military background. Years from now, after I have left the presidency, I will be a combat veteran of the U.S.," Hamlin says.

"Do you going, Mr. President, reduce the value of or demean what they do?" Lowenstein asks.

"No, what I do provides value to their mission, dedication, commitment and professionalism. They train each day, knowing they could be deployed anywhere in the world. I assure you, I will compliment their service and job duties by accompanying them in a foreign policy endeavor when needed. Mr. Lowenstein, you seem very ambitious about the need to attack the Iranian Government. Believe me, they've earned the right to be removed from office. Are you willing, right now, to join me in this mission?" Hamlin asks. He took the extraordinary effort to slow down his speaking in the last two sentences. Lowenstein lowered his head and refused to answer the question for some time.

"Mr. President, are you sure? I mean, you don't have a pilot's license. How does your wife feel?" Vice-President Touter inquires. By his tone he was completely unaware of Robert Hamlin's newest hobby.

"Yes, I'm sure because it's the right thing to do. I began flying because there is always the risk these events we're discussing could occur. Our troops prepare, each day, for such circumstances. I would never commit our troops to do anything if I wasn't willing to serve myself. For the record my wife doesn't know about me learning to fly in a military aircraft. Some prior Presidents hid girlfriends from their spouses. I chose to pursue a hobby that serves a public purpose, but hid the news. Didn't want to share the information for fear it would scare her," Hamlin answers in a clear and firm voice.

"Whether someone learns how to fly is not important. The real issue is the foreign policy actions of the Iranian Government. They have clearly violated the international agreements they signed. Their word means nothing and their signature means even less," Kevin asserts. After speaking he turns toward Robert Hamlin. He wanted to express his clearly support his best friend's statements. Privately, however, he was very concerned about President Hamlin's decision.

"Thanks. We all have a job to do. We're going to continue to monitor this situation. Secretary Newby, I want you to prepare with the Joint Chiefs of Staff a plan of action for attacking these locations and any convoy that steps foot on that property. I look forward to reading it tomorrow morning.

"Peter Thomas; Get some sleep. Around 2 or 3 (am) I want you to resume contacting your sources. They are 7-8 hours ahead of us. Let's see what they're hearing at that time.

"Bill, commence communications with our personnel in the region. Let's see if they are learning the same info as what Peter's sources have come across. If they're not hearing what other people are, I want you to report that, also.

"Rob, I want you to meet with your staff. I'm directing the NSC to filter through what various sources are reporting. Pete and Bill, you are to report to Rob's staff for a more thorough debriefing, starting at 7 (am) Eastern Time. Rob, I want the NSC to prepare a written report that is to be updated every six hours starting at 1 (pm) Eastern Time. However, if something of importance happens, we want to know immediately

"We're not going to take any military action unless we're absolutely sure what the Iranians are planning to do. However, I want to make two points very clear: If the information that Peter's sources allege is proven to be true, our military will be ordered to intervene. We will not hesitate to defend the security interests of the U.S., our allies, and honorable law-abiding countries across the globe. Also, if our sources learn and confirmed by our satellites that trucks are moving from these manufacturing facilities, I can assure you that the threat will be eliminated. Any such convoy or one truck will be destroyed and the facilities will never again be usable. Let us pray," Hamlin declares. Several of the staff members are slightly caught off guard because he had never led such a prayer with his staff. Kevin, who he has known for eight years, is completely in awe.

"Dear Lord, please grant our intelligence sources the wisdom to professionally do their jobs. Please grant the Iranian Government to understand the full weight of their decisions and the actions that will result. Please protect our servicemen and women in the performance of their duties. With your help, common sense and the law-abiding nations of the world will prevail. In this we pray. Amen," Hamlin offers. A few staff members are seated there, not knowing what to say.

"Mr. President, one last question. What are you going to do tonight?" Mike Harnett asks. Everyone turns to look at him, surprised at his boldness, but glad that someone did.

"We have a state dinner tonight at the White House. I am meeting with my wife around 10 (pm) or so. Then I'll be making the rounds, contacting many of you. The bottom line is this: We all have a job to do. We all work for the American people. I'm not changing my schedule tonight or tomorrow morning so as not to alert the press that something very serious may be occurring. Whether we are here, at home, or overseas flying in an aircraft, we have this to do: Protecting the American people is our #1 duty. We will never permit the Iranian Government to threaten the security interests of the world. That includes the transportation of oil in the world economy. Isn't that right, Mr. Speaker," Hamlin says.

"Yes, Mr. President," Speaker Williams Rhodes replies.

"Thank you. May God keep watch over the United States of America," Hamlin states. He stands up to leave and the other staff members in attendance immediately rise to their feet. The time is now 6:35 (pm).

Kevin rushes to the door to exit so he can interrupt Bob Hamlin's departure. "Mr. President I wish to speak with you," Kevin says in a rather terse (mean) tone.

"I know you do, but I'm on my way downstairs to attend the dinner. I'm sure you wish to discuss the flying lessons, but I decided to do this during the transition period. I vowed I would never commit the use of U.S. Troops if I was not willing to go myself," Hamlin asserts in a clear but calm demeanor.

While they are talking they continue to walk past various security checkpoints. "I respect you for wishing to '*Be all you can be*' Mr. President, but this is serious. This isn't like playing with toy soldiers when you were a kid. You're flying affects millions of other people. Not just the American people, who you are obligated to protect, but the safety of the troops. Don't you realize that?" Kevin angrily questions.

Right then Bob Hamlin stops and turns toward his friend. He pauses before speaking to clear his thoughts. "Kevin, you're my best friend. I value and respect your opinion. That said, I've already answered why I'm doing this. We all have a job to do: You, me, our troops, and the people who were in the same meeting that just ended. Please, let me do this. I know it's dangerous, but it's the right thing to do," Bob says. He stops to move closer so only Kevin can hear what he's saying. "Listen, you know me better than anyone but Tracy (his wife). Deep down, you know why I am stepping forward to do this. We are confronted by a dangerous enemy. Yes, I'm scared too. Those planes go pretty fast. That said, the Iranians knew what they were doing. They've known, all along, that someday they would get caught. Their banking on us not knowing and more importantly not doing anything about it. Taking out these materials we discussed is the morally and politically right thing to do. I'm going to be there," Bob Hamlin declares.

"This action is not about becoming some action hero, Mr. President. There are people trained to do this who practice that every week. Let them do it, please!" Kevin pleads with his friend.

"I'll visit you tonight after the dinner, probably around midnight or so. Be sure to get some sleep. Also, don't forget to pray . Amazing things happen when we turn to God and ask for His help," Bob Hamlin replies to his closest friend.

Later that night, Bob Hamlin had returned to the private living quarters for the First Family. Located on the second floor in the White House, the President's family enjoyed a very spacious living area. Tracy Hamlin, Bob's wife, had already cleaned up and was preparing to go to bed. Bob enters the room. She had sensed something was wrong throughout the evening. However, she had some important news of her own to share.

"Hey Bob, it's good to see you," Tracy says.

"That's odd. You've never said that before," Bob replies.

"...about being good to see you? Well, you never tell me how your day was anymore. So, I decided to try another approach," Tracy offers with a smile.

"Let's just say we have another issue overseas to deal with. Another nation that thinks they're on the world stage and we won't respond" Bob whispers. "Anyway, that's not important. As you know I have a very complicated job. You said earlier you wanted to talk about something."

"Is it a good time?" she inquires.

"It's as good a time as any," Bob responds with a smile.

"Do you have any plans tonight?" Tracy asks.

"Yes, there are people at the National Security Council who are working on a major issue. I told a few of them I would stop by around midnight," Bob declares.

"Serious?" she says.

"It's serious enough to go over there. It's, also, important enough not to change my schedule. Doing so would let the press know something is up. However, at this moment, it's not serious enough to hear what news you wanted to tell me," Bob offers while standing.

"Well, I have a hard time getting time in your schedule, so here it goes. You might want to sit down. Bob…I'm pregnant," Tracy declares.

While on the edge of the bed, Bob sits there in complete surprise. "Wow. After the news I heard today, that's amazing" he says with a smile. You know, timing is everything. Wow, that's news. Being president I came to expect that nothing would surprise me anymore. Was I wrong…I mean, I'm happy for you, well, us. Are you sure?" Bob questions.

"Yes, I bought three boxes and took the test six times. I didn't want to share the news and not be sure. After all, having the President's time is very important and limited," Tracy says with a smile.

"I'm going to be a father? I mean, the greatest goal I had in life a few short years ago was being a political consultant…Now I'm the President and I'm going to be a Dad," Bob says with a smile in complete shock. "Want a hug?" Bob inquires.

"Of course I do. And Bob…I wouldn't want anyone else to be the father of our children. That's plural," Tracy says with a smile.

"We're going to have twins?" Bob asks.

"No, it'll be one baby at a time, Mr. President. That said we're going to have at least one more child" Tracy replies with a smile. Her and Bob are sitting on the edge of the bed, in a deep embrace.

"I committed myself to participating in the mission, if and when the day comes. Now, I'm going to be a father…What do I do?" Bob asks to himself, not knowing what to say.

"I know you have to go. Go be the President," Tracy says.

Bob stands up, walks toward the door, turns around and faces his wife. While smiling he says, "I love you, Tracy," as his wife smiles back at him. He exits the living quarters, proceeds down the stairway, and stops. He briefly sits down in a chair located in the hallway and says a few words of thanks in prayer. "Thank you, Lord, for this news. You know how much Tracy wants to be a Mom. Help me in the days ahead. Amen," Hamlin states.

Afterwards he sits down and calls the Prime Minister of Israel. Their phone conversation lasts for about one hour. At times, it's very acrimonious, but it ended with both men in agreement on what to do. "Nobody said this job was going to be easy. Give us the strength to do what's right," Hamlin whispers after putting down the phone.

He stands up and proceeds to walk down the hall to join the meeting of the National Security Council in session. Before entering the room Hamlin pauses to observe each person in the room.

Chapter 9:
Protecting the Safety of the World

"Good evening, Mr. President" Kevin says as President Robert Hamlin enters the room and joins a meeting of the National Security Council in progress. Everyone present stands. All military personnel are saluting, the remaining employees are all on their feet.

"Ladies and gentlemen please be seated. Earlier this evening I asked many of you to get some sleep. From now on I'll have to order you to do so. We need you well-rested to do our jobs. However, since many of you are here, what's our status?" Robert Hamlin asks in a clear and firm voice.

"It's bad news, Mr. President. It appears that Pete Thomas' sources may be correct. Some of our people in the area (Middle East) are providing similar information regarding the status of the weapons program and more importantly the intent of the Iranian Government, sir" Bill Ashton, Director of the CIA, reports.

"Well, same status here, Mr. President. Pete Thomas, as you can tell, is working the phone, with his sources. They are holding to their story of the status in Iran. I'm sad to report that additional individuals we have relied on for information in the past are confirming the intent of officials of the Iranian Government," Rob Lowenstein, the National Security Advisor declares.

"Get Defense Secretary (Karen) Newby on the phone, please," Bob Hamlin states in a firm voice.

"Good evening, Mr. President. I regret to say my sources have confirmed the allegations from earlier," Pete Thomas asserts.

"Same here, Mr. President," Mike Harnett from the National Security Council says.

"Roy (Blanchard) please do me a favor. Get Speaker William Rhodes on the phone. We're going to have a conference call ASAP," Robert Hamlin affirms.

"Mr. President, I have Secretary Newby on the phone," Bill Ashton says.

Hamlin walks over to him and takes possession of the phone. "Ms. Secretary, I'll have Bill fill you in with more details…It appears from numerous sources that the intelligence first conveyed earlier today is being verified. As soon as we get Speaker Rhodes on the phone, we're having a conference on the issue," Hamlin states.

"Yes, Mr. President," Secretary Karen Newby provides.

Hamlin deactivates the speaker phone and whispers into the receiver. "How are plans going with the (military) initiative that we discussed today? Do you and the Joint Chiefs feel we can begin, on Friday?" Hamlin inquires.

"Mr. President, I believe we can meet that goal," Newby replies.

"Can we be ready without the media and the rest of the world learning what's happening before the first 'gift package' (cruise missile) is delivered?" Hamlin inquires.

"We'll do our best, Mr. President," Newby answers.

"I need better than our best, Karen. You're incredibly good at what you do, but I need everyone there (the Pentagon) to understand this is not a chat room exercise. Be firm and tell them the subject they are discussing is not to leave that room tonight. We'll bring you into the conference call after you announce what I just said at your location, understand?" Hamlin inquires.

"Consider it done, Mr. President," Newby responds.

"That's what we want to hear. God speed to you Ms. Secretary," Hamlin says as he places the call back on hold. "Ladies and gentlemen, please wrap up your (phone) calls. We're having a meeting in five minutes. Plan accordingly."

"Yes, Mr. President," the individuals present say intermittently.

"What are you going to do?" Kevin asks as he pulls President Hamlin aside.

"It's not good…not good at all. You're my best friend. There's few people I'd want here more right now than you," Hamlin says.

"Are you going to start a war?" Kevin angrily asks.

"Wait a minute. The Iranian Government signed the Nuclear Non-Proliferation Treaty. They agreed, verbally and in a written format, never to develop a nuclear weapon. It appears that is not the case" Hamlin replies as Kevin folds his arms in disgust. "Kevin, regardless of what we decide today, I need you on board. The number one job of what we do is defending the U.S. and its people."

"Mr. President I have Secretary Newby back on the phone" Bill Ashton says.

"Thank you. Kevin, there is no greater duty than what I just said. The Iranian Government will not attack the U.S. or any other nation on our watch," Hamlin states as he walks past him.

"Ladies and gentlemen, can we please be seated. Thank you...We are joined tonight by Secretary of Defense Karen Newby from the Pentagon on the speaker phone. Wish to express my appreciation for you all being here at this late hour. Some of our pundits would say it's our job. I would reply that it's our responsibility. Although I was not here with you, I was here in spirit. We had a state dinner for the Prime Minister of India. We wouldn't want to cancel the dinner for a number of reasons. One being, I didn't wish to cause a panic with the media about any pending events on the world stage.

"Also, want to make two things absolutely clear. As you all know what's said here stays here. On occasion, we need to be reminded of this. No need for support groups with our friends or 'pillow talk' with our significant others. We work for the American people. Not just the voters and those who are civic-minded. We work for every American citizen, regardless of their race, creed, social status, level of income, or orientation. Our responsibility is to protect the United States of America from all enemies, foreign or domestic. We will follow through on that goal," Hamlin asserts in a loud and clear voice. "Now, Pete Thomas, will you please tell everyone present what you have learned over the past five hours."

"Yes, thank you Mr. President. We had a spirited discussion earlier. I am thankful for the opportunity to be here. When I returned to my desk, here, I learned I had several voicemail messages. I called and spoke with each of these same sources whose information prompted our initial talk earlier today. I am sad to report each of them are holding firm. In fact, it appears the Iranians may push the situation by moving the uranium very soon," Pete Thomas declares.

"How much time do we have?" National Security Advisor Rob Lowenstein inquires.

"Toward the end of the week…Sunday at the latest," Thomas answers. Before providing the last part of his answer, he made direct eye contact with each person in the room.

"Are you sure?" Vice-President Touter asks.

"Sadly, yes," Thomas says.

"What about the Israelis? Have we inquired as to how they feel? Do they know what we know?" Karen Newby, Secretary of Defense, asks.

"They won't wait a day longer than they have to. If they suspect the Iranians are going to move the uranium, they won't wait for an e-mail from us to tell them the news," Mike Harnett, a member of the National Security Council, answers.

"No, we have not notified the Prime Minister of Israel what we have learned. I made a decision to not tell anyone, even the state of Israel, until we decided what to do" President Hamlin says.

"Why not? Are they not our strongest ally in the Middle East?" Vice-President Touter asks in an elevated voice.

"Like Mike (Harnett) just said. If Israel knows, they won't wait for our permission to attack. Remember what happened when Israel feared that Iraq was close to completing a nuclear reactor in the early 1980's? It's (the reactor) no longer there," Hamlin asserts.

"They're our closest ally, Mr. President" Touter firmly states.

"No one in this room tells their spouse everything they do for various reasons, including not wanting to answer certain questions. Until we're sure what we're going to do, we don't tell any nation including the state of Israel, anything," Hamlin answers.

"But," Touter interjects.

"Absolutely not. If Israel's intelligence sources are that good, which they are, they probably already know," Hamlin angrily replies…"When we're ready, we'll share our information and our expected course of action, we'll tell them" Hamlin says in a calmer voice.

"(Defense) Secretary Newby, Have you explored with the Joint Chiefs (the heads of the nation's four services of the Armed Forces) a plan for how we would address the situation?" President Hamlin asks.

"Yes, Mr. President. We've been actively pursuing a plan regarding the issue in Iran. We have directed three to four satellites on the locations we believe, with the greatest likelihood, where the Iranians would have the uranium stored at. If we see any trucks show up there and move ten yards, we will destroy the entire convoy pending your order. If and when any truck moves, the location, the buildings, people, and trucks above ground will all be fair game," Secretary Newby answers.

"And what about the facilities located underground?" Hamlin inquires.

"Anything at that location where a truck moves, whether it be above or below ground, can be eliminated pending your order, Mr. President," Newby replies.

"Understood. Have we reviewed our naval strength in the immediate region, near the Persian Gulf?" Hamlin inquires.

"Yes. According to the Naval Secretary, we have one entire Carrier Group in the Persian Gulf now. We have a second group in the Mediterranean Sea and a third in the Indian Ocean," Newby answers.

"Please move the group that's presently in the Mediterranean to the Persian Gulf. Move the group in the Indian Ocean and have it replace the one we're moving out of the Mediterranean… Do we have enough submarines in the immediate area?" Hamlin asks.

Yes, sir. That won't be an issue," Newby responds.

"We want to remove their ability of them moving the uranium but I don't want our troops to be sitting ducks in the water. What poses the greatest risk of safety to our troops on those ships?" Hamlin inquires.

"Well, the Iranian Government has dramatically improved their missile defense technology over the past three years. As everyone knows, they successfully launched a modified version to their surface to surface missile. If our ships are in the Gulf, they'll be pretty easy targets," Newby responds.

"Vice President Touter, if we launch an air assault against their nuclear facilities, will the Iranians attack our ships?" Hamlin asks.

"In a heartbeat, sir. You could bet on it," Touter answers.

"Secretary Newby and the Joint Chiefs and...anyone else here...Is there a way to convince the Iranian Government to not attack our ships in the water?" Hamlin inquires. Surprisingly it's dead silent in the room. For thirty seconds, you could hear a pin drop.

"You know it's awfully quiet in here. You all heard my previous question, right?" Hamlin asks. A chorus of "Yes, Mr. President," is heard over the intercom and from within the room.

"Ok, then. What can we do? I don't need to hear what makes me feel better. I need to hear your opinions now and not next week. This is not feel good time. The Iranians have played games for the past twenty years. We have information about their missile technology and the development of a nuclear bomb. They have threatened to destroy a few nations on this planet when they have developed the weapon (a nuclear bomb). They threw out the inspectors from the IAEC (International Atomic Energy Commission). They've deceived the international community. They've openly violated agreements they've signed. They've deceived a lot of presidential administrations since 1979. I don't know if they are *'the greater Persia in some end of the world'*, scenario. I do know this, however: The game is over.

"I'll ask a second time: since the Iranian Government refuses to play nicely within the established, international rules of order, how do we eliminate this threat posed in their facilities without them attacking American Troops on land on water or in the area or who may be on 'maneuvers' later this week?" Hamlin clearly asks.

"Mr. President, I have an idea. It's not a court order and it may not answer your question, but it provides a basis, a starting period, for debate," Bill Ashton, CIA Director, declares.

"Go ahead, Bill, you have the floor," Hamlin replies in an upbeat manner.

"(National Security Advisor) Rob Lowenstein and I were talking about this very topic and, in fact, this very scenario one month ago. We don't want anyone to think we're crazy. We debated this very issue about the Iranians' commitment to attack for several hours one night over some beers," Bill Ashton says as he is interrupted by President Hamlin.

"Bill, were the two of you sober a few hours after the discussion began?" Hamlin inquires.

"Yes sir," Ashton replies with a laugh. In fact, I know we were both sober enough to remember the details of the pros and cons of what to do and how they (the Iranians) would respond in kind," he answers.

"Ok. Tell us what you think," Hamlin orders.

"We agreed that they would not attack our troops or Israel for that matter, but only by a fulfilling one clear condition," Ashton says.

"And that requirement is what?" Hamlin asks.

"That you would have to convey how any attacks on any troops from our nation or upon Israel, would guarantee the end of Iran. We agreed that the Mullahs (the religious leaders that govern the country) have very strong beliefs and are great at encouraging young men to give up their lives. However, the Mullahs would never commit themselves to pay the ultimate penalty," Ashton declares. The tone in his voice was very clear.

"What are you saying?" Hamlin asks with a look of disbelief on his face.

"Mr. President, Advisor Lowenstein and I discussed how the Mullahs have successfully recruited children to run through mine fields. However, I have never seen one Mullah run through a mine field or attack Lebanon and attack Israeli soldiers," Ashton offers.

"And your point is?" Hamlin exclaims.

"We are of the opinion, Mr. President, that when push comes to shove, they'll cave in. However, on *one* condition: you have to convince them that if any soldier is threatened or hurt or killed, that the entire nation of Iran will be obliterated. That it will cease to exist and will be ended forever. You have to convince the

Mullahs that you'll destroy their nation with nuclear weapons and that they'll be killed themselves. At that point and *only* then will they give up their technology and won't harm any other countries' soldiers or people."

Hamlin had asked the Vice-President to play the role of devil's advocate beforehand. What Touter didn't know was that this time he would have to be the one to tell the Iranians of the pending attack. After all, Hamlin would be in an F-16 Fighter Jet participating in the attack. "That's taking quite a risk, gentlemen. Playing games with the possibility of a nuclear war when we don't know if they have developed a bomb or not," Vice-President Touter says.

"Mr. Vice-President, for twenty years the U.S. has been kind, respectful and even patient in encouraging the Republic of Iran to comply with the rules of law and with the treaties that they sign. According to my sources, with all respect, they have failed," Ashton says.

"Mr. Vice-President and President Hamlin, I must concur with the Director of the CIA (Mr. Ashton). We debated this very issue one night. We, also, followed up with additional discussions over the past few weeks. It is my opinion, from the individuals I've talked to in the Middle East and from other persons, some in this room, that Iran has not lived up to their end of the bargain," Rob Lowenstein, the National Security Advisor, adds.

"So, Mr. Lowenstein, how do you really feel?" Touter asks.

After a slight delay in response, Lowenstein gives his response. "The word of the Mullahs from the Republic of Iran means nothing sir. I would not believe them if they swore to me they were lying," Mr. Vice-President."

"I must add one more time to be clear Mr. President. The Mullahs have to believe that you are calling to risk their destruction by nuclear weapons. If not, they won't be afraid to order their Armed Forces to defend themselves, including the attack upon American Troops located on bases in the region or on ships in the Persian Gulf. In fact, if you're not willing to use the full arsenal of weapons at our disposal, including a nuclear bomb, then I must urge you not to attack," Lowenstein declares.

"You just made a good argument for attacking their nuclear weapons program, now you're backing away?" Hamlin inquires.

"No, Mr. President. Mr. Lowenstein and I believe there is enough (probable) cause in the evidence that they have a nuclear weapons program. In fact, we need to destroy their technology before they use it on any country, including us. I just added the firm belief that you must convince them, unequivocally, how you *will* use a nuclear bomb or they'll fight back. If we attack, they will be perceived as the victim by the world community. The Muslim nations will conclude we were out to take over that part of the world all along...To avoid an armed conflict, the Mullahs have to believe their destruction is at hand if they defend themselves," Ashton responds.

"I'm trying to build a consensus here," Hamlin inquires. "Mr. Lowenstein, do you agree with Bill's analysis?"

"Yes, Mr. President," he answers in a clear voice.

Hamlin deactivates the speaker phone and talks to (Defense Secretary) Newby, "Karen, it's me. I value your judgment more than anyone in this room," he affirms.

"Thank you sir. I do my best" Karen responds.

"We need to be right on this issue; we don't need your best. Can we get the ships from the carrier groups into the proper positions by Friday night? I know the Israelis may not wait that long, but I have to try. Tell me how long will it take to be ready to launch (an attack) using cruise missiles and have enough warplanes available?" Hamlin asks.

"Mr. President, such an attack would take weeks, perhaps months, to prepare for," she answers as the President cuts her off.

"We don't have months. The Israelis may wait days, maybe a week. What if they declared the war would start tomorrow. Would we wait a few weeks until the Armed Forces were ready? We spend more than $400 billion a year on our national defense. The taxpayers expect single mothers to be accountable to an audit to remain eligible for food stamps, if asked," Hamlin says in raising his voice. Tell me what can be available come Friday night our time," he asserts. There is silence in the room as President Hamlin does not say anything, but is writing some diligent notes from the dialogue over the past half hour.

"My God, you're seriously considering launching an attack Mr. President?" Vice-President Touter asks in disbelief.

"Mr. Vice-President we are going to defend this country. I'm trying very hard to build a consensus for this week...Look I wasn't going to say this but here's the bad news everyone. I called the Prime Minister of Israel before our meeting. Everything Rob (Lowenstein) and Bill (Ashton) alleged about Iran asking to move the uranium was recently verified by their intelligence forces. Worse, they aren't prepared to wait very long. Apparently, they've known (about the uranium and recent missile test) for about five days. They were going to attack (Iran) tomorrow," Robert Hamlin declares.

"They were going to do what?" Touter inquires. He is completely shocked by what he just heard as are the other individuals present.

"The Prime Minister told me that their country had planned to launch an air strike, possibly with nuclear weapons, tomorrow. I told him that I had a meeting scheduled with the National Security Council and Joint Chiefs of Staff in less than one hour," Hamlin asserts. I begged, yelled, and shouted at him, for obvious reasons, not to begin the attack. After some active discussion, Israel's Prime Minister promised that his country would not attack this weekend. Luckily, he stated he would urge his Cabinet to wait until Monday," Hamlin answers.

There is dead silence in the room. Nobody spoke for about two minutes. "In the mean time, what are we going to go? We'll need weeks to prepare (as Karen says)," Lowenstein offers as he is interrupted.

"We don't have weeks. We have a few days...I told him the U.S. would lead the attack on Saturday morning," Hamlin replies.

"What? You're going to start World War III!!" Touter yells.

"No, Mr. Vice-President, World War III would have started tomorrow. Luckily Israel has decided to let us lead the attack...I can assure you of this: if we don't fix the problem this weekend, Israel will attack on Monday. They are located within the range of the missiles' capability that Iran has. As the Prime Minister told me over the phone, Israel doesn't have the luxury of being able to wait. If they lose one war, it's over for them. It's that simple!" Hamlin shouts in response.

The room was very quiet for a few minutes. After a brief delay, "Mr. President, you got to know me very well during the last (presidential) campaign...I'm a team player, sir. I'll do what you need. I may not agree with what we're doing, but I trust you. I don't agree with the sudden urgency to attack nor do I like being boxed into a corner. However, I believe you. You said the Prime Minister has delayed the attack until Monday, correct? Vice-President asks.

"Yes, Mr. Vice-President, that is correct" Hamlin calmly answers.

"Israel waiting threatens their safety. Doing so gives us chance to help them. I'll take your word for it. I hope and pray, like hell, that you're right...What do you want me to do sir?" Vice-President Touter questions in a quiet and humble tone.

Twenty seconds later, President Robert Hamlin addresses the room. "We're at a difficult crossroad. Regardless of who would be here in this room, we were given the responsibility to lead by the American people to defend our nation after the prior election. I've spoken many times of how great our country is...We all know and believe it, but there are rare times, like now, when we have to show it. I don't recall the global community voting to have us be the leading policeman in the world. However, I also know Iran has made tactical decisions over the past twenty years to pursue developing a nuclear weapon. It's not a boating accident that we're at this juncture.

"It's time for the good people of the world to lead. I don't believe in deploying our troops unless I was ready to go myself. I'll be 30 years of age next month. Earlier this evening I learned that my wife is expecting our first child. It would be very convenient to opt out and not go. However, I made my decision when I began training two months ago. I decided I would be part of any such attack, if needed. As Former President Harry Truman once said '*The Bucks Stops Here*'," Hamlin declares as he sits up in his chair.

"I'll be leaving tomorrow night to join my squadron. We've been training for this very mission.

"Here's what we're gonna do. Rob and Bill discussed how the Iranian Government needs to believe that we'll eliminate them. Waiting untiol will give us an extra day, Vice-President Touter will break diplomatic protocol and call the Iranian President at 2 (am) in Teheran (the Iranian capital). He will announce at 2:30 (am) that American warplanes will be attacking the nuclear production facility at Narvaez and anything else that's within a mile of the facility. They will be joined by cruise missiles, with conventional weapons. Secretary Newby you are to work with the Joint Chiefs to make this happen. Is that understood?" Hamlin asks.

"Yes, Mr. President. It'll be hard on short notice, but we'll meet the challenge," she responds without hesitation.

"You have an extra day. I know, we can meet the objective. Remember this everyone: the Nation of Israel was going to attack *tomorrow*.

"Sam (Vice-President Touter)...You've got a more difficult task. You have to convince them (the Mullahs) and the Iranian President that we're serious and that their ambitions are about to end. In fact, here's an idea. We'll have a cruise missile hit the Intelligence building right before you place the call. By the time the President of Iran gets on the phone, he'll know someone just attacked his capital. If he is hesitant to agree to your demand, let him know our satellite is tracking the phone call and that a cruise missile is about to destroy the building where he is at. We'll have a second cruise missile hit the target across the street when he's on the phone with you," Hamlin says.

"Mr. President, what if he doesn't agree? Remember, he'll have a translator and there could be a language issue or a time delay," he replies.

"The President of Iran speaks English. He knows what an American-made cruise missile will do. Regardless of his religious beliefs are, if he wishes to avoid viewing, firsthand, American firepower destroy his country, then he is to comply with our desires. Secretary of State (James) Marron will work with you. You two shall determine the necessary words to educate him that he is to convince the Mullahs to give up the technology or we'll do it for them. He is to do as he's told," Hamlin states.

"What if he doesn't agree after the second explosion?" Touter inquires.

"The Iranian President needs to understand that if he does not issue the order, then and there, to surrender the technology that he'll never live to see the destruction of the Republic of Iran. Throughout history there have not been too many leaders who were in the position to make decisions that save their country from immediate destruction. He doesn't want to be the first...Your assignment is to persuade him not to attack any American soldiers or ships or he'll be responsible for the deaths of millions of his own people, starting with him and his home," Hamlin declares.

"One last question: Where will you be? What are you going to be doing?" Touter asks.

"We'll make arrangements to be available to tell him what is going to happen. I will be with my squadron assisting in the attack upon Iran. We'll be one of the first units delivering the message in the bottle. As I stated before, I'll never ask our troops to be deployed overseas that I am not prepared to do myself.

"That said, we all have a lot of work to do. I've learned firsthand, about the power of prayer. God can do many things in our lives. Many times, we just have to ask Him. Please join me in prayer... Dear Lord, grant us safety in our mission. Please use your power to convince the leadership in Iran that it is in everyone's interest to comply with treaties and rules and signatures. Keep our troops and ships safe in their travels and locations. Please encourage our enemies and other nations not to strike or oppose our actions. This weekend, we are only enforcing treaties and agreements that have been disregarded by the Republic of Iran. Lord, thanks for your protection and the blessings we have in our nation over the past two hundred plus years. Sometime we don't always express our gratitude for our safety, wealth, and security...At this hour and time, we need you more than ever. We ask all of this in your name. Amen. Our Father, who art in heaven, hallowed by thy name. Thy kingdom come, thy will be done as long as it is in heaven... Amen.

"The meeting is adjourned. Get some sleep. We have vital work to do. Remember this in all that you do the next week: The American people depend on us. They elected us because they believe in our abilities to defend this country and our allies. God has kept watch over us for a long time. Pray that He continues to extend his guiding hand for our behalf. May God bless the United States of America," Hamlin says in a clear and firm voice.

Chapter 10:
Transition to the Attack

"Hello Major. I'm President Robert Hamlin" he declares while offering to shake his hand.

"Mr. President. Wow, it's a surprise to meet you. What brings you here?" Major Tom Jackson asks in a low tone.

"Major, I'm here to fly with your squadron. We have important business in the week ahead. Are you ready for any assignment?" Hamlin inquires.

"Yes sir! We prepare for any contingency all the time. It's our duty to be ready," he responds.

"Good. We're going to need your help and leadership. We have a special mission in the near future," Hamlin says. The two of them walk away toward Hamlin's flying partner Colonel James Dillard.

"Mr. President I'm kind of concerned. What brings you here to Ankara, Turkey," he asks. There is a great deal of uncertainty in his voice.

"Major, you'll be debriefed, as will I, in the days ahead. Let's just say your experience and training is about to be tested. In college we have classes and then tests at the end of the semester, right?" Hamlin asks.

"Yes, Mr. President," Jackson answers.

"Well, let's just say this is final exams week in your senior year. Never mind that…Here's a better example. Remember your anxiety when completing flight school and Officer Candidate School?" Hamlin says.

"Yes, I do" he responds.

"Well then, its final exams week. Remember what you learned, throughout your career, about duty, your assignment, and your responsibility to the unit. It'll serve you well. In fact, I'll need your help in the next few days," Hamlin declares.

"By the way, is it okay, Mr. President, if I didn't vote for you? After all, I was born and raised in a military family. Didn't think you were the biggest supporter of the Armed Forces," the Major says with some hesitation.

Hamlin smiles at him. "It's okay. Believe me, I understand. However, next week when this is all over, it won't matter. Remember the events at hand. You won't be able to vote for me in the next election anyway because I'm not running for re-election. However, somebody else will run. Can you promise me you'll remember that Major?" Hamlin asks.

"Yes sir…You already know you won't be running for re-election?" he asks.

"Of course. I made that announcement during the last campaign after Senator (Al) Howard from Louisiana died. There are a lot of reasons why, but saying I would not run helped me (to win)," Hamlin offers.

"I'm from Louisiana. I liked Senator Howard. He seemed like a nice man," Major Jackson says in response.

"He was a great man. I was so blessed to meet him a few years ago. He came to Chicago and to my district and helped me get elected to the U.S. House almost five years ago. Miss him a lot," Hamlin says as a tear forms and begins to roll down his cheek. "Man, I could use his help this week."

"I'm sorry sir. Hey, there's Colonel Dillard," Jackson says as he salutes. Dillard immediately stops and salutes President Hamlin.

"At ease, both of you. Colonel Dillard, I thought I mentioned some time ago that you were not to salute me anymore," Hamlin says as he extends a salute and a handshake to his training officer while smiling.

"I'm sorry, Mr. President, but it's a requirement to salute. If an officer sees me and feels I didn't extend the proper respect to the U.S. President or an officer he'll have my (behind)," Dillard says as he is cut off.

"If that happens, call the White House and the officer in question will be politely contacted by me. Is that understood Colonel Dillard?" Hamlin says with a smile.

"Yes, Mr. President," Dillard quietly replies. "By the way, I was notified ten minutes ago that you were coming. However, I was ordered to act surprised when I saw you. Since we ordinarily train at Andrews (Air Force Base), located not far from Washington,

D.C.), I didn't have to pretend…I am surprised. Is this part of our training?" Dillard innocently asks.

"No Colonel. I'm sorry to report that events have transpired in the last week that are very serious," Hamlin replies as he turns. He turns and extends his hand outward. "Follow me Colonel. Jim, both you and Major Jackson will be receiving your assignments very soon. Let's just say that this is not a training exercise. It's the real thing," Hamlin replies with a serious look on his face.

"How real?" he inquires.

"I made a promise that I would never commit American troops into a hostile situation unless I was willing to go and fight myself. Well, I'm here and you're my training officer. We'll be flying together the next few days… The bottom line is that there is some important work to do," Hamlin answers in a firm voice.

"The fact you're here means it is serious. Wow… Wait, were you training with me because you knew this would happen?" he inquires.

"No, actually we just learned about some intelligence activities that may be happening. However, it appears that our sources are correct about some important national security matters. No, I didn't know when we began training together, Colonel, the entire team, our squadron, is going to need your help. We have a very important mission to do. I'm very proud to have the opportunity to fly with you. In fact, I trust you, which is not easy to say when you're the President. However, this isn't a training exercise nor is it a political campaign anymore," Hamlin whispers. He has a very firm look on his face when sharing the information.

"I'm here and I'll do my best sir, I'm a little nervous only because of the unknown," Dillard offers.

"That last statement you made shows you trust me. Colonel, there's a lot of danger in life. Hell, you already know because you're a fighter pilot for a living. I just learned my wife is pregnant. But I wanted to keep my promise on this issue about deploying our troops. I haven't slept much the past few days," Hamlin says while yawning.

"You'll be fine sir. I'll make sure you return home safe and sound next week," Dillard declares with a smile.

"Thanks. I'll do my best to help you keep the plane safe and not get hit. After all, we have some buildings to 'greet' next week," Hamlin says.

"Red Eagle…Red Eagle, can you hear me? This is Home Plate, over," states Colonel Bill Meyers. He is calling President Hamlin from a base in Afghanistan. Hamlin and Colonel James Dillard's plane is flying in formation with their squadron. Their target is a nuclear facility located in Narvaez, Iran. He was the only military officer authorized to contact their plane in flight for two reasons. One, he would be calling President Hamlin and two the safety of their entire squadron.

"Yes, Colonel this is Red Eagle (Hamlin's code name given for this mission). "Go ahead, Sir," Hamlin replies.

"Yes, Red Eagle, I have been told to tell you the Secretary is on the line. When you begin talking, I have ordered to terminate my communication. Is that understood, Red Eagle?" Colonel Bill Meyer inquires.

"Yes, Colonel that is affirmative. Go ahead and send the call through," Hamlin says.

Red Eagle, this is Karen Newby, can you hear me?" Defense Secretary Newby questions.

"Yes, loud and clear Ms. Secretary," Hamlin answers. A click is heard in the background, meaning it is only them talking. "Go ahead and preach the good news," Hamlin states.

"The Vice-President is about to make the call to the other leader (the President of Iran). We just learned the first mission was successful in greeting the target (two F-14 Fighter Jets were ordered to destroy the Iranian Intelligence building, located across the street from the Iranian President's residence)," Newby announces.

"Excellent news, Ms. Secretary. We are traveling as scheduled and are, approximately, 15 minutes from the start of the party (from their target)," Hamlin declares. "Feel free to put a shout out to the tourist guide." The coded language here means the Iranian President was to be called. While they were on the line a second call would be submitted to Hamlin's plane. That way, the Iranian

President would be immediately notified when the nuclear facility at Narvaez, Iran, was hit.

"Yes, Red Eagle, we will be making the call in two minutes. I'm ending our dialogue. Prepare to receive the second 'message in a bottle'," Newby says.

"That is affirmative, Ms. Secretary. Good luck in your discussion. I'll await the next letter (call)" Hamlin responds in terminating the call.

Six minutes later, as scheduled, Vice-President Touter places the call to Iran. It takes about five minutes for the Iranian President to get on the phone, approximately twelve minutes after the call between Secretary Newby and President Hamlin.

"Good morning, Mr. President. My name is Sam Touter and I am the Vice-President of the United States of America," Touter declares in a firm voice.

"What do you want?" President Ranjive Ramneini, the President of Iran, says. He is very rude in his tone.

"I can assure you that this phone call is very much worth your time, President Ramneini at 2:15 (am). I didn't mean to awake you," Touter says as he is interrupted.

"You didn't awake me. I woke up because the building across the street was destroyed. Do you happen to know anything about that?" Ramneini angrily yells.

"Yes, Mr. President. The United States Military, about twenty minutes ago, hit your Defense Ministry. I've been assured it no longer exists," Touter replies as he is interrupted.

"You're damn right it was hit! The building is on fire. Do you know how many innocent people you just killed?" Ramneini shouts. "Wait a minute. Where is your President? Why is he not calling me?"

"Well, Mr. President, I don't know how many innocent people work at the Defense Ministry. I do, however, know this. Your nation has been diligent in violating agreements with the international community over the past twenty years," Touter replies.

"Who are you to question us? The U.S. has been supporting one country (Israel) that has stolen land from our friends," Ramneini yells.

"I'm very glad, sir, you're wide awake. You see, pilots of our Armed Forces are about to attack your nuclear facility at Narvaez. I'm calling you at this time for you to convey how the Republic of Iran will not be harming any foreign troops or ships in international waters or there will be severe consequences," Touter proclaims.

"I can assure you the Islamic Republic of Iran can and will defend itself. Soon, we will have the ultimate weapon. Please tell me, what consequences will happen in our attempt to defend ourselves?" Ramneini asks in a rude manner.

"Mr. President, it's actually very simple. If one weapon is directed at any foreign soldier or ship, regardless of where they are located, whether in Iran or not, we will destroy Teheran tonight with several nuclear weapons. I can assure you, the Republic of Iran will never be able to use a nuclear weapon," Touter responds in a firm and clear manner.

"Our air defense system is fully capable of allowing us to defend ourselves. We have prepared for this gallant day!" Ramneini answers in an angry tone.

"Once again, Mr. President, I must declare our intent. The United States of America, today, will be enforcing the agreements of the world community. Your nation signed these agreements and agreed to comply with the rules that prohibit nuclear weapon development and proliferation. In less than five minutes, Armed Forces will destroy your nuclear facility in Narvaez," Touter declares.

"We have been developing nuclear materials for peaceful purposes at more than 500 locations throughout the Islamic Republic of Iran. You will never dictate to our country what we will or will not do!" Ramneini shouts.

"Mr. President, I assure you, the commitment of the United States of America to enforce international agreements began a few hours ago. Here is what is going to happen. In three minutes your nuclear facility at Narvaez will be destroyed. Additional attacks at hundreds of locations will occur within the next hour. Each facility will be hit and destroyed. At that time, you will be notified to comply with an international monitoring agreement. The Republic of Iran will be notified when and where you are to surrender all remaining nuclear materials and research products. You will, also, talk to your country's citizens on television your willingness to comply with these provisions. If you do not, Teheran will be hit with one of several nuclear devices three hours from now. You have less than three hours to send, in writing, your agreements to these principles. If not, you will never live to know about it. These terms are not negotiable," Touter says in a clear and positive manner.

"That's not going to happen. You are very arrogant, Mr. Vice-President, in thinking that your Armed Forces can defeat us. The people of the Islamic Republic of Iran have prepared for this day. Our air defense system is perfect. Our nuclear technology, developed for peaceful purposes, will soon be ready to defend the world from your horrible country. We will not agree to your arrogant proposal. Where is the President? He is the person I should be talking to!" Ramneini declares.

"Sorry to hear that, Mr. President. President Hamlin will soon be joining us. Karen (Secretary Newby) please dispatch the call to Robert Hamlin, President of the United States of America... President Ramneini, I can assure you that I am speaking with you under the direction of Robert Hamlin, the President of the United States. You're agreement with this order is mandatory," Vice-President Touter firmly declares. At this time their conversation is interrupted . A series of loud explosions are heard in the background.

"What is that noise? I demand to know what's happening!" Ramneini shouts. There is a strong sense of fear in his voice.

"Mr. President, this is Vice-President Touter still. As I mentioned earlier, the nuclear facility at Narvaez is being destroyed at this time. The loud explosions you hear are a clear sign that your defense system has failed to stop an air attack occurring right now. Soon you and I will be joined by President Robert Hamlin. He is in one of several aircraft over Narvaez at this time," Touter answers.

"That is impossible. We have spent billions of dollars on a system to stop your arrogant country from even thinking about such an attack. Our air defense system was recently tested as being near perfect...What do you mean President Hamlin is part of the attack?" Ramneini asks. His tone reveals he is angry, mainly because he cannot obtain any information about what is happening from any other sources than Vice-President Touter.

"Well, President Hamlin is participating, personally, in the attack. Before he joins us, live, I wish to make two things clear. One, you will be unable to receive communications from your field commanders soon. A separate mission is underway that will severely undercut your capacity to be updated by your defense commanders. Two, President Hamlin wanted me to update at this time the declaration that no foreign troops, ships, or aircraft will be fired upon or harmed in any way. No American or other foreign troops or other countries' citizens will be injured or attacked. The Republic of Iran will peacefully surrender any capacity, items and research to develop a nuclear weapon or materials regardless of intent or purpose," Touter proclaims. The tone in his voice reveals he is very serious.

"Any such proposal would come from the U.S. President himself, not some lackey," Ramneini asserts.

"THIS IS AN IMPORTANT MESSAGE," is heard by both parties. "This is Major Bill Meyers of the United States Air Force. I have received orders to notify you that President Robert Hamlin is on the line. I will hang up as soon as you can hear his voice," Major Bill Meyers declares.

"Good morning President Ramneini. My name is Robert Hamlin and I am the President of the United States of America. I am flying with a squadron of several aircraft, property of the U.S. Air Force. Several operations are underway led by the U.S. Armed Forces that will impede and end the Republic of Iran's ability to defend itself. Can you hear me President Ramneini?" Hamlin inquires in a firm voice.

"We will never surrender to your arrogant country," Ramneini replies.

"It is with a firm intent Mr. President that I'm notifying you that such a decision has already been made for your country and its existence in the next few hours. You see, the Nation of Israel was going to attack the Republic of Iran yesterday. Their intelligence sources knew before we did, that you were creating a nuclear bomb. Also, your missile tests were ahead of what we projected. I successfully convinced the Nation of Israel to postpone, by a few days, any foreign intervention in your country. If our discussion had not been positive, I assure you, the Republic of Iran would have been sent back a few centuries by now. We are, at least, allowing you the option to survive. As I stated earlier, various operations are well underway to end your ability to produce a nuclear weapon. If you do not comply, a nuclear attack will commence on Teheran. If it begins, you'll never live to know about it.

"The simple math is this: you will send to the United States a declaration to surrender all such materials within three hours or we will eliminate the city of Teheran and other parts of your nation. At that point, you don't want to know, what's next and what will occur to the Republic of Iran. Submitting a declaration to surrender all nuclear items and research materials is not negotiable," President Robert Hamlin says in affirming what Vice-President Touter had previously said. At this moment, a huge explosion is heard down the street in Teheran. It was clearly audible to all three persons talking.

"What was that? What are you doing?" Ramneini shouts.

"Mr. President, as I mentioned a number of operations are underway to impede your ability to produce a nuclear weapon or attack American servicemen and women in this mission. The noise you heard was a building being destroyed to further this mission. I don't know which one was hit because I'm not there. However, in flying near Narvaez, I can assure you that there are hundreds of aircraft being utilized to end, forever, any potential that such locations will produce any nuclear material or anything of value," Hamlin says.

Both Hamlin and Touter hear voices of several people speaking to the Iranian President. Spoken in Farsi, they did not understand what was being said. Ramneini, after a delay, resumes talking. "I was handed a notice that states how several targets were being hit by American warplanes and cruise missiles," Ramneini whispers.

"That is correct, President Ramneini. I promise you that your ability to produce a nuclear weapon is ending today. The air defense system that you spent a lot of money on isn't working very well. Rest assured today that the Republic of Iran has been judged to have violated agreements it signed regarding the proliferation and development of nuclear weapons... Today begins a new order," Hamlin slowly declares to President Ramneini.

"In fact, the rest of the world will soon learn that the rule of law and international agreements will be complied with."

"Here's something to consider: say we give the technology next month?" Ramneini says as he is cut off by Hamlin.

"Mr. President, the game is over. You have three hours to make a decision. If you don't understand perhaps the Israeli military flying over here, destroying your air defense system, ending your defense posture and killing millions of people would provide better clarity for you. I don't really think that being embarrassed by the Nation of Israel would really play very well to other nations... We are providing you three hours to submit a declaration to forfeit and surrender any and all nuclear technologies. Failure to comply will result in the obliteration of the Republic of Iran three hours and thirty minutes from now. I am leaving this conversation because my aircraft has to return to the mission of enforcing international nuclear arms development agreements, many of which you personally signed, all of which the Republic of Iran has violated. Once again, you are to discuss the resolution of the declaration with Vice-President Touter. After all, if my plane is shot down, he'll be the one you'll be communicating with... It's over President Ramneini. "We're going back to rejoin our squadron. Major Dillard you are permitted to engage our list of targets again," Hamlin says.

"Yes Sir!!" Major Dillard shouts.

"May God bless the servicemen and women of the United States of America today. Give us the strength to complete our assignments and face fear knowing that we have every moral and military right to be here today," Hamlin says in prayer as the call is terminated.

"President Ramneini this is Vice-President Touter again. I will call you back in one hour. I doubt you will receive much information from your commanders. However, it will also permit us to know how effective we've been. Once again, let me assure you, Mr. President, the destruction of your nuclear capacity is not limited to Narvaez. When I terminate our call, I was told by President Hamlin to order the next mission to begin. They include hundreds of additional sites where we believe you are producing or researching how to create a nuclear weapon. As President Hamlin previously said, it's over. I'll call you back in one hour," Vice-President Touter proclaims as he terminates the phone call.

President Ramneini briefly sits there, stunned, from these developments. It is now 2:35 (am) Teheran time. "Get me our generals and tell them to get their (bottoms) in here now!" he screams to an aide at the presidential palace in Farsi.

Back at the White House, a lot of activity is underway. Meetings to implement the battle plans, modified at the Pentagon over the previous days are now being discussed. "Yes, this is Vice-President Touter. Please get Defense Secretary Newby on the line," Touter says to a staff member.

"Yes, Mr. Vice-President, we have Secretary Newby on the line. Go ahead sir" the staff member replies two minutes later.

"Secretary Newby, this is Vice-President Touter. I just got off the phone with President Hamlin and Ramneini," Touter calmly says.

"How did it go?" Newby asks.

"Not sure. President Hamlin and I were both firm and clear to the Iranian leader about what was happening in his country and what was expected of him. He has three hours to send the declaration about the materials. I'm calling him back in one hour with an update on what's happening. Therefore, we are to carry out the plan in the theater of Iran, as planned, for the next 50 minutes," Touter offers.

"Yes Sir, we will proceed as scheduled. How is President Hamlin?" Newby inquires.

"Pretty calm, from what I could hear. I'm sure he's pretty excited with the attack. I hope he's alright," Touter whispers.

"He'll be fine Sam. You know Bob; not much affects him. He doesn't fly in F-16 fighter jets everyday. However, rest assured: he's flying with the best pilot we have, bar none. When I learned he was being trained for this, I was besides myself in disbelief and then anger. Here, one of the most dangerous missions we have today of destroying a nuclear arms facility and he volunteered for it," Newby says.

"He's stubborn Karen. It's going to be his downfall. Don't get me wrong. I have a great sense of admiration for him. In fact, I'll never be able to repay the trust he showed me to be his running mate. Nevertheless, I can't figure him out sometimes. Now we learned two days ago, Tracy (his wife) is pregnant. Unbelievable," Touter offers.

"Hey come on. He's a person of his word. He truly believes he shouldn't deploy our troops overseas into a hostile situation unless he's willing to go himself. That said, there was no way he was going to let Israel attack Iran. God knows, it would have started World War III," Newby replies.

"It may still happen. Ramneini still has to submit the declaration or we launch the (nuclear) attack against Teheran, as planned. There's not much margin for error," Touter says with some fear in his voice.

"I know; Look, I'm sure you and the President conveyed clearly to Ramneini what he has to do. Remember, Ramneini went to the effort to develop a nuclear bomb. He violated the agreements that both his predecessors and he signed. Iran has put the world in this situation today, not us. We patiently waited, what, ten years for their compliance. We finally learned and verified a week ago that they were cheating the entire time period. Worst, our intelligence sources were able to ascertain how close they were to developing a weapon and how much better their long-range missile became. All of this confirmed by (the nation of) Israel."

"Sam, we were lied to and misled. If we do nothing, Israel would have been attacked within a few months. We will carry out the plan in the theater today and beyond," Newby answers.

Vice-President Touter had been updated over the past forty-five minutes. The various bombing assignments have been very successful in destroying their targets. There had been no planes lost and no pilots missing. The cruise missiles had been incredibly accurate. With the exception of the attack on Narvaez, the other pilots had been assigned to observation / status detail, meaning what the cruise missiles did not destroy, their planes were assigned to 'finish the job'.

An hour after their last conversation, the Vice-President calls Iranian President Ramneini back. "Mr. President, this is Sam Touter, Vice-President of the U.S. calling again," Touter declares. His voice is firm and direct.

"Yes, Mr. Touter, I hear you," Ramneini replies. The tone in his voice is sad and withdrawn, lacking confidence.

"Oor enforcement (bombing) campaign is going very well. In fact, it's going better than expected," Touter states. He is trying very hard to be respectful, despite his knowledge that the attacks have been very successful. "It's going so well that I doubt you're receiving much information from your commanders. Have you had an opportunity to contemplate the issue referenced in our last discussion?"

"Yes… We are not yet prepared to agree to the declaration. In our system (of government) we need approval from a variety of people, including several religious figures. It's not like your dictatorship, Mr. Touter," Ramneini offers. The spite in his tone is clearly evident.

Touter pauses to gather his thoughts before speaking. He is livid but does not wish to dignify Ramneini's statement with a display of anger. "Mr. President, with all due respect, you just demonstrated a clear lack of knowledge of the American political system. First, we have a President and Vice-President in the United States. We are elected, together, as a team. We have an Electoral College system, where electors vote for a presidential candidate as determined by who won specific states. The system is not perfect. However, unlike in your country, both males and females have the opportunity to run for public office. Every person of the U.S. has an opportunity to register and vote. Also, everyday citizens determine who governs the country, not religious clerics.

"Religious figures in the U.S. have no greater or less impact on choosing candidates. In fact, they have absolutely no input on what military targets are selected and struck. I assure you, the only person I report to is the President of the U.S. We don't need, nor would we ask for, the blessing of a cleric, minister or priest, regardless of their religious affiliation to do our jobs.

We are very proud of the democratic system we have. Our Constitution is patterned and emulated by other emerging democracies across the globe. It is a living Constitution, complete with various amendments added over time. We move forward over time, not backwards, Mr. President. In the U.S. we also honor our commitments. The signatures on the treaties are a tangible demonstration that we agree to legally abide by the terms within the document. It means we'll keep our word," Touter proclaims. His tone was incredibly calm, just at the time when it was most needed.

"Even if our clerics agree to the terms, which they probably won't, getting approval for such a declaration takes time. You see, we do have a system that is indeed democratic," Ramneini replies.

"However, your country is very different. Your country is a theocracy, Mr. President. Your religious leaders have known for a long time actions that they supported, such as not abiding by the terms of international agreements and proceeding with intricate plans to develop a nuclear weapon, would result in a confrontation some day. Your nation agreed not to construct a nuclear bomb... Today, your time is up. Remember what President Hamlin said: 'Israel was scheduled to attack and destroy the Republic of Iran this weekend.' President Hamlin, the person who you view as a dictator, has spared the lives of millions of Iranian citizens, thus far. You have two hours now, Mr. President, before the ultimate penalty is rendered against your citizens. You may want to notify the clerics the clock is ticking if they truly love their people. I will call back in two hours. You will want to have a more clear answer at that time," Touter declares as he hangs up.

"How am I going to convince our religious leaders of the importance of complying with the American declaration?" Ramneini asks.

Over the next two hours Vice-President Touter has a number of phone conversations. He calls numerous officials across the world, including the leaders of Russia and China. These not only are leading military powers in the world, but are also large trading partners with Iran. Touter politely explained to them the situation in Iran, what Israel had planned to do, and notified both what would occur if Iran did not comply with issuing a declaration and surrendering the nuclear materials. Needless to say, neither were pleased. In fact, both had broken the world arms embargo that existed for Iran by selling various missile and air defense technologies. Touter had revealed to both nations how their investments had been failing miserably, much to their disappointment. American cruise missiles and hundreds of aircraft were successfully destroying hundreds of military targets across the country without much opposition. He, also, was receiving first-hand account information from President Hamlin on the success of eliminating Iran's ability to produce nuclear weapons near Narvaez.

"Not only are the targets being hit, but the explosions and fires here are unbelievable. The other pilots are telling me, from their experience of what they see, whatever is underground at these locations is also being destroyed," President Hamlin affirms.

Two hours later, Touter contacts Hamlin. They both agree to call Iranian President Ramneini. "It's time," Hamlin says.

"Yes, Mr. President. Hopefully Ramneini has notified the clerics the game is over," Touter responds.

At approximately 5:45 (am), Vice-President Touter calls Ramneini. "Mr. President, this is Sam Touter, the Vice-President of the United States again. Robert Hamlin, President of the United States, is joining us on this phone call. He is flying above Narvaez participating in the mission we previously discussed," Touter states.

"Yes...I'm here, now joined by my defense council. There are, about, twenty generals, military commanders and spiritual (religious) leaders in this room who are participating (in this phone call)," Ramneini replies as he is cut off by a cleric in his room.

"I am terribly sorry, but I cannot understand why you are doing this. We are a loving and peaceful people in Iran. There are religious shrines you have destroyed that were hundreds of years old. What you've done today is wrong, legally and morally wrong," he shouts.

"Gentlemen, my name is Robert A. Hamlin and I'm the President of the United States of America. You have my personal assurances that every target hit today had a military purpose. Two of the shrines hit today had military items that included tanks and rocket propelled grenade launchers moved onto their sites during the past week. I know because I personally approved the target list from the intelligence presented to me. If I'm wrong, I'll be the first to apologize. In fact, I won't wait for your nation's apology about spending billions of dollars buying military items, in clear violation of the international arms embargo. Nor will I wait for your apology about appropriating billions of additional dollars developing a nuclear weapon... If I'm wrong, you'll hear my apology first, if your nation still exists for a few hours from now," Hamlin declares in a firm and clear voice.

"This is wrong, just absolutely wrong. You had no right to attack our facilities," a general shouts.

"The Republic of Iran had no right to violate the Nuclear Non-Proliferation Treaty. This is very important, but it's only one of several agreements nevertheless that your nation's leaders and scientists violated. By signing, you agreed to comply with. It is with great sadness that I announce the game is over for the Republic of Iran. The international community, the U.S. included, has allowed your country to repeatedly evade, ship, flaunt, and violate the terms of the agreements you signed. Your word means little to me because your signatures mean even less. Thus, the world community had every right to enforce these agreements today," Hamlin affirms in a clear but calm voice.

"Mr. President, we need time to secure support for what you wish. We need more time," Ramneini says as Hamlin cuts him off.

"You've had enough time Mr. President. Everyone in that room where you're at has been provided *years*, not hours, to support agreements that various current and previous leaders of the Republic of Iran signed. In fact, I'm sure some of the negotiators to these treaties are present and can hear my voice.

"Here is your one and only option: President Ramneini, as we discussed, various military exercises are underway to diminish your nation's ability to pose a threat to other countries. You are to go on national television in Iran within the next 45 minutes and announce you are surrendering any and all items and technology pertaining to nuclear research and development and missile technology. That includes every missile and nuclear atom you have. Since you're already on extra time, I want to hear a reference about culpability and how the agreements were consistently ignored. If our analysts do not see you on your television network within 45 minutes, I will issue the launch codes in 50 minutes to destroy Teheran. Vice-President Touter told you beforehand and I am repeating the status now: it's over. As I previously mentioned I was able to convince the nation of Israel to delay such an attack until Monday," Hamlin says as he is interrupted.

"We would destroy them if they dared to think about such an attack," one person yells.

Hamlin pauses before answering. "What would your nation have done against ten nuclear warheads…or maybe twenty? Your air defense system is being destroyed this morning in the same manner Israel would be successful if they attacked. I assure you: Be grateful the issue was not left to them. If they had the choice, we wouldn't be having this discussion…You now have 45 minutes. This should not take long. Do not underestimate our resolve," Hamlin says as he hangs up. A huge explosion can be seen directly across the street, no more than 50 yards away. The presidential building shakes from the blast.

"It's gone," a general yells after running to the window. "It's completely flat…," another person shouts after the dust settles enough to see. In fact, many windows in their building are destroyed from the impact of the blast.

Forty-five minutes after the conclusion of their prior phone call, President Ramneini appears on national television. It is approximately 6:40 (am) local time in Teheran, Iran. He begins by reading an Islamic prayer. He is speaking in Farsi, the national language, but a language expert is immediately translating the content of his speech for President Hamlin and the entire National

Security Council. "Many of my fellow citizens were awakened early today. Our nation was notified that decisions were made to destroy Teheran, our beautiful city, and other targets unless we were to comply with suggestions to forfeit our nuclear research program. I'm here to announce that the Islamic Republic of Iran is culpable for and at fault for what's occurring. Our military undertook efforts to develop a nuclear bomb. We were very close... within weeks to being able to test a weapon that would have altered, forever, the balance of power in the Middle East.

Today, now and at this time, the Islamic Republic of Iran will be surrendering nuclear research materials to the control of foreign nations," Ramneini says. Outbursts and cheers of happiness are heard from the Pentagon to the White House to President Hamlin's plane. Robert Hamlin sought confirmation from the translators to confirm what Ramneini was saying. It took nearly three minutes, with all the shouts, cheers, and hugs being offered. Meanwhile, the Iranian President was taking the time to explain what was done and that surrendering the materials should begin to save his nation from annihilation.

"Mr. President, you did it," Touter shouts. Normally, a very calm man, he is overcome with emotion.

"No, Sam, you are to be congratulated. You were the one who called him and got his attention. Put out the order to suspend all military activities in Iran. Tell them to have our troops return to where their missions began today, immediately. However, I was reminded of something...God saved us all today. God intervened and convinced Ramneini to do what was right. God is all powerful and can do anything. God continues to bless our nation," Hamlin proclaims. A gentle tear begins rolling down his cheek as Robert Hamlin smiles in praise and thanksgiving.

Chapter 11:
A Song of Thanksgiving

When President Robert Hamlin returned to the air base in Afghanistan, bedlam broke out. Emotions ran high as word filtered out that the Iranian Government had agreed to the U.S. declaration to surrender their nuclear weapons program. Each pilot was enthusiastically welcomed as their planes landed. At a quickly organized victory rally, Hamlin let go of his normally reserved demeanor to lift a beer in his hand to praise his fellow servicemen and women of their contributions.

"Hell yea we won today! The entire world community won today!" Hamlin shouted into the microphone as those present yelled, clapped, and jumped with excitement.

Two hours after the pep rally ended, a much more calm President Hamlin was seated in a small room. Arrangements were made for him to address the nation, live, about the events of the day. It was approximately 8 (pm) Eastern Standard Time. He chose to keep wearing his Air Force pilot's uniform. "I want the world community to understand the United States' resolve to enforce international agreements. If such actions offend some people, then that's too bad. If they had been doing their job the past ten years, today's events would not have been necessary" Hamlin whispered to a staff member who questioned his decision to wear his military-issued uniform for this broadcast. At 8 (pm) exactly, he began talking.

"Good evening everyone. I am speaking to you from a secure location in Afghanistan. Nearly eight hours ago hundreds missions were commenced from various nations within the Republic of Iran. Intelligence was received nearly one week ago that Iran was very close to the development of a nuclear weapon. They had been successful in testing a long-range rocket over the past few months. Iran was prepared to begin the final tests to add a nuclear warhead to this advanced missile. Efforts were undertaken to verify the allegations that Iran's capability to build a nuclear bomb was enhanced and that their long-range missile technology was greatly improved. Through the intelligence capabilities of the U.S. and our allies, the allegations were confirmed.

"In fact, as part of this process, it was learned an ally of the U.S. had planned to resolve this situation outside of agreement by others in the world community. In those conversations, it was decided the U.S. would single-handedly pursue missions to enforce the compliance by Iran not to have a nuclear weapons program.

"It must be unequivocally announced the nation of Iran is solely responsible for today's military actions. For more than twelve years they have signed various international agreements that mandated their compliance with not pursuing the development of a nuclear bomb. No one forced them to sign these agreements, (a list of which will be provided to the media tomorrow). In fact, Iranian leaders boasted, several times, how they could be trusted because they had signed such documents. Copies of such statements will, also, be provided to the media tomorrow.

"From our aggressive analysis of such agreements, from conversations with our allies over the past week, from discussions of sources of intelligence in the region and the use of various high-tech technologies in the past week I am sad to report there was clear and substantially documented evidence of flagrant disregard to comply with these agreements. Sadly, this had been done over the course of a number of years. In fact, compliance was not just ignored; it was violated, repeatedly, in hundreds of locations after the expenditure of billions of dollars, by the Republic of Iran.

"As Commander-in-Chief I have a moral and legal responsibility to defend the people of the United States. Being President, also, has other responsibilities to the international community and our allies. Over the past few days, I chose to fulfill those duties. It was my decision to attack. I personally approved the targets selected by Defense Secretary Karen Newby. I examined the intelligence data gathered from the information supplied by various sources. I did not take this responsibility lightly. In fact, as former President Harry Truman once said, '*The Buck Stops Here.*'

"Hundreds of missions were undertaken today to destroy the ability of the Republic of Iran to develop a nuclear bomb. I can safely announce that all our planes, pilots and servicemen and women are accounted for. From my appearance you can ascertain that I personally participated. Additional missions will begin soon to inspect and determine the success of the missions at destroying their targets.

"As part of this effort, Vice-President Touter began communications with President Ramneini of the Republic of Iran. Some time later, I joined the discussions with the Iranian President. Due to the professional diligence of Vice-President Touter, Defense Secretary Newby and thousands of others, the government of Iran has verbally announced and submitted a written declaration to surrender and forfeit all technologies in the production of a nuclear bomb and the means to deliver such weapons. Shortly after receiving the verbal and written commitment from the Iranian President, I ordered that all military exercises would be suspended.

"I want to express my acknowledgement to the thousands of servicemen and women who participated in today's military exercises. They not only performed exceptionally well, they were perfect. Their diligence and professionalism is second to none in the world community.

That said, I want to issue a word of caution. Our work is not done. In fact, it is just beginning. We still need to obtain from the Iranians any and all materials for the production of a nuclear bomb. We need to inspect the damage of our military strikes executed today. We need to educate the Iranian Government that their signature on international agreements does mean something. We, also, need to encourage other nations in the world community that assisting various countries in the production of a nuclear bomb will not be tolerated, ever again.

"Today begins a new order. Yes, our military exercises were successful. The real work will come in verifying that the technology will be surrendered to the U.S. We have to confirm that the sites where such production was alleged to be occurring is where, in fact, it was happening. We have to run samples for the material in the air and at the physical locations. This will enable us to verify the intelligence learned. A year from now, we'll also be able to ascertain if such production efforts have resumed. Let me make this very clear: as easy as we entered Iran today and immediately stopped bombing, we can just as easily return. We will be clearly conveying our thoughts to other nations that helped Iran in the development of nuclear weapons they aren't off the hook either.

"I end on one last note. A few days ago I learned that my wife is expecting our first child. Children are born every day to families across our nation and throughout the world. A lot of people across the planet get upset when the United States is acting like, in their opinion, the world's policeman. However, world peace requires a commitment by everyone, each nation, to follow the rules of law. Countries, including the United States, must comply with international agreements that they voluntarily sign. This pertains to each country on the planet. Not just the nations that want certain military technologies, but the nations that violate international agreements that prohibit their sale and manufacture. Until that day arrives, the U.S. will remain diligent in the enforcement of such agreements. It is each county's responsibility to ensure that we find a way to live together for the future of our children.

"May God continue to keep watch over our troops, our citizens and our nation. May God continue to bless the United States of America. May God encourage you to hug your family members tonight, particularly your children. Thank you for listening. Amen," Hamlin declares after finishing his address. He leaves the air base via fighter aircraft, flies to England to visit with U.S. troops there and returns to the U.S. on Air Force I.

Seven months later, Robert and Tracy Hamlin are at the hospital. Tracy has given birth to their firstborn son: Matthew Robert Hamlin. At a press conference with the First Family, President Hamlin was answering various questions about their child, the nation, and the world at large.

"What do you wish for your son, Mr. President?" a reporter from the *Washington Star* inquires.

"I've thought about this over the past few months…I want my son to be more tolerant, patient, and care-free than me as I grew up. I want him to have fun, but learn from every incident that happens. Last, as every other parent desires, you want your child to be a good person, want to help others as they grow older and be active in a charity and their church. I, also, understand that'll be a few years from now, but you want to make sure you raise your children properly. You, also, want your child to live in a world that's safe with a great future," Hamlin replies.

"Mrs. Hamlin, is there anything you wish at this time?" a reporter from the *Phoenix Gazette* asks.

"Yes, I'm very happy our child is active and healthy. Since Bob is up late at night, frequently, being the President, I want him to help with the feedings at 2 (am)," Tracy answers with a smile for the reporters' benefit.

"Mr. President, any comment on your wife's response to the last question," the same reporter asks in a follow-up question.

"Hey, look how time has flown today at the Hamlin Family press conference. I'm sure I'll be up late, again, tonight. You know, sometimes I hear baby talk from the world leaders in the early morning. Perhaps I'll put our son on the phone so he can express his opinion," President Hamlin answers as many in the room begin to laugh.

"Do you wish to identify any such leaders, by name?" another reporter questions.

"Won't be sharing any names or specific countries today, but thanks for asking. After I've left office, I'll be glad to share the information" Hamlin answers to the cheerful group with a smile as laughter fills the room.

One year later, President Hamlin is meeting with his political advisors. He had previously announced he would only serve one term. In the monthly political strategy sessions, a number of 'spin doctors' (political consultants who work for specific candidates during an election campaign who try to put the best spin on a situation) and key members of the U.S. Congress are at the meeting to try to alter the agenda.

"Yes, Mr. President, it's time to put the team back together," Tom McPike, Senate Majority Leader from Michigan says.

"I'm sorry. We have a great working leadership with the Congress. What team are you referring to?" Hamlin replies.

"You're re-election effort, sir. The midterm election was months ago. It's time to move forward. Your poll numbers look good. Just say the word and we're ready to go," he answers with a big smile, pumping his fist.

"Yes, Mr. President. You've surprised even your critics. The bid for a second term looks better by the day. The economy is strong. Even our manufacturing sector is finally picking up. And the fact you're a war hero now even increases the positives. I had my doubts in the beginning, but you've proven me wrong," Roy Blanchard, Hamlin's Chief of Staff, enthusiastically offers as he is cut off.

"We can stop the dialogue now. There's not going to be a movement to draft me. I made clear in the first campaign I'm not running for a second term. This is it. I gave my word to my wife, the voters, to Lillian Howard (who recently passed away), the media, and critics of me and to American people…In fact, I am supporting Karen Newby. Notified her yesterday of my decision when she expressed her desire to run in the future. I told her she can run now. She's qualified, she has the energy level needed, the enthusiasm, and the experience to be the U.S. President," Hamlin answers.

"Come on, Mr. President, you can't give up the greatest job in the world. You've earned the right to disregard what the general public thinks. You protect them. Look what you did in Iran. They need you. After all, people expect their elected officials to lie to them. Honesty in government, come on," one of the congressmen present says as many in the room start to laugh.

Robert Hamlin is sitting there with a look of disbelief. He was fearful this would happen, but still found the statements to be incredulous. "With all due respect, gentlemen, the issue is moot. In the first presidential campaign, I announced I would not run for re-election. In fact, one of the reasons I won was people were willing to give me the benefit of the doubt; a fresh start. After Senator Howard died, people gave me the opportunity to lead, govern and tell the truth. At the time the media and critics across the nation didn't believe me. It appears now that the view of ignorance has extended to some in this room," Hamlin calmly says.

"Come on, Mr. President. As the congressman stated, people don't trust elected officials in the U.S. You could change your mind. In fact, here's a scenario. In order to continue to enforce the agreement with Iran, you announce you'll be running for a second term" Senator McPike offers as many verbally offer their approval with 'Here-here' and 'absolutely'.

"Strike one. Won't happen," Hamlin answers.

"A second term to continue the work started. A second term because the nation needs you," Chief of Staff Blanchard enthusiastically adds.

"Strike two," Hamlin offers.

"You leave me no alternative, Mr. President. I'm calling House (Republican) Speaker William Rhodes," McPike adds.

"Call whoever you want. I'm not running. That's Strike three," Hamlin angrily replies. The tone of his voice surprised even experienced Washington politicos. Hamlin had a reputation for getting upset, but he never expressed it, even to his strongest supporters and campaign staff.

"I told you guys that he wouldn't run" Kevin, his closest friend joins in. "Bob, I know you're a man of your word. You're too honest, even to a fault. Will you, at least, listen to what they have to say?" Kevin pleads.

"No, I won't. Contemplating the issue only makes the decision tougher and opens the door to reversing my stand. Making the offer to serve one single term helped me earn the respect of the American people. Keeping my word and not running will demonstrate my intent, to both the American people and others in this room," Hamlin affirms.

"President Hamlin, I have House Speaker William Rhodes on the phone," Blanchard announces.

"…Good afternoon, Mr. Speaker," Hamlin offers in his response after pausing.

"Sounds as if there's trouble in paradise; Knowing you, as I do Mr. President, the only issue that startles you is when you're asked to do something when you've already decided you can't. You guys wouldn't be having, by chance, any discussions on the next presidential election are you?" House Speaker William Rhodes asks.

After a delay of twenty seconds or so, Blanchard offers, "Why yes, Mr. Speaker, that's exactly what we're talking about."

"Yes, Tom Pike here...The President won't budge from the decision against running for a second term."

"Fearful we'd be having this discussion... Mr. President, we'd be honored, on my side of the aisle, if you didn't run. Then we could take back the White House (U.S. Presidency). However, it's different with you, Sir. You see, I trust you. I've learned firsthand you're a good man who keeps his word. The nation has accomplished a lot under your leadership. You work well with everyone I know, including me, regardless if they deserve your respect or not..."

"I'll keep it simple, Mr. President. If you run, I can promise, right now, in front of several witnesses, nominal, I mean token to minimal opposition, to a successful bid for a second term. You've earned the right to run for a second term. You, to be honest, have done a great job leading our nation. You'll be re-elected. If you don't run, Republicans will nominate a strong candidate, someone who can win," House Speaker William Rhodes declares.

"I appreciate your support, Mr. Speaker, but I'll respectfully decline. Besides, I'm endorsing Defense Secretary (Karen) Newby," Hamlin answers.

"Yea, okay," Rhodes says, in between his statement he is trying not to laugh. "I appreciate you wanting to keep your word, Mr. President. Believe me, I do (laughing). But come on, Mrs. Newby?" he questions while laughing.

"Yes. Secretary Newby was a great Congresswoman, she's been a fantastic Defense Secretary and she'll be a great presidential candidate. In fact, I assure you, she's extremely well-qualified," Hamlin asserts in a raised voice.

"Yea; sure she is," he responds. Most of the staff is surprised at the Speaker's opinion and how he is laughing at the U.S. President. The women in the room (Newby was not present or participating in the conversation) are very put off by his demeaning responses.

"Mr. Speaker. I've been honest with you about my decision. However, I have a question. Would you like to explain to everyone listening, particularly the women present, why you're laughing regarding Secretary Newby's qualifications," Hamlin angrily inquires.

"Well, Mr. President, we've had 46 presidents to date, all men. That's 46-0, a shutout. Zero for the office. None. Do you see a pattern there?" Rhodes responds in a condescending manner.

"Someday, we'll have a woman president. In fact, after working with her for the past two years I can assure you, there are few people more qualified for the position. That's very few. Personally, I don't care what gender she is. I know she'll be a great president," Hamlin declares. The women in the room applaud his remarkable compliment.

"There's a difference between governing and getting elected Mr. President. You, more so than anyone, know how difficult it is getting elected president. Won't happen for Secretary Newby," Rhodes says.

"I'll be out working very hard for her. Harder than I did for myself," Hamlin confidently offers.

"Bring the cavalry, Mr. President. You may be campaigning, but your name won't be on the ballot...She's not you," Rhodes jokingly adds, without hesitation.

Sixteen months later, it's the last weekend of the campaign. President Hamlin has been campaigning across the country, non-stop, for the past three days. "Man, I love political campaigns," he confessed to a number of national reporters. He had been campaigning on and off for the past six weeks. However, the poll numbers never seem to get better than a five point margin of defeat.

"If you were running, this would be a blowout sir. In fact, Governor Timothy Crawford would not have even entered the race...You can campaign all day, sir, she can't win," one reporter from the *New York Tribune* offers. Timothy Crawford was the Republican Governor of Michigan.

"Why is that? She's eminently qualified. She's well-educated... Hell, there are more women voters than men," Hamlin yells in response.

"Well, that (yelling) incident one month ago didn't help. She's a woman, sir," the reporter offers in a whisper.

"Come on, Tom...You have a mother. Last time I checked, she's a woman," Hamlin says with his voice elevated.

"My mother isn't asking men to elect her to be the first female president. Besides, my mother is deceased, Mr. President," the male reporter answers.

"...I'm sorry. It's just frustrating. It certainly isn't due to a lack of effort. Yes, she's made a few mistakes but she's a great candidate. I'm very proud of her," Hamlin decries.

"Problem is she can't afford to make mistakes, Mr. President... Fair or not, she's being held to a higher standard because she's a woman," he responds.

President Robert Hamlin truly made an incredible effort to help Karen Newby get elected. However, she was defeated in her run to be the first woman elected as president. She lost 52-47 percent, with a third party candidate getting about one percent of the vote. She won sixteen states but lost in the Electoral College 320-228.

With the Defense Secretary standing near him, Robert Hamlin was quoted as saying, "The economy is strong. The economic factors are all positive. We are in a more secure world today, thanks to the efforts of leaders like Karen Newby. Yet, still she lost. The only factor that can explain why she was defeated today is because of her gender. America is not ready for a female president yet. 230 years after the U.S. Constitution was written, we still see the eye of discrimination, alive and well," Hamlin answers to the nation.

Chapter 12:
A New Chapter

It's January 20th and Governor Timothy Crawford has just been sworn in as the next President of the U.S. Robert A. Hamlin, his wife Tracy, his son, Matthew, his parents and in-laws, and several staff members are en route flying home to Midway Airport in Chicago. It is his last flight aboard Air Force I. At the airport, approximately 35,000 people await his arrival, most from the South Suburbs of Chicago. They were permitted to gather on the tarmac adjacent to the gate because of their size.

Once the plane lands, it taxis to where the crowd is gathered. After a brief delay, for security reasons, the ladder is pushed to the plane. The door opens and the crowd starts cheering. Bob, Tracy and Matthew Hamlin are all standing at the top of the ladder, waving and smiling to a very vocal crowd. A chant begins of '*Four More Years*' after they descend down the stairs. The chant continues until President Hamlin has reached the podium set up.

"Hello Chicago and the great citizens of the state of Illinois" Hamlin shouts as the crowd roars its approval. About two minutes later, Hamlin resumes speaking. "On behalf of Tracy and our families, we wanted to say thank you. Thank you for your loyal support when I was a Congressman, voting to elect me as your President and for choosing to support Karen Newby in her presidential bid two months ago.

"I know you'd love to hear a long speech about governmental policies, national security or how we stopped Iran's bid from being a nuclear power" Hamlin says as the crowd resumes cheering. However, it won't happen today. We're going to go inside and greet every single one of you who came today. In closing, I wanted to say thanks for the past four years. I'm 33-years-old now and we have the rest of our lives as private citizens to look forward to." Tracy begins to jump up and down in approval as Matthew tries to run away, being a curious two-year-old..

Twenty-two months later, Robert Hamlin was speaking at a series of fundraisers for a Democratic candidate in Illinois for the

U.S. Senate. Over the course of a month's time, Robert Hamlin's schedule included stops in Chicago, Alton, Arlington Heights, Aurora, Bloomington, Bolingbrook, Bourbonnais, Cairo, Calumet City, Carbondale, Centralia, Champaign, Charleston, Chicago Heights, Chicago Ridge, Country Club Hills, Crystal Lake, Decatur, Danville, Deerfield, DeKalb, Downers Grove, DuQuoin, Edwardsville, Effingham, Elgin, Elmhurst, Evanston, Freeport, Galena, Galesburg, Geneva, Gurnee, Hinsdale, Joliet, Kankakee, Lake Forest, LaGrange, Lisle, Lombard, Macomb, Matteson, McHenry, Mendota, Moline, Mt. Prospect, Mt. Vernon, Naperville, New Lenox, Niles, Normal, North Riverside, Oakbrook, Oak Lawn, Oak Park, Orland Park, Ottawa, Palos Hills, Park Forest, Peoria, Peru, Plainfield, Princeton, Quincy, Rantoul, Rock Island, Rockford, Rosemont, Saint Charles, Schaumburg, Skokie, Springfield, Utica, Tinley Park, Tuscola, Urbana, Vernon Hills, Vienna, Watseka, West Dundee, Western Springs, Wheaton, Wilmette, Winnetka, Woodridge, Yorkville, and back to Orland Park, where they now lived. At each stop, the message was the same, '*Keep America Moving Forward.*'

Subsequently, Bob and Tracy joined thousands of others at the victory party for Congressman Joe Taylor. He was successful in his bid to become a U.S. Senator and won by a 54-46 percent margin. His margin of victory was an excellent performance for a Democratic candidate in a particularly strong Republican year. "In concluding, I want to thank former President Robert Hamlin. His assistance was instrumental to our win tonight. In a night where Democratic candidates are losing across the nation, we won by eight percentage points. Thank, Mr. President" Taylor shared with the crowd at a hotel in Matteson, Illinois, the site of prior victory parties of Robert Hamlin.

The following March, Hamlin was in Los Angeles, California, speaking at a charitable fundraiser. He, Tracy and Matthew had just returned from a three week vacation to Florida with all their immediate and extended family members. "Bob, I know you like politics but this vacation was great. I hope our time together lasts forever. I had a fantastic time," Tracy whispers to Bob as they flew from Orlando back to Chicago.

"Me tool; Politics is great but you and Matthew are the best thing that ever happened to me," Bob replies with a smile and kiss.

At the end of his speech, a staff member walked up to the podium and whispered in his ear, "Mr. President, there's a problem. We have to leave immediately," he sadly offers.

"What wrong?" Hamlin replies.

"Mr. President, please come with me. You have a phone call," he reiterates with a serious look on his face.

"Sir, please follow me. We've made arrangements for you to take the call," Rich Pavlich, a staff member traveling with Hamlin says.

They go leave the room and hurry outside the ballroom. The individuals refuse to answer Hamlin's questions and they soon arrive at the room where the phone has been set up.

"It's for you sir," a second male staff member aide sadly says.

"Who is it?" Hamlin asks as they refuse to answer. "Yes, it's Robert Hamlin. How can I help you?"

"President Hamlin, my name is Doctor Roger O'Malley at Randolph Hospital in Naperville, Illinois. I'm terribly sorry sir but I have some bad news to share," he says.

"Bad news?... What's wrong? Who is hurt?" Hamlin asks with a raised voice.

"Sir, your wife Tracy collapsed this afternoon. She was rushed to the hospital here. It appears she had a problem breathing and passed out. We tried our best but we were unsuccessful. Despite repeated efforts of our staff over twenty minutes' time, we couldn't save her," Doctor O'Malley calmly describes.

"What do you mean, couldn't save her? She's only 34 years old. Is she dead?" Hamlin asks with disbelief.

"Yes, she passed away today, Mr. President. She died around 4:15 (pm) Central Standard Time, about thirty minutes ago," O'Malley replies. He hears the phone fall to the ground at the other end. "Hello. Hello...Is anyone there?"

"Yes, doctor, it's me again (the staff member). President Hamlin is still here, but he's really shook up...He's panicking," he states.

"Okay. I want you to stay with him. Send someone else, have them yell to get a doctor. Just stay with the President...If he sits down, then just be there with him. If he is anxious and wants to walk around, then stand and do it with him. Don't leave him" O'Malley offers in a compassionate tone. In the background, they hear Hamlin yelling "Oh my God! No! No! I can't believe this happened."

"Where is the President's son? Does anyone know where his parents are?" the staff member asks. Hamlin, meanwhile, was now having a panic attack.

"Their son is here. They're trying to contact the parents on both sides of the Hamlin Family, but until now we can't find anyone. He's really shook up. He was with Mrs. Hamlin when she collapsed. He traveled with the Secret Service, but was not in the ambulance in route to the hospital. Once again, I'm very sorry about the events today" Doctor O'Malley says in a somber mood.

After a brief pause the conversation continues. "Okay, here's what we're going to do. Keep calling the President's parents and his in-laws. I will contact the President's best friend, Kevin Chapin, and fill him in. He lives in the Chicago area. If worse comes to worse, he can pick up Matthew. He'd be able to locate Mr. Hamlin's parents... I'll make sure to stay with the President," Pavlich sadly declares.

"How is he doing?" O'Malley asks.

"Not good sir. He and his wife were very close, even more so over the past year after he left office. They never seemed happier than they had over the past few months. She was a wonderful person and he's a great person, including that he's a fantastic Dad and husband...Let me let you go. We've got to have President Hamlin get to the airport. Thanks for your help Doctor," Pavlich replies with a tear flowing down his cheek.

"I'm very sorry. Give me your cell phone number so I can reach you if things chance here regarding locating the son's grandparents," Doctor O'Malley says.

"Okay, we'll do...Hey, Bob, I need to talk to you," Pavlich offers. During this time, Bob Hamlin is seated on a chair, crying. He has his body facing the adjacent chair, overcome with emotion.

"Bob, I just got off the phone with the doctor. They are having problems locating your parents. Apparently, Matthew was with your wife when she collapsed" Pavlich says.

"Oh my God; He saw the whole thing?...How could this have happened?" Hamlin yells. His face is white, with fear. He looks like someone has who may be going into shock.

"Bob, I'm terribly sorry. I don't know the circumstances of what happened or certainly not why. I'm going to contact the airline and see if we can catch an earlier flight home. I'll make sure they are reserved in first class and that we board the plane last. That minimizes the knowledge that you're on the plane and reduce the likelihood someone will want to talk with you. We'll see what we can do to get some privacy" Pavlich says.

"Thanks," Hamlin whispers after a delay. His voice is barely audible. He's physically there, but mentally, his mind is somewhere else.

Pavlich walks away (from Hamlin) to call the airline. He successfully makes arrangements to catch a flight home earlier, saving an hour. Subsequently, the phone starts ringing about two hours later, after they had reached the airport terminal. "Hello," he answers.

"Yes, it's Doctor O'Malley again. I wanted to personally convey some good news. Kevin Chapin is here. He is on the phone with the President's parents. He has offered to stay here and watch Matthew until the Hamlins arrive. Finally...some good news," O'Malley quietly says.

"Yea, it is. Did you wish to talk with President Hamlin?" Pavlich asks while walking away.

"About what sir?" O'Malley inquires.

"Thought you may want to share some insight as to what happened. He's really shook up, as I would be if I was in the same situation," Pavlich says.

"Yea, sure, let me talk to him," O'Malley replies. Pavlich hands Bob the phone.

"Yes, this is Robert Hamlin," he quietly shares.

"Yes, Mr. President it's Dr. O'Malley again; I think I have an idea what happened, but I'd rather wait to discuss it until the autopsy is completed. However, I have a question. How has your wife been the past week? Has she complained of any pains anywhere?" O'Malley asks.

After a brief delay, Hamlin replies "she's been fine. Had a doctor's appointment just two to three months ago and everything was okay...She had been complaining of pain in her legs the past few days," Hamlin answers.

"How bad was the pain?" O'Malley persists.

"Real bad; her leg was warm the past two to three days and discolored, red. Today I convinced her to make an appointment... She was supposed to go later today," Hamlin responds as he starts choking up.

"Mr. Hamlin, I'm very sorry. With your permission, I'd like to start the process of an autopsy, for you and your family. At least we'll have a better idea what happened and why. We'll have some paperwork to sign when you get home. With your permission, we can have the medical examiner start first thing tomorrow morning. I'll need you to come here and sign some paperwork. That way you can pay your respects to Mrs. Hamlin," O'Malley offers.

"Yes sir, go right ahead. I'll be there tonight," Hamlin says.

"I'll wait until you get here tonight, Mr. President. I really respected your family when you were in the office. You and your wife are good people," O'Malley offers.

"Thanks...I appreciate your kind words, but you don't have to stay for me. Go home and get some sleep," Hamlin declares.

"I'm a doctor, Mr. President. Many times we work 24 hour shifts. I'm on a double shift so I'll be here all night," O'Malley shares.

"Yea, I'm used to 24 hour shifts too...It's just not fair. Tracy put up with a lot in my political career. We were really enjoying our time together. I just can't believe she's gone," Hamlin says as another tear rolls down his cheek.

That night after arriving at his parent's house, tears freely flowed from Hamlin while hugging his son and parents. "Where's mommy?" his son Matthew asks, not sure what's happening in the busy world around him.

His parents begin to cry, again, as Robert Hamlin picks up his son. Fighting back a new set of tears, his response was delayed for what seemed like forever. He leans toward his only son, just shy of his third birthday. "Matthew, Mommy isn't here anymore. She received a phone call from God earlier today. God told your Mommy that he misses her and wants her to come home...to be in heaven," Hamlin replies. "When will she be coming back to us?" Matthew inquires.

After another delay Bob tries to answer the question as he fights back tears. "She's not coming home, son. I don't know what to say... She was fine this morning, but something happened and she's no longer here. We can't talk to her anymore," Hamlin answers while doing his best not to cry.

"But I want to hug Mommy. I miss her," Matthew says while crying.

"I miss her too...I wish she was here still. I guess God needed her more than we did" Hamlin sadly declares. They both hug each other, tears freely flowing from everyone present.

Two days later Dr. Roger O'Malley, Dr. Peter Smith, the county coroner, and Robert Hamlin were at Randolph Hospital in Naperville, Illinois. A press conference was scheduled to announce the autopsy results in three hours. However, the doctors wished to personally notify Hamlin of the news beforehand.

She died of what?" Hamlin asks with disbelief.

"Your wife, Tracy, had complications from Deep Venous Thrombosis. In the medical profession it is commonly known as DVT. She had several blood clots that had gone from her legs into her lungs. The clots travel to the heart and lungs in the same bloodstream. The veins, of course, return blood back to the lungs and heart. Her right lung was severely affected. In particular, her left lung stopped working completely. Hence, she collapsed and died from what is called a pulmonary embolism. A blood clot (thrombus) breaks free from the wall of a vein and travels to the lung. The clots stopped the blood flow from the deep vein into her lungs," Dr. Smith replies.

"How common is this? How would anyone know they had this?" Hamlin inquires with sadness.

"It's too common. There are 60,000 people each year who die from pulmonary embolisms. About 600,000 people are hospitalized each year from them. It's estimated around two million people in the U.S. each year develop DVT. "The symptoms, for most people, are pretty clear. The legs become swollen and change to being red in the calves or thighs. The same area that is discolored also becomes warmer. For adults, they may have a leg cramp during the night while sleeping. Most often they'll have swelling in the calves. The sad truth is about one-half of people are not aware of any symptoms. Your wife's legs were full of DVT or thrombus. Did she complain of any pain in her legs over the past two weeks?" Dr. Smith inquires.

Hamlin pauses before answering the question. "Yes, she had been saying her legs were very sore the two to three days before she died. She made very clear she was in pain. That very morning I told her to make an appointment to see a doctor. I received a voicemail where she stated she was going to see the doctor later in the afternoon…Was there anything that could have been done to save her?" Hamlin asks in a frustrated manner. A tear starts to roll down his cheek.

"Tough to tell. If she had gone to the doctor in the morning, he or she would have seen obvious symptoms of DVT. Her legs were swollen and colored red. They could have ordered a venous Doppler of her legs and they would have found a large amount of thrombus in her thighs. They would have immediately admitted her as a patient…But, that's a lot to get done in just a few hours. The truth is we'll never know," Dr. Smith answers.

"Did she suffer? Was there a lot of pain?" Hamlin whispers.

"Probably not; she may have had difficulty breathing for a number of seconds. She may have felt really uncomfortable for a very short time period, but then she collapsed. At that point, she probably didn't feel anything," Dr. Smith acknowledges.

"To build upon what Dr. Smith said, it's hard to tell. For a number of moments…It could have been 10 or 30 seconds, she probably couldn't breathe. After that, probably no feeling at all because she passed out," Dr. O'Malley offers.

"How did this happen? What created the clots?" Hamlin asks.

"It's different with everyone Mr. President. With some people the thrombus forms from immobility: not being able to walk after surgery, trauma, and frequent airline travel. Other people are genetically prone to having a coagulation disorder. They may have gene mutations, such as Factor V Leiden or deficiencies of Protein C or something else that is inherited from their parents," Dr. Smith answers.

"You both flew frequently, sometimes taking long airline flights. Many people form clots during a long flight. For most people, nothing happens to them. The thrombus will frequently get absorbed into the bloodstream and disappear. However, in some people, the clots grow. Combine a long flight where your legs are immobile for too long with a genetic blood disorder that they're born with; for some people the clot grows and moves to the lungs or heart. If left untreated, it's deadly.

It's kind of like a severe thunderstorm watch in the lower extremities. During a severe thunderstorm watch, many times nothing happens. However, on occasion, a severe thunderstorm forms with lightening, strong winds, or a tornado," Dr. O'Malley describes in a somber tone. The sad part is we can't issue the thunderstorm watch if the person doesn't recognize the symptoms. All too often, it's too late to help them.

"She never had a chance did she? There was nothing that could have been done?" Hamlin asks sadly.

"Not in this case, Mr. President. If she had seen a doctor yesterday, maybe; I'm terribly sorry," Dr. O'Malley replies.

"We know how to treat the patient, Mr. President. We even know how to stop the clots from forming, but only after we recognize the person has a potentially serious health condition with the clotting factors. However, most of the time we don't know who to treat until some event happens, such as major surgery, a bad fall, or they come to us with leg pain," Dr. Smith answers.

"How do you treat someone who has a blood clot?" Hamlin inquires.

"Depends why we think they have a clot. If we fear one could form, for example, after they have a hip replacement, we have them take a prescription that is an anti-coagulant (a medicine that minimizes clot formation). If there is swelling below the knee, we generally start them on the medicine and restrict their activities, but they are sent home," Dr. O'Malley states.

"What if the symptoms are seen above the knee?" Bob inquires with a look of fear on his face.

"Then we normally send them to the hospital to get a venous Doppler. We perform an ultrasound on both legs to determine where the clot is and its size. If it's above the knee it means the clot is traveling and we admit them into the hospital. We attach them to a heart monitor so we can watch their vital signs. We start them on an IV to thin out their blood. We may also do a chest x-ray to determine if any clots have broken free and traveled to the lungs," Dr. Smith explains.

"What if the clots are in the lungs?" Hamlin questions.

"Then our patient will be a guest at the hospital for about a week. We keep the patient hooked up to various machines, including a heart monitor. That way if the heart starts beating faster or even stops we can rush in and save their life. If they're not here we can't help him or her. By the time they realized there was a problem, if they recognize they need help, they'd collapsed or died by that point. We can do a lot more if they're a patient here," Dr. O'Malley offers.

"I told her to go to the doctor the day she died. Tracy told me her legs really hurt and I was out of town. Damn; I should have been more persistent in telling her to go to the doctor...If I was in town, I would have taken her to the hospital myself," Hamlin whispers. Tears are now flowing from each eye.

Two hours later Dr. Smith, Dr. O'Malley and Robert Hamlin were at a table in the auditorium in the hospital. They were joined by the parents of both Robert and Tracy Hamlin and Kevin Chapin, Hamlin's best friend. After introducing himself, Chapin began reading a prepared statement.

"On behalf of the Hamlin Family, I wanted to thank everyone for your thoughts at this time. Thousands of e-mails, letters, and cards were sent by you, the American people, to show your compassion. Robert Hamlin has promised to personally reply to every single one of them in the future. As you continue to pray for your elected officials to make good decisions please pray for our family, and in particular, our son Matthew.

"Tracy was a wonderful, loving, kind and beautiful human being. We were all touched by her enthusiasm, compassion, and persona. She will be missed dearly by everyone.

"Funeral arrangements will be announced tomorrow. They will be held in the Chicago area. Thank you again. This letter was signed by both families of Robert and Tracy Hamlin."

"Now, I will turn over the press conference to Roger O'Malley and Dr. Peter Smith. Dr. O'Malley was the attendant physician here at Randolph Hospital when Tracy Hamlin arrived at the hospital. Dr. Smith is the Coroner of Du Page County, Illinois. He and his staff performed the autopsy. They will be talking during the remainder of the press conference," Kevin says. He stands up to join the family members, located at the side of the room.

"Good morning, my name is Dr. Roger O'Malley. I am the attendant physician of Randolph Hospital. I am joined here with Dr. Peter Smith, the Coroner of DuPage County. "I wish to explain the findings of the completed autopsy of Tracy Hamlin. A few hours ago we verbally shared with Robert Hamlin the conclusions of the report regarding her death. Mrs. Hamlin died from complications of Deep Venous Thrombosis. That's spelled D-E-E-P. Second word, V-E-N-O-U-S. Last word, T-H-R-O-M-B-O-S-I-S. She had several blood clots in her left leg. The thrombus, also, traveled to her lungs and she suffered a Pulmonary Embolism, spelled P-U-L-M-O-N-A-R-Y. Second word E-M-B-O-L-I-S-M. The blood flow to her lungs was cut off. She collapsed and never regained consciousness. She was dead upon arrival at Randolph Hospital on Monday afternoon, March 16th. Various technologies were used to determine the cause of death, including a venous Doppler, for an ultrasound of the deep veins in both legs.

"The details of the autopsy report are available, upon written request, to the media organizations present here, per permission of the Hamlin Family. The videotape evidence and ultrasound pictures are not available. Quite frankly, unless you are a physician or a radiologist or technician performing the venous Doppler, you wouldn't be able to understand what the pictures showed anyway. However, with the written permission of the Hamlin Family, we are going to show the documentation and explain what we seen in the pictures and film of the legs and chest x-rays as best we can today. The pictures and reports were explained to former President Robert Hamlin when we explained the cause of death to him within the past two hours" Dr. O'Malley declares. Over the next fifteen minutes he and Dr. Smith proceed to show the ultrasound and x-ray images on an overhead projector.

Afterwards, they both sit down. Dr. Peter Smith begins describing what DVT is. "Sadly, more than 200,000 people die each year from complications of DVT. Complications from blood clots cause strokes, heart attacks, and pulmonary embolisms. Symptoms may include leg pain, tenderness, swelling or discoloration of the affected area. They generally form in the lower limbs, generally the calves, within the deep veins. They then travel into the thighs and too often to the lungs or heart. Half of the time, no symptoms are provided. Thousands of people, each year, die from this health condition.

"It's caused by immobility of the legs from extended periods of time. It will occur from a lack of activity after major surgery, a long airline flight or just sitting too long. Most often, such individuals also have genetic factors that make them more likely to form blood clots. More information can be learned from many websites in using a search engine. In fact, a list of them has been prepared and will be made available when we're concluded," Dr. Smith describes.

For an additional thirty minutes they entertain questions about the autopsy and DVT. One reporter asked Hamlin if he has any thoughts to share. "This has been hard on everyone, particularly our son Matthew. It's very complicated. It's amazing the damage something so small, as a blood clot, can do...You know, being President is a very powerful position. You can affect the lives of millions. You can order air strikes to destroy targets. But when it comes to a small item like a blood clot, you're powerless," Hamlin answers with a great deal of sadness.

"How has it been the past few days?" one reporter asks.

"It's been horrible. You can never plan for this. There's nothing that anybody says that makes you feel better. I'll just say this: Everyone has been wonderful the past few days. We really appreciate everyone's prayers and thoughts, but it doesn't affect the outcome. I would have given up my political career to have her back. As you know, I did not seek a second term. I kept my word; I promised Tracy that I would spend more time with our family. That said, there's no job in the world, even being the President of our great nation, that's worth losing your best friend, the best wife, the best mother you could possibly ask for," Hamlin says in a lowered voice. When completing his answer, he covers his face and begins to cry.

A few days later the funeral of Tracy Hamlin was held. Both the funeral and burial were held in Orland Park, Illinois. The location was selected on the grounds of the Hamlin Presidential Library. It was the first event where Robert Hamlin, well known as a fantastic public speaker, yielded to someone else to talk. For months, he cancelled his public appearances. He fell into various bouts of depression over the loss of his wife. Regardless of the numerous conversations about how it wasn't his fault, he couldn't move on.

A few months later he decided to join a small group at his church. He just felt he needed to give closure to his wife's death with people who shared his religious faith. When Kevin Chapin asked why he replied, "I pray everyday, man. But I just don't understand why her. Maybe some people of faith will help me know that it's okay if we don't understand…That's what I can't get over. When I was President, I could call anyone in the world about an issue and I'd get an answer, right away. Here, with God, it doesn't work that way. I know he answers my prayers. Maybe I'm not listening to him."

After attending meetings over four months' time at his church, he decided it was time. Seven months after the death of his wife, Robert Hamlin says, "It's time to step up and move forward. I may never get over the loss of my wife but it's time to try." He calls Kevin Chapin and notifies him he has decided to try and raise money to find a cure for DVT. He makes an appointment to meet with Steve Barnes, the Executive Director of a national organization doing research to find a cure for DVT.

Hamlin flies to Ann Arbor, Michigan, location of a facility for DVT research. He intentionally did not want to fly to the national headquarters of the group. "I've viewed enough websites, read enough pamphlets and discussed the seriousness of the problem over the past month. I want to see what we're doing to find a cure. I want to ask questions of the doctors and researchers who are examining the blood of people facing this health issue. I want to talk to, the people firsthand, who if we raise enough money I can ask can we cure this problem, forever. Most importantly, once a cure is found, I want to pursue how we make the medicine affordable. If I'm raising the money needed to find a cure, we can make the medicine. I want people who are more likely, due to surgery or genetic factors, to take a pill with the daily vitamin so other people don't have to endure the loss of their loved ones due to blood clots. We ended polio. We put a man on the moon. We won the Cold War. We can end blood clots," Hamlin affirmed in a phone conversation with Steve Barnes.

In Ann Arbor, Michigan, Robert Hamlin meets with Steve Barnes at the Marriott Hotel. They spoke in a private room about the problems DVT causes. "I wish to help your organization find a cure. I mentioned in a prior phone call about the accomplishments our nation has achieved. We've overcome greater hurdles as a country. We've won two major wars. We created a nuclear bomb to end the second one. We've had periods of great internal conflict. You know what? We've become even better as a country because of it. We can do this" Hamlin asserts. The look in his eye and the optimism of his face reminded Steve Barnes when Robert Hamlin was the President encouraging the nation to stop Iran's nuclear ambitions.

"Mr. President, you're a good man. I didn't vote for you when you ran. I thought you were too young. But how you handled yourself as the President was amazing. How you led the attack in

Iran. How you chose to leave office, to keep the promise you made to your wife… You're a good person. It'll be an honor to work with you, sir," Barnes offers.

"Well first the promise was made to the American people, including my wife. Please Steve, my name is Bob. That's what my friends call me, But, I'll be honest with you; the last eight months weren't easy. I learned how your wife died and the internal conflict you had in a medical journal a few weeks ago. I was very impressed how you handled things… To confess, I had to get over some issues also. I may not get over the loss of my wife for some time. However, I'm now mentally prepared to try. A few months ago, I began to give God a chance to help me. I realized that doing it alone wasn't working. I reached out to some people of faith in my small group at church. It's amazing what God can do, working through other people, if you let him. I'm here to be a soldier in the battle to find a cure against DVT and blood clots" Hamlin positively says.

"That's quite a story. It'll be great to work with you. Thanks again" Barnes replies as they both smile.

"Good. Let's go to the (research) hospital, shall we?" Hamlin asks.

"Yes sir," Barnes responds.

A few blocks away was the site where this national organization for DVT conducted it's research effort to find a cure. Steve Barnes took it upon himself to request the presence of several of the premier scientists and doctors that were diligently pursuing a cure against DVT. They were gathered in a room anticipating the arrival of Hamlin, accompanied by a few Secret Service Agents and Barnes. After they walked in and introductions were made, the meeting began.

"I wish to thank you for taking time out of your schedule to be here today. What we do here is very important. I know you all have projects with deadlines pending. However, today is a special day. We are really blessed to have with us former President Robert Hamlin. So, let's put our hands together and greet our special guest. At this time, please welcome President Robert Hamlin. Every person present stands and demonstrates their respect for Hamlin's presence. The applause lasts for more than two minutes.

"I wish to thank you for that kind introduction. Wish I could learn what I'd done to earn that. My Mom would be very proud. In all seriousness, your support is greatly appreciated," Hamlin offers with a smile. Based on the events of the past few months it should not be that difficult to figure out why I'm here…However, in addition to losing Tracy, I do have one regret, which pertains to the fact of not getting involved sooner. The truth is my wife was not the first person in my life who died from complications of DVT. As you know, former President William Crowe died from this silent killer. What you may not know is that former Senator Al Howard, who asked me to be his running mate and is the one person responsible for my success on the national political stage, also, died from DVT. He died from a heart attack caused by a blood clot that went through his lungs and into his heart.

"More importantly, hundreds of people die every day from complications from blood clots. It takes away people, one half of whom has no clear symptoms that something is very wrong. It kills grandparents, parents, brothers and sisters. Sadly, it cuts short nearly 200,000 lives each year. We learn how this is affecting the professional sports world, also. The only good thing affecting famous athletes is that it helps raise public awareness for a very serious medical condition.

"You all personally know the severity of this problem. You do research, valuable work, trying to create medicine to treat Deep Venous Thrombosis. I'm here to issue a new challenge today: we need to find a cure to prevent blood clots from forming," Hamlin proclaims in a loud and clear voice. The doctors and researchers present begin to stand and clap. "I'm here to announce that you'll never have to worry about the monies to fund the various research projects of your organization. I am making myself available, as your ambassador, to raise the necessary monies to find a cure. In return, I am requesting two things: No, I don't want my name on the building or a parade. I want you to find a cure for DVT within five years and I want the medicine to be affordable. I'll help raise whatever amount of money is needed. I don't care what the cost is, but I want it done. That's right about what I said: *within five years.*"

"I don't want to hear excuses about time or money. Steve, in fact, told me about an article recently published in a prominent medical journal. It stated how a cure for DVT would be identified in ten years. That's great news. However, if my math is right that's two million people who will still die. Ten years is not fast enough. We need a cure discovered within three years to have the medicine tested so the vaccine, as a pill or a shot, is ready for the general public to buy in five years time.

"Now, don't tell me it's not possible. We've accomplished more difficult tasks. We won the Cold War defeating the Soviet Union. We put a man on the moon. We found a cure for polio. We eliminated the threat of Iran's ability to create a nuclear bomb and threaten world peace. Hell, we even elected a 29-year-old person President of the U.S.," Hamlin says with a smile. "Therefore, I know firsthand the U.S. has successfully accomplished far more difficult challenges.

"Steve Barnes described to me a variety of the research projects being pursued. They sound very worthwhile. I know you all care about your duties. I, myself, don't do anything with less than a 100 percent effort. Steve believes it'll take about 20 million dollars to accelerate the research efforts in our goal to find a cure. You can count on me to raise the money to help you fulfill the mission of finding a cure for DVT. Thank you for your time today. May God bless you all in this effort," Hamlin asserts. The attendees begin to enthusiastically applaud.

"Is there anyone who has any questions?" Steve Barnes asks.

After a delay the one person who really wasn't clapping clears his throat. "Yes, Steve, I have a question for the former President. Yes, Mr. Hamlin, will there be a press conference soon? I'm hoping you're not just here to view yourself on television. After all, it's been a few months hasn't it?" Dr. Lawrence Ream inquires while leaning back in his chair.

Everyone else present in the room is sitting there, in shock. A few of the scientists, several of whom have been flustered in their efforts to work with Dr. Ream in the past, are really upset. However, no one wants to be the first to speak up. "Dr. Ream, I think we need to talk after the meeting," Steve Barnes replies. The look of anger is clearly visible on his face.

"Steve, let me see if I can help. Do you mind?" Hamlin questions. Steve Barnes slowly nods his head in approval because he's had it with Dr. Ream's disrespect for other people he feels are intellectually below him.

"Dr. Ream, I presume?" Hamlin inquires.

"You presume correctly. I am, in fact, Dr. Ream," he replies.

Robert Hamlin proceeds to stand up and walk over and sit next to Dr. Ream. "I was wondering how the air quality was on this side of the room. Now I feel better knowing it appears okay. Dr. Ream, I read your recent article about the potential of stem cells and finding a cure for DVT. It was an excellent piece. It was absolutely brilliant and incredibly well documented. Great job," Hamlin says.

"Well, thank you," Dr. Ream answers. A huge smile is seen on his face.

"You're incredibly intelligent. I'm sure you attended the most prestigious colleges in the nation. You're truly talented," Hamlin offers.

"I attended Harvard for my B.S. in Chemistry and UCLA for medical school. I graduated from both schools at the top of my class," Dr. Ream proclaims.

"Yes, that's fantastic, but I don't understand something. I mean, you have the brilliance of a doctor and the intelligence level of a genius. You just use a synapse to allege something so erroneous that the others here view you as rude or worse, as an a------ (seven letter curse word.). Can you help me understand how that could happen?" Hamlin asks. The tone in his voice was as clear as the sincere look on his face. Everyone begins to laugh and clap enthusiastically. Dr. Ream's face is turning red with anger.

Hamlin leans forward with a smile on his face and says, "Dr. Ream, you possess some incredible gifts from God. However, I've met more odd and threatening people than you. For example, you may want to review the deposition of how I 'pacified' the guy after an assassination attempt on my life in Louisiana," Hamlin whispers. "You know, seven years ago some genius was talking smack to me in a jail after he was arrested. I had warned him he should shut his mouth and wipe that stupid look off his face. He didn't. When he ran at me I kicked him in the family jewels. The field goal was good because the ball or his balls sailed through the uprights. I'm a human being, just like the other 25-30 people here. Dr. Ream, you're going to learn that just because you're an academic and scientific genius doesn't give you the right to be rude" Hamlin conveys without a smile on his face.

At this point Hamlin stands to continue talking; "I want to thank Dr. Ream for his steadfast support of the research performed here. He has graciously promised to be a team player in our efforts to find a cure for DVT. Thank you, Dr. Ream, and thank you all for your dedication, diligence and professionalism. Together, we can succeed in providing a cure for this silent killer and create longer life spans for the American people and others across the world. Thank you, for your time today and beyond. May God bless you all in this effort. Amen," Hamlin declares.

Over the next six months, Robert Hamlin toured the nation. In addition to speaking across the country, he participated in countless interviews with radio and TV stations. All the media outlets were very accommodating in their desire to interview Hamlin. He used the opportunities to educate the American people about what DVT was and the importance of finding a cure. A typical exchange went as follows:

"That's right. 200,000 Americans each year die from complications of DVT," Hamlin states.

"How does it happen? What are the symptoms?" a talk show host would ask.

"What happens is blood clots form in the deep veins, usually in the calves. They travel through the vein toward the heart and lungs. The typical symptoms are severe pain in the calves or thighs. The skin will be discolored and will feel warm. You may, also, have a leg cramp in one of the calves during the night. Half the times a person will have no symptoms," Hamlin offers.

"If someone has these symptoms what should they do?" the interviewer inquires.

"You should *run* to the doctor's office, immediately, if not sooner. DVT is not to be taken lightly. Go to the doctor. If they recommend you go to the hospital, leave right away. Don't worry about packing a travel bag. Let someone else do that for you. Sadly all too often, people ignore the warning signs that they have DVT. They hesitate to see the doctor by thinking their decision 'it's just a little pain, it'll go away'. Everyone; it doesn't just go away. As we know, the vein returns blood toward the heart and lungs. If the blood is moving in that direction, so is the blood clot. If the clot makes it to the lung, you may have a pulmonary embolism. Here, the clot is blocking your ability to breathe. If it goes to your heart, you could have a heart attack. If it proceeds to your brain, you could have a stroke. None of those options are very good. Therefore, to prevent their occurrence, you proactively have to go to the doctor to seek treatment.

"Is this how your wife, Tracy, died?" the host asks in a serious manner.

"Yes. Tracy Hamlin, former Senator Al Howard, and former President William Crowe all died from complications of DVT. Tracy died from a pulmonary embolism and had several clots in her lungs. Her left leg was full of thrombus material. Both Senator Howard and President Crowe had heart attacks caused by blood clots. It hurts knowing these three people all died from the same issue," Hamlin answers.

"That's why you're here today?" the host asks.

"Sadly, bad things happen to good people. I'm here as part of a much larger effort by countless individuals to raise both awareness and money to find a cure for DVT. Hundreds of people across the nation work, each day, as researchers, scientists, and volunteers to discuss this issue. This does not include the thousands of medical professionals, doctors and nurses across the nation treating people afflicted by this terrible medical condition. The bottom line is we need the financial help of the American people, your listeners, to accelerate the research process to develop a cure," Hamlin provides.

"How much money is needed for a cure to be created and how close are you?" the host inquires.

"Simply put, I'm here to help raise whatever money is needed. The goal is 20 million dollars and I think we'll be able to successfully reach that by the end of the year. My own personal goal is to assist so that amount of money is raised in six months. The harder part is finding a cure. Some recent articles in prominent medical journals described how some researchers believe we can have a cure available to the general public in ten years. Recent research by scientists, particularly Dr. Lawrence Ream, has been incredibly valuable toward understanding how a blood clot forms. Recently, prominent advocates how mentioned how if enough money was raised, we could cut that (time period) in half to five years.

"The bottom line is this. There are more worthwhile and established charities in the world whether it is your church, fighting homelessness, helping people afflicted with Cancer, MS or any other disease. There is no shortage of worthwhile causes that need help. In fact, if I may, there are many needs that are never met, such as donating blood, visiting someone in the hospital, helping out at a food pantry or cooking at a pancake breakfast. There are countless other needs across our great nation that will always need help.

"I talked about these issues in my first congressional campaign. The need for volunteers was there then as it was beforehand and as it is today. It will, also, be here ten years from now. Enough said; I'm going to continue to ask people to find some cause an charity and do the best they can to help. Yet, at the same time, pick something that's fun. There's no rule that says that charity work has to be tedious, hard, or boring. The benefits and joy you bring to other people when you help them can't be measured in dollars and cents. You know, seeing a smile on the face of someone you help is priceless," Hamlin declares.

"Well, Mr. President, I voted for you seven years ago when you ran for the presidency. I was hopeful that in thinking that you could make a difference. I'm proud to say that you're a good man, your wife was a wonderful person, and you've got a great family. I'm reminded again, today of your character and positive contributions. We're all better off from your leadership as President and in your charitable efforts to find a cure for DVT" the host proclaims.

211

"Thank you for the compliment. I'm just sharing my time, talents, and treasures with others. Believe me, I'm not perfect and I'm glad the researchers and scientists let me raise the money that allows them to do their jobs. I, like countless numbers of Americans, I just want to be part of the answer in improving the quality of life for people who aren't as lucky as I am," Hamlin offers with a humble tone.

Six years to the month after Tracy Hamlin died and 27 million dollars later, the Centers for Disease Control (CDC) granted approval for a pill that became a cure for Deep Venous Thrombosis. Robert Hamlin refused to participate in the press conference where the good news was announced. His office issued a press release that just said, "On behalf of the thousands of Americans who died each year from complications of DVT and their surviving loved ones, thank you for your thoughts, support, and donations. A special note of thanks goes to Dr. Lawrence Ream from the Society for Blood Research and DVT who developed the cure. Without his and countless other's help, this day would not have been possible."

Chapter 13:
One Campaign Ends, the Next Begins

In the future, just after turning 45-years-old, Robert Hamlin is contacted by former Vice-President Sam Touter. He resides outside of Atlanta, Georgia. The Democratic National Convention is scheduled to begin in two weeks. With three major candidates, none of them could secure a majority of the delegates to win the nomination. He was asked to attend a private meeting at a hotel with a few members of Congress and some prominent party fundraisers. Robert Hamlin believed he was traveling there to give his input for a compromise on one of the three candidates.

"Mr. President, it's an honor to see you again. You look great. Have you been working out?" Vice-President Touter asks with a smile on his face while extending his arm for a handshake. Both persons did not always agree during their administration, but Hamlin and Touter personally liked each other. In fact, they always hugged each other after their initial greeting.

"I feel great. I try to exercise now and then, but never as much as I should. More importantly, you look great. I can tell you have been exercising. Good for you," Hamlin replies.

"Mr. President I believe you know everyone here," Touter offers as he personally escorts Robert Hamlin around the room. "If there is anyone you don't remember, let me know. Believe me, they all know who you are," Touter whispers to his friend.

"Damn, you're a great guy. Thanks for the invitation. I'm hoping we can make some progress on determining a nominee," Hamlin positively says.

"Oh, I think that'll happen too. In fact, I think coming to a consensus is well under way" Touter hints with a shy smile.

"What are you talking about?" Hamlin naively questions.

"I'll make this really clear. If I told you the truth, you wouldn't have come to this meeting. The fact is the purpose of everyone present is to select a compromise candidate to become the (Democratic) nominee for President...It's you," Touter says as he continues to walk to his seat at the table. Hamlin immediately stops walking and is frozen at that spot.

"If we can have everyone be seated we'll be able to get started… Thank you for coming today. Mr. President, we would be honored if you could join us," Touter says.

"What the hell are you doing, Sam?" Hamlin asks while whispering to his former Vice-President. The entire time he was trying to smile so as not to reveal any surprise or anger toward Touter.

"Once again, Mr. President, if I told you the truth you wouldn't have come. Ken Seals from the United Auto Workers approached a few members of Congress a few weeks ago and offered your name as a possibility to run. The three current candidates (two were members of the U.S. Senate and the third was a former Governor) would not budge on their candidacies nor were they willing to ask either of the other two to run with them as a ticket. Thus, we're here seeking someone else to run to unify the party. You're the person," Touter answers.

"You got to be kidding me!" Hamlin replies.

"No I'm not. Ken Seals, members of Congress, and some major players (fundraisers) in the party are very serious about resolving this issue. The candidates won't but we will. You're the one common name that is repeatedly suggested," Touter says.

"Mr. President, we're glad you could join us here today. I suppose you're quite surprised," Seals offers.

"That's an understatement," Hamlin answers with disbelief.

"Mr. President, sir, we have a problem and we need your help. The three current candidates won't agree amongst themselves on what to do. More importantly, I don't think any of them can win anyway. Maybe one could win in another year against a weaker candidate. However, President Mike Stephens is way ahead in the polls," Seals says.

"What makes you think I can win? What entitles me to run this year? After all, the other three candidates have been running for a year or two now," Hamlin declares. It's evident he doesn't like the idea of him being drafted.

"Who thought you had a chance sixteen years ago? I didn't. In fact, I lobbied against your candidacy with Senator Howard. Then, low and behold, you won. Quite frankly, we're all better for it. You were a great leader, but more importantly, an even better man Mr. President. Everyone here is willing to work to help you win again," former Senator Steve Ramsey of Colorado offers.

"Come on. I can't run. It's different now. My son is almost 12 years old. Who would watch him? Hell, there's twenty reasons, at least, not to run," Hamlin retorts.

"Well, there are countless reasons why you should. In fact, you can begin with three reasons right off the top," Ramsey says.

"And they are?" Hamlin asks.

"The three current candidates provide three reasons by themselves. Enough said; A fourth reason, quite frankly, is you. Nobody is a better campaigner. In fact, no one ever left the White House after having done a better job. I opposed your selection then. I categorically support it now," Ramsey declares as the individuals present begin to clap. One by one, they begin to stand to show their agreement with Ramsey's statement.

"Mr. President, we need you. I know this is going to be a tough race. President Stephens is very popular, but he's done nothing to help working men or women or (our) union members. I don't expect him to ask for my endorsement. However, I do expect him to care about the loss of manufacturing jobs the past four years. He seems to oppose any effort that helps the auto industry. He naively thinks these problems get solved by themselves.

"You, on the other hand, clearly understand the impact of manufacturing jobs and the world economy. You know better than anyone what impact a plant closing has on the local community. To be blunt, he doesn't act because his genius advisors (he was being sarcastic) feel that any action, benefiting the manufacturing sector, is an undue interference in a capitalist economy. Hell, Ronald Reagan put together a legislative package to save Chrysler in the early 1980's. Stephens is like a ghost: no substance," Seals shouts. A number of the others present begin to clap.

"Mr. President, we can't wait four more years for President Stephens to get it. It's time to unify on a candidate. It's time for new leadership at the White House...It's time for you to return to the political arena," Touter says.

"I've been out of this for over six years," Hamlin suggests.

"Politics is like riding a bike: You never forget. It's the rush you never can fight or ignore. Just because you've been out of the loop, Mr. President, doesn't mean you can't regain the focus or the energy," Ramsey declares.

"Why don't you run Steve? Why don't you use your talents to put together a campaign?" Hamlin inquires.

"I'd lose, sir. Nobody wants this face (of arrogance) on the national scene. My best days are behind me and my best days weren't very good," Ramsey replies. Laughter fills the room from the people present.

"Sure you were. You and Roy Blanchard (his Chief of Staff) put together bills with (House Speaker) William Rhodes that worked to help people, move our economy forward and allow everyone a turn," Hamlin states.

"I was, also, taking turns with female lobbyists, staff members and friends. Politically, I'm untouchable. If I had a chance for the office that time and opportunity ended many years and several women ago," Ramsey responds with a touch of sadness. Silence fills the room at this time.

"Mr. President, if I could interject. There are a lot of reasons I could state having worked with you, each day in your administration, as to why you should govern again. Notice I didn't say run. I said govern. Here's the best reason I can offer: you voluntarily gave up the greatest job in the world twelve years ago. Countless other persons and I tried to lobby you to reconsider. However, you gave up the office to keep your word. You believed it was so important to keep your promise about serving one term that you gave up the most powerful position in the world: being President of the U.S...I just wanted to let you know that if you decide to run, I'll be there for you because you've earned it," Roy Blanchard, his former Chief-of-State says in a polite, but firm manner.

"I can't run. I don't have the fire anymore," Hamlin offers.

"Yes, you can run. You can get the fire back Mr. President. It's just taking some verbal and emotional sticks of wood and a lighter to create the fire" one congressman from Georgia says.

"Mr. President, we need your help. However, you deserve our assistance and support. We're here for you if you need us," another congressman from Ohio jumps in.

"What does it take for you to run, sir? You're the only person who can unify our party. There are about 30 people here. If asked for our second choice, excluding the three current candidates, we would probably have ten, maybe twenty names offered. After all, we're Democrats. We rarely agree on anything," Blanchard says. Everyone present begins to laugh. Some even applaud.

"Bob, you have to let her go" Touter says from out of the blue. Everyone instantly becomes quiet and turns their attention toward Vice-President Touter.

"What?" Hamlin asks. To say he has a surprised look on his face would be an understatement.

"There comes a time when you have to move on. You chose not to run for re-election to keep your promise to her. You raised millions of dollars to help find a cure for a disease that killed thousands of people. It, also, killed her. Believe me, I know you loved her. She was worth every ounce of energy you had and gave. I know you both had a great time in the few years before she passed away, but there comes a time when you have to move forward" Touter says. It was so quiet, a pin could drop.

"What makes you think anything about this issue pertains to Tracy?" Hamlin angrily asks.

"It's all about her. You don't date. You don't even have an interest in other women," Touter proclaims privately to Hamlin in a whisper.

"That's ridiculous. How can you even think that?" Hamlin yells.

"I know women who have called you. They weren't calling to discuss the weather. They had a romantic interest in a good looking widow who has his whole life ahead of him. I know because I gave several of them your phone number. They call, but you don't express any desire in pursuing them. It's not about your son or other commitments, Mr. President. If you intend to move forward with your life you have to let her go" Touter whispers to Hamlin.

"Mr. President, we need you. You're the only one who can give us a chance of winning back the White House. I don't know what you're thinking and I sure as hell can't imagine losing my wife. However, I do know you have a lot of class…I pray for you every day because I know you give of your time and efforts to improve the quality of life for countless people. Raising the money to find a cure for DVT is just one example. You do other events, each week that have helped thousands of people…It's time we helped you," Blanchard calmly states.

"You were one of the greatest presidents we've ever had, Mr. President. I would say the best, but that would be disrespectful to others who held the office. I know you have a great deal of respect for other individuals who held the title of President of the U.S. You single-handedly stopped the nuclear weapons program of Iran. In fact, you participated in the attack. I can't recall a president ever doing that while in office. You dramatically improved the position of the U.S. in the manufacturing segment of our economy. In fact, your efforts made us more competitive in the world marketplace. You put us back in the game of world trade and gave our nation, again, a chance to compete and then you left office," Tom Ransford states in praise. He was from Youngstown, Ohio and the leader of a steelworker's local of the national union.

"Just say the word. We'll be there for you sir," Seals shouts.

"We all know this is a big surprise for you Mr. President. We're sorry we didn't provide you with more notice. We'll need an answer relatively soon," Ramsey offers.

"Well how soon? I mean if you want an answer right now, I can provide it immediately, if not sooner. If you value my time, thoughts, and family… you'll give me through the weekend," Hamlin retorts.

"Let's do this, Mr. President. Call Sam (Touter) on Sunday night with your answer. That'll give you a little more than five days. That way, if you decline, we still have a week. That'll give the campaigns more time to reach a consensus (for one candidate or another) although I don't foresee any progress there…I'm hopeful that you can pursue this opportunity. We could use your help. In turn, you deserve ours," Blanchard politely says.

"Thanks. I think we can handle that. I apologize for not being more ready. I was caught off guard today, but that's okay," Hamlin says.

"I apologize for being personal Mr. President. I wasn't trying to offend you. I'm sorry if I did," Touter whispers to his friend.

"I know Sam; the sad truth is you're probably correct about what you said" Hamlin acknowledges.

"Sometimes we need a push from the ones that know us best," Touter states with a smile.

"The one person who knew me best died 9 ½ years ago…There have been a few moments when I questioned whether all the political success was really worth it. If mean, I lost time I could have spent with Tracy," Hamlin answer as he stands up and begins walking to the door. Touter stands up and escorts Hamlin to the door.

"Mr. President, what you did was worth it. God worked through you to bring optimism and a better life to millions of people in our country. Hell, you improved the safety of the world. People are better off because of your leadership… Bob, we need your help now. I helped organize this event because our nation needs you, again. The nation desires the leadership of God's humble servant," Touter declares.

"You mean God's *less-than-humble servant*…I'll think about what you said. However, remember that my son is almost 12-years-old. If he says no, there's no further debate or discussion on this, ever," Hamlin proclaims.

"If he says yes, we'll help you win, Mr. President," Touter says as he salutes.

"I didn't say yes to the question. If my son says its okay, then I'll think and pray about it. It depends on what God says. If he says no, then it won't happen," Hamlin answers

"I'm asking God that he says yes!" Touter exclaims.

"I'll call you on Sunday night. Have a good weekend Sam," Hamlin affirms. He proceeds to walk out the door. In doing so, the attendees are applauding, chanting his name HAM-LIN, HAM-LIN, HAM-LIN.

Later that evening, Robert Hamlin arrives back home in Orland Park, Illinois. He sits down with his son, Matthew, at the dinner table.

"Hey Dad, they showed some information about the upcoming Democratic (National) Convention in Atlanta. The report stated you were there today and attended a meeting of the delegates. What was the meeting about? Did you give a speech to cheer people up?" Matthew asks.

"Yes, son, I did go there. Was invited to attend thinking that we would settle on a candidate" Bob offers. "However, why would they need to be cheered up?" Hamlin questions with a serious look of interest.

"The report also showed how President (Mike) Stephens is ahead by fifteen points over the nearest candidate. The biggest lead is 22 points. Whoever runs, the commentator said, will be defeated badly," Matthew replies.

"That's not very optimistic, but you're probably right...Hey, I need to talk to you about something very important about the election," Hamlin offers.

"What's up Dad? Are you gong to be traveling a lot for the election? I mean, if these people that are running are all going to lose why do we have to help them?" his son innocently questions.

"This doesn't get easier over time, but I really need your advice on something; I'm going to run an idea by you and I want to hear what you think, ok? Hamlin inquires.

"Ok..." Matthew tentatively replies.

"Former Vice-President Touter invited a lot of very important people to the meeting to talk about the convention. Much to my surprise, they asked me to consider running for president this year," Hamlin states.

"Wow, that's really cool Dad! What's it like to be President?" Matthew asks. From his tone he is very excited.

"Well, everyone gets to know who you are. You have no privacy. Your life is an open book. It's a lot of responsibility. Get to fly anywhere you want in a really cool plane that's very big...

You probably don't remember when we lived in the White House because you were pretty young. You got to fly on the plane with us a few times," Hamlin responds.

"That's great. Wished I remembered it...Why did you stop being president?" Matthew sadly asks.

"Initially I was asked to run as the running mate of Senator Al Howard of Louisiana. He was someone I really respected in politics. You could say he was my mentor...He died during the campaign from a heart attack. Months later I was notified that it was caused by blood clot," Hamlin answers with a lowered voice.

"Like Mom?" Matthew sadly asks.

"Yea; real close. Your Mom had some blood clots that traveled to her lungs, which is called a pulmonary embolism...It was a tough time for all of us. Having you in our lives was the best thing that ever happened to me. However, losing your Mom was horrible, "Hamlin mentions. "Not going to say it was a happy time because it wasn't.

"After I became the (Democratic) presidential candidate, I made a promise to serve only one term in office. We won the election in a huge upset. There are a lot of reasons why we were successful. However, I still believe to this day that we won because I made that promise. It's important to keep your word, son," Hamlin proclaims.

"Weren't people upset? Weren't you popular (at the end of the term)? Would you have been reelected?" Matthew questions.

"The people at the meeting today clearly felt upset twelve years ago. Most political experts felt we would have been easily re-elected. Our approval rating was pretty high. We did a lot of good things to help people. We helped make the world a safer place... When I left office a lot of (Democratic) political activists weren't too happy," Hamlin replies.

"Hey, Dad, I don't like politics too much, but I know it's important to you. I like hearing your speeches. You make a lot of sense, much more than other leaders today. You have a lot of emotion. It's like a football game. People get really excited when you talk," Matthew shouts.

"Well, thanks, "Hamlin states with a smile. "I firmly believe a quote I once heard that *'there can't be fire in the pews if there's ice at the pulpit'*. The speeches are a lot more interesting when the speaker shows they care. However, let me ask you something; you said a few minutes ago it wouldn't matter who ran because they all would lose. Why would that be different with me?" Hamlin asks with curiosity.

"Well, you're my Dad. You can do anything...About the election I was talking about the other people. You can win Dad," Matthew states.

"What about President Stephens? Do you think he's doing a good job?" Hamlin asks.

"He's doing nothing...Look, I've heard say once how much respect you have for the office of being President, but he doesn't care," Matthew sadly replies.

"Come here son," Hamlin states as he and Matthew hug each other. "The president is a good man, but he's ineffective. He does a poor job at motivating people to work with him. There's a lot of problems that aren't being addressed because he's a poor leader, not a bad person...I'll think about it (running for the presidency) on one condition," Hamlin shares.

"What's that Dad?" he asks.

"You have to stay here most of the time. The school year starts again soon. I don't want to take you away from your activities, the school work or your friends. You're still young. I've tried very hard to make sure you had a normal childhood. I haven't always succeeded, but we try...If that's okay, with you, I'll consider running," Hamlin declares.

"Alright! I'll do whatever you want Dad to help, but I have a request too" Matthew whispers.

"Yea, what's that?" Hamlin asks in response with a grin.

"If you win, you have to get married again. You're a great Dad, but I want a Mom. All my friends have a Mom...You need someone too," Matthew innocently states.

"Okay. I'll think about it; I promise. However, that's only if we win. I'm pretty busy with various projects. It's hard to be married to me. Your Mom was one of very few people who could have done it," Hamlin declares.

"That's not cool Dad. You'll have to come up with a better excuse than that," Matthew says.

"Yea, you're right. You deserve better than that. I'll pray tonight about me running and we'll talk about it again tomorrow," Hamlin replies. Both members of the Hamlin Family smile as they walk toward the kitchen.

Two weeks later on a Wednesday evening, Robert A. Hamlin was nominated to run a second time for the U.S. Presidency on the second ballot at the Democratic Convention. As a tribute to his old friend, Hamlin selected former Vice-President Sam Touter from Georgia as his running mate. Later that evening a news reporter from a national television station asked him if they had a chance in the election against President Stephens

"Yes, we can win and we will," Hamlin replies when asked of his chances against the incumbent president in the general election in November. "Remember, we did (win) this once before. We can do it again. The American people need help and we're here to assist them. May God help us in this effort" Hamlin offers with his arm extended waving to some of the delegates in the audience.

Chapter 14:
Presidential Campaign (Take) Two

"So as to renew the effort of our successful campaign from twelve years earlier, we start again on another bus trip across America. Some time has passed, but the challenges have not. Yes, we start out way behind in the polls. (Some polling organizations placed them twenty points behind incumbent President Mike Stephens). Yes the race is going to be difficult, but it's worth the fight," Hamlin shouted. A crowd of nearly 20,000 people was gathered in an arena in Downtown Atlanta for his acceptance speech.

"Yes, the experts have us way behind again. Hey, where have we heard this before? Wait a minute, it sounds like the last time Vice-President Touter, Georgia's very own, and I ran together. This time they can't say we're inexperienced or not qualified. Why? We've had the jobs before and we performed very well. We all know how that race turned out. We're ready for another victory," Hamlin shouts as the crowd cheers.

"We begin our journey tomorrow by heading to Tennessee, Kentucky, Arkansas, and Missouri and then back to my home state of Illinois. The challenges before us are much like they were twelve years ago.

"We still face the threat of a nuclear attack, although the enemy may have changed.

"We still have schools that are not performing and an educational system that relies too heavily on property taxes generated from the market values of the homes where you live.

"We still face challenges of a legal system that is not fair by income or race.

"We still hear talk about stronger sentences for criminals, but few states provide enough resources for their prison systems.

"We have high gas taxes, but still have far too many roads and bridges that need serious repairs or have to be replaced entirely. One bridge collapse is one too many.

"We still hold telethons for areas destroyed by national disasters, but fail to help people rebuild their communities. We

224

have billions allocated for construction of the areas destroyed by tornadoes last spring in Missouri, Illinois, and Kentucky, yet they are tied up in red tape. We're not going to repeat the bureaucratic snafus that happened after prior hurricanes.

"We have millions of people in America who want to help their fellow Americans afflicted by disease, disaster, or bad luck. However, we have a president who recently said '*it's their job to pull themselves up.*' It may be their responsibility, but everyone needs help at time. We know the largest corporations in the country receive tax breaks. They receive such assistance from the federal government and then lay people off to keep the shareholders happy. When are they going to pull themselves up and do what's right?" Hamlin challenges the audience as they cheer wildly

"We still have millions of Americans who attend church services and seek spiritual leadership. Yet our nation's leader fails to go to religious services unless there's a camera rolling to catch him leaving a church (building). Amazing; He then has the tenacity to talk about family values. He asks Americans to help each other when he has no clue what community means.

"What do all these issues have in common? Here's the answer: talk. The entire past four years have been talk about this, talk about that, support for this, support for that. What we need is action, determination, sincerity, results, and accountability," Hamlin proclaims to the cheers of thousands.

"Some of our wealthier friends in America may be asking 'why is this important?' Wasn't Hamlin talking about these issues years ago? Of course, it's important. It's even more of an issue if it affects you. A few months ago, several large tornadoes hit the Midwest, including my home state. In particular, some upper income communities in Plainfield, New Lenox, and Joliet close to where I live in Orland Park, Illinois, were severely damaged. The parts hit were not Section 8 Housing. These are towns with people of upper-income levels who have large homes that required obtaining big mortgages for the owners to buy. Just like the victims of the hurricane that destroyed entire neighborhoods of New Orleans (Louisiana), they are still waiting for payments from their insurance companies and the government.

"Sadly, yes I was talking about comparable problems twelve years ago. If you think the issues of nuclear proliferation, rebuilding our communities, funding our schools, fixing bridges, or improving our legal system are important, you'll still be here four years from now wondering why, what, and when. We know who the president is and the when is now. There will be a commitment to fix these issues by changing the occupant who resides at the White House," Hamlin shouts. The crowd roars its approval.

Forty minutes later, Hamlin concludes his speech. "Sixteen years ago you trusted a 29-year-old Congressman from the suburbs of Chicago to be President. No one gave Vice-President Touter and I much of a chance. We were running against an incumbent President, the polls said the lead was insurmountable, and the pundits didn't believe that change was possible... Well, we're back, we're rested, and we're ready for Round Number Two. We're going to campaign, non-stop, and discuss the issues that affect the quality of people's lives," Hamlin states in a loud voice as the crowd feeds off his energy, cheering in an enthusiastic manner.

"Here, repeat after me. I am (echo) a winner (echo). I am (echo) a winner (echo). I am (echo) a winner (echo). We are (echo) together (echo). We are (echo) together (echo). We are (echo) together (echo)," Hamlin proclaims in a firm voice as the audience is repeating his words. They begin clapping loudly showing their approval.

Minutes later Hamlin resumes his speech. "In closing, this is going to be a difficult campaign. Nothing in life comes easy, even when you've previously been elected President. Believe in yourselves and do the best you can. Senator Touter believes in you and so do I. May you please bow your head in prayer.

"Dear Lord, thank you for bringing us together tonight. You know we never live up to your expectations. Keep watch over us all in the days and months ahead. Please help us in this mission. In the spirit of democracy, please help us all, the American people, to discuss the issues in an educated and responsible manner. Please help Vice-President Touter and I to be truthful with the American people as we communicate our vision.

"Thank you for the opportunity to serve in the past. Assist our volunteers and supporters to speak from the heart about a country we can always believe in. As always, may Your will be done; and all of God's people said Amen," Hamlin offers in praise and thanksgiving. Balloons began to fall from the ceiling. Hamlin walks around the stage, acknowledging various members of the delegates by state, across the nation. He returned to the podium, greeted by Vice-President Touter and they raised hands smiling at the delegates.

Throughout the next three months, the election polls tightened. The race was becoming closer by the day. Hamlin and Touter campaigned, exclusively, in 23 states. "We began seventeen points behind in our tracking polls. However, if we focus our energies and money in 23 states and win 21 of them, we'll win with a total of 280 votes in the Electoral College, ten more than needed to win. The margin of error is very small. We have to win 21 of the 23 states. If we fail, we'll lose," Touter explained to a group of fundraisers.

Speech after event after appearance after fundraiser, they crisscrossed the country. Hamlin and Touter, together, were campaigning constantly. When in a Southern state, they had campaigned 10-14 hours per day. Two weeks before the election, Hamlin appeared in Charleston, West Virginia. The state was in striking distance for the Democratic candidates because they trailed by only five percentage points, just outside the margin of error. They made a total of six stops in one day, appearing live on various radio and TV outlets.

"I love what coal can do" Hamlin proclaims to about 150 coal miners and their families as the people present cheer wildly. "Let me tell you why. In my home state we have a famous museum in Chicago. One of the exhibits features a coal mine. At the end of the tour there's a map which shows the abundance of coal located throughout the entire state. Even more so, there's no shortage of coal across the nation. That said, I'm really disappointed after the effort by our nation to find alternative energy sources. We are more dependent on foreign oil now than four years ago when the President took office. In fact, at the end of our term twelve years ago when we left office, it was the last time our national share of imported oil for our domestic energy needs had declined. Get this, the source of our energy needs from imported oil *decreased*, which was the first time since the end of the Nixon administration.

"Why is that important? It's an issue of national security and it helps the environment and creates good paying jobs here in the U.S. Yes, it impacts our national security because the countries we are buying oil from are nations with large percentages of their people who don't like us. That doesn't bode well. Also, we can remove more coal today with newer, environmentally safe technologies. Since the price of oil per barrel is so high, it's profitable to remove coal and oil from the ground. We all win. Both Illinois and West Virginia have large deposits of coal. Simply put, with these new technologies we can protect the environment and create good paying jobs. This should be and can be done," Hamlin declares as the crowd cheers.

However, despite several campaign appearances in one day, the tracking poll in the state showed Hamlin had only gained one percentage point. The same was true in both Kentucky and New Mexico. Three days later, Hamlin spent the entire day with the polls showing he was trailing 46-43 percent. On a Thursday, five days before the general election, he made campaign appearances in Louisville, Lexington, Bowling Green, Frankfort, Paducah, Murray and at Cincinnati's International Airport (which is located north of the Ohio River within Kentucky itself). Yes, a statistical tie but he only gained one percentage point. It was a valiant effort, Robert Hamlin sat down with three staff members late Friday night in Atlanta, Georgia, to discuss the poll results.

"Quite frankly, it looks bad," Kevin Chapin, Hamlin's best friend and former college roommate declared.

"Yea, I'm terribly sorry. I have to agree with Kevin. It doesn't look good," Roy Blanchard, Chief of Staff in the Hamlin Administration offers.

"I counted votes on hundreds of (legislative) bills, Mr. President. It's over," Tom McPike, former Democratic Majority Leader of the Senate confirms.

"How can you say that? I won elections in the past when no one thought we had a chance. We have three more days left in the campaign," Hamlin replies.

"I'm sorry, Bob. We spent two entire days this past week in two must-win states. We gained a total of two points, combined, and we spent a *lot* of time campaigning there," Kevin says.

"Kevin's right. It's not that it was a bad idea. We all decided by consensus, that we would go to West Virginia and Kentucky (for the entire day). However, we're still losing these two must-win states. We can't get to 270 (number of electoral votes needed to win the presidency)," Blanchard adds.

"Wait a minute…we had two states we could lose," Hamlin answers.

"We gave up on New Mexico and Missouri last week. The simple math is we have to run the table and win Michigan, West Virginia, Kentucky and Georgia. If we lose one state, it's over" McPike asserts.

"Does that mean we just give up? We have one weekend left. Is there anything we can do?" Hamlin inquires.

"Well, we have to win these four states, while not losing any of the remaining seventeen. I suggest we have you spend every hour in Michigan, West Virginia, and Kentucky. We'll keep Touter in Georgia. We'll have you travel to West Virginia tomorrow morning first, then to Kentucky and Michigan. Sunday, we'll reverse the order, but still depart from Atlanta," Chapin suggests.

"I agree. Sounds like a plan," Blanchard says.

"We're all on board. We may lose, but no candidate will ever outwork our nominee. You're the best campaigner I've ever seen Mr. President" McPike asserts.

Just then, a staff member walks into the room and delivers some papers to Kevin Chapin. Immediately after reviewing it, he tosses it on the desk toward Blanchard. "Damn. Just as I feared," Chapin angrily declares.

Blanchard picks up the (same) papers, reads them for five seconds and throws them back across the room. "Damnit," he yells while shaking his head.

"What's wrong?" Hamlin questions.

"It's (President) Stephens' schedule the next few days. They're keeping him only in Georgia and West Virginia, exclusively through Tuesday, just like we feared," Chapin whispers.

"How's that bad?" Hamlin inquires.

"Remember, he only has to win one of the four states. We need all four...They're obviously reading the same poll numbers we have. By keeping (President) Stephens in Georgia, it forces us to spend additional resources on TV ads and to keep you here for additional appearances. The more you're here, the less you're in West Virginia, for example. You can't be at two places at the same time. You're a great campaigner, Bob, but you're not a magician," Blanchard explains.

"I thought Sam (Touter) could win the state, freeing me up for West Virginia?" Hamlin questions.

"Touter's lived here his entire life, sir. Our poll shows it's a statistical tie here. We can win in Georgia, but that's with you being there a lot, the next few days. If you're here, you're not in the other states," McPike asserts.

"Come on. I've won every race I've ever been in. He won't outwork us the next four days. He sure can't beat me, straight up, on the campaign trail. We can do this. We were down by almost twenty points three months ago when we stated. It's now a tie. Fourth quarter in a football game... Hey, who's with me," Hamlin asserts in a positive manner.

After smiling and saying good night, the remaining staff members depart. They agree Robert Hamlin will give a press conference at the airport in Atlanta, Georgia tomorrow morning, then travel to West Virginia. Alone, Hamlin turns toward one of his two escapes (plus exercise): prayer time.

"Dear Lord, please give our staff the strength to believe in themselves. Please soften the hearts of undecided voters to hear our message. Please encourage our supporters to turn out and vote. Please give me the energy to push forward the next four days. Through you, all things are possible. Amen," Hamlin affirms.

The final weekend begins on a positive note. President Stephens' plane arrived on time in Atlanta. However, the second plane carrying media representatives covering his campaign was delayed due to severe weather. Several lines of severe thunderstorms swept from Louisiana through Georgia, grounding their plane. Thus, the President's press conference was delayed three hours because only four media outlets were there to cover it. The Hamlin Campaign saw an opportunity and jumped on it.

"Welcome everyone to the final weekend. It's been a great campaign and we're here to continue the dialogue. We'll be spending a lot of time the next few days here. People from the South have always been incredibly generous and hospitable with my family and our staff and I thank you all.

"We're at a crossroads here in America. There are several challenges the American people face. Our dependence on foreign oil; A declining manufacturing base, from textiles to coal to autos to steel to textiles again." (From the content of the sentence, Hamlin was reaching out to people employed in those specific industries in Georgia, West Virginia and Kentucky). "Worse, there's a perception among young people that our future won't be as good as the past.

"There are times when you and I have questioned our elected officials and their decisions. However, throughout my life I have never lost faith for the ingenuity of the American people. We put a man on the moon. We send continue to men and women into space and probes to Mars. We find and develop medicines to improve the quality of people's lives. We encourage researchers to find cures for diseases and health conditions, including Deep Venous Thrombosis. We produce new technologies to make our manufacturing sector more competitive and extract coal while protecting our environment.

"I stand here today to issue another challenge to our citizens. We can dream again. We can develop technologies to improve our economy. We can create new jobs in our manufacturing and health care sectors. We are still the great dreamers. I still believe in you, but you have to believe in a few key things. You need to understand the value of what hard work can accomplish; you have to have faith that we can be successful; and last, you have to place value in finishing what we started. We have three days left before Tuesday. It's time to complete our campaign and cross the finish line, victorious. On to West Virginia," Hamlin proclaims. He acknowledges the media members present, smiles, departs the stage, and follows his campaign staff to the gate to board the plane.

Throughout the weekend, Hamlin focuses on his campaign's message. Feeding off the energy, he briefly naps on his various flights. Flying each day from Georgia, he travels to West Virginia to Michigan to Kentucky or vice versa. Come Monday night, he achieves the impossible: he is within distance of winning all four states. He leads in two: Michigan and Kentucky, by four percentage points. In Georgia, he is winning by two points, both statistical ties. It's decided to make additional appearances the next day, even on Election Day, one in each state.

The plan is to speak at a rally of coal miners in West Virginia at 2 (am) on Tuesday morning. Fly to Atlanta for a pep rally, live on all the morning TV shows at 7:30 (am). Fly to Michigan for a lunchtime campaign stop in downtown Detroit and then a last appearance at the University of Kentucky at 4:30 (pm), just before the polls close. Political pundits across the nation are all amazed over how Robert Hamlin has run this race. "Does he ever sleep?" one commentator states.

Through it all, President Mike Stephens remained confident. "The bottom line is we only have to win one state. President Hamlin has to win all four. Good luck in West Virginia," he offers in a demeaning manner.

"Hamlin should be able to win West Virginia. Democrats lead Republicans by a 4 or 5 to 1 margin in party registration," one reporter from the liberal newspaper *America Now* expresses.

"A Democrat, yes, but the fact is West Virginia is not Illinois, sir. The only thing they share is an abundance of coal mines and steel mills. As Hamlin will soon learn, many of those have closed and his campaign ends today," Stephens declares with a smile.

One reporter from the *Minneapolis Meteor* assigned to President Stephens campaign whispers "you did nothing to stop the mines of the mills from closing; that's absolutely nothing, sir."

Come election night, it's nip and tuck, just as everyone projected. All other 46 states come in, as projected, for either Hamlin or Stephens. At 11:45 (pm) Eastern Standard Time, the pundits give Kentucky to Hamlin. At 12:30 (am) Hamlin is declared the winner in Michigan. Around 1:30 (am) Hamlin is awarded Georgia. He leads the total number of popular votes cast by 400,000. However, at 3 (am) the magical story ends.

"Yes, Tom Peters here live from Charleston, West Virginia. Every media person covering these two campaigns is here in this building. Vote totals have been coming in slow all night. I can, at this time, report two issues. One, President Stephens leads the state by about 13,000 votes. It's been close all night, with no candidate leading by more than 20,000 at any given time. In fact, all the votes have been counted, except for 15,000 absentee ballots. It appears that President Stephens has successfully fended off an aggressive challenge by former President Robert Hamlin" Peters asserts.

"Tom, this is Blaine Randolph here in the studio. We've been trying to analyze what happened across the nation all night. What President Hamlin achieved is simply remarkable. We had him eight points down in national polls just three weeks ago. At the beginning of the race, he was so far behind in some states by more than 20 points. In fact, he was losing Georgia and Kentucky each by at least 18 points in our polling, yet he won both states today. However, the greater story is what happened in West Virginia?" Thomas asks.

"I don't know. Staff members at Hamlin's campaign had him losing both West Virginia and Georgia by four points in their own poll data. Hamlin pulled out a miracle win in Georgia tonight in winning by about 45,000 votes. In fact, it's a major tribute to Sam Touter, Hamlin's former Vice-President. He lived here the past week, never once leaving the state. Remember he was the Governor and Senator here many years ago. He urged his constituents to give Hamlin and his team another term. He, also, knows how to count votes and called in the chits. Congratulations are clearly I order to the (Hamlin) campaign staff here tonight.

"West Virginia is another matter. The state is overwhelmingly Democratic, but leans toward Republican candidates in presidential elections. For example, in 2000 the incumbent Democratic Senator here was re-elected here with 80 percent of the vote. However, the Democratic presidential nominee still lost the state. Hamlin didn't have the political operation in West Virginia that he had, in say, Georgia. It's amazing how a former Democratic Congressman from Illinois had incredible electoral success in key Southern states, winning Louisiana again tonight for example. However, he lost West Virginia twelve years ago and he lost the state again, tonight," Peters says.

"Was there anything Hamlin could have done here?" Thomas inquires.

"Well, remember this. He was way behind when he was nominated a few months ago. Yes, he was the president years ago. Yes, public opinion polls revealed he was very popular when he left office. Yes, similar polls showed he was incredibly successful as a leader. His wife, Tracy, died suddenly from complications from blood clots. Then, he goes out and raised, what, almost 30 million dollars to find a cure for DVT, I believe. President Hamlin is a good man and I'll admit, was a great President. President Hamlin successfully hit his stride in the final weeks of this race. In fact, the latest numbers showed he won by popular vote by almost 350,000 votes. However, credit should be given to President Stephens. He had a large lead because he is very popular. Hamlin successfully hit at him, hard, on a number of issues, but you still need 270 Electoral votes to win the presidency. Current numbers show a 271-268 victory for Stephens in the Electoral College," Peters states.

"Yes, let's discuss that point you just made. It appears another presidential candidate has lost in the Electoral College, yet won the popular vote. Any chance, you'll see a call to action by the U.S. Congress to amend the U.S. Constitution to change how we elect our President?" Peters questions.

"Not a chance. There have been more than 600 attempts to amend the U.S. Constitution pertaining to the Electoral College and they've gone nowhere. The same thing happened in the Year

2000. There weren't any nationwide efforts, mass protests, or huge lobbying efforts to change our presidential election process back then. Safe to say, it won't happen now. Secondly, it's very hard to amend the Constitution. We've only had 28 amendments to date (the last one, remember, added before Hamlin's political career began eliminating age discrimination. Thus, since 1790, we've had 18 amendments. That's about one every twelve or thirteen years or so," Peters replies.

"Tom, hate to cut you off, but we're going back to Chicago. We've been notified that President Hamlin, defeated in his bid for a second term tonight, is at the podium. No advance warning of this was given and it is now 3:40 (am) Central Time. We now join President Hamlin's concession speech in progress," Peters announces.

"Thank you everyone. I wish to make a very short speech. Ten minutes ago I made a phone call to President Mike Stephens. I know, firsthand, how to receive a victory phone call on election night or the following morning. I've been blessed to receive a few of them. However, this is the first time I made the congratulatory call," Hamlin says as the crowd begins to boo.

"Everyone please, we have nothing to be ashamed of. We were losing months ago in our own polling, big time. We stuck to some key issues, we were consistent, and we talked about them, often. We even won the popular vote by more than 350,000 votes when our own poll data had us losing just one week ago. Simply put, we ran a great race. We worked incredibly hard and nearly pulled off a huge upset. However, it didn't happen.

"I called to offer my support to President Stephens. I called to congratulate him and his supporters on a victory. I, also, notified him that the issues we pursued in this campaign are not just going to go away, nor are we," Hamlin proclaims. The crowd begins to cheer very loudly.

"One last thing before we call it a night. I have been blessed in my life. I won the Illinois State Lottery and a lot of money. I married a wonderful woman that God chose to take from us and join him in heaven. I have a fantastic son, Matthew, here with me tonight. Hey everyone, do you think Matthew has a political career in his future?" Hamlin asks with a smile. Matthew turns toward his father, with a tired and shy look on his face.

"We helped find a cure for a disease that killed thousands and thousands of people each year. We were nominated for office to be President of this great nation sixteen years ago. We enjoyed years of prosperity afterwards due to some changes we made in our economy. We have tried to make a positive difference in people's lives. After all, I didn't find a cure for DVT. I was part of a team that found a cure that saves thousands of lives each year. We disarmed Iran from being a nuclear power. We have a lot to be proud of, my friends," Hamlin states as the crowd begins to cheer very loudly.

"I've been told there's 20,000 people here tonight in downtown Chicago. It's almost four in the morning. Think they can hear you in Evanston?" Hamlin asks with a smile. The crowd begins to loudly cheer and yell his name HAM-LIN, HAM-LIN, HAM-LIN, HAM-LIN.

"Do you know we won Georgia again tonight? This man right here, Vice-President Touter, spent the entire last week there and won us the state. Mr. Vice-President, it's been an honor to work with you," Hamlin says. He and Touter stand and give each other a big hug. "I'm sorry, but I'm very tired. I didn't sleep much the past week. Thank you all for your support. Thank you for your prayers when Tracy died. Thank you for helping to make me the luckiest man in the world. I am incredibly blessed," Hamlin says as he is trying to fight back a tear. He raises his hand, smiles one last time, salutes and waves to the crowd, as he and Touter leave the stage to go. The crowd continues to cheer, but Hamlin doesn't return for an encore.

Hamlin begins to walk down the long corridor as Kevin Chapin catches up to him. "Don't you have anything to say about what happened in West Virginia tonight?" Chapin angrily asks.

"What do you mean?" Hamlin asks in response.

"They stole the election! They took it right out from under you. Aren't you mad or hurt? Doesn't it bother you?" Chapin inquires in an angry tone.

"I was hurt when Senator (Al) Howard died. I was really hurt when Tracy died. I've already been President before. This is water under the bridge, buddy," Hamlin replies.

"Bridge? Get real, Bob. They stole the race today from you in West Virginia!" Chapin declares.

"Kevin, I didn't win West Virginia last time, remember? I don't know what it is. I talk about coal mining and the steel industry and creating jobs, yet we lost that state twice. Here, I talked about things to improve their quality of life and they voted against me, again. God help them because I apparently can't...Face it, we lost," Hamlin states in a depressed voice.

"Done? What are you talking about? Bob, you just won the popular vote to be elected President, a second time, by more than 350,000 votes. Doesn't it bother you?" Chapin asks in disbelief.

"You told me (last) Friday that I was going to lose. We were trailing by 4-6 percent, in our own polls. I spent the whole weekend doing two things: One, campaigning as hard as I could to prove you wrong; Two, writing in my head a concession speech that you heard tonight," Hamlin offers as he slowly turns toward his friend. "It's over, I'm done."

Slowly, Hamlin resumes walking down the corridor as Kevin walks behind him. After a minute, he joins Robert Hamlin and walks alongside him.

"Hey, I'm sorry...Is there anything that can get you back in politics?" Chapin politely inquires.

"Nope...Wait, there is one thing," Hamlin replies.

"I'm listening," Chapin answers.

"Congressman Ronald Owens. If he is ever nominated for the Presidency, you won't have to ask me to run. I'll be first in line," Hamlin proclaims.

"Ronald Owens? I heard he's running for the U.S. Senate next year in Florida. Wait, what's wrong with him?" Chapin asks.

"He's a tool," Hamlin responds.

"What?" Chapin inquires in response while laughing. "You've never referred to anyone in politics in that manner.

"Well, we have our policy differences with President Stephens, but he's a good man. Deep down he's honest, sincere, and a good guy. I'd even call him a friend, but he's lazy. Owens... we were sworn into office together into the Congress, what, sixteen years ago? I'm sorry, but he's a phony. I've seen the good and bad in this business and he's the worst. I wouldn't believe him if he swore to me he was lying. He's living proof that most humans only use a quarter of their brain capacity," Hamlin replies. Kevin begins to laugh hysterically.

"Come on. He can't be that bad!" Kevin declares.

"He's worse. Like I said, he's a tool," Hamlin asserts with a straight face.

"That was quite a story" Emily whispers as their bus pulls into Cullerton, Illinois, home of Central Illinois University.

"Yea, I'm sorry. It was a really weird dream," Bob replies.

"Let me ask you this: Why can't you just be like everyone else? Get real, buddy. How are you going to make friends or be elected President telling people stories like that?" Emily asks. "Most people would run away from you after hearing about that dream."

"But, you're not leaving" Bob responds.

"No, I'm not. Do you know why? Emily inquires.

"No why? Bob innocently questions.

"I listened because different, but sincere. You're the kind of person that others could believe in" Emily answers as she reaches to hold his hand.

"I do the best I can. Running to be President is like the *Epitome of Motivation*," Bob says while looking into her eyes.

"Is that your pick-up line?" Emily asks while laughing.

"No, it's just an expression of the dedication I have toward any project I participate in," Bob answers.

"I'm glad we met today. Glad I made the effort to listen, but you have to lighten up a little," Emily offers with a smile.

"I'll see what I can do," Bob replies as he begins to smile. "*Let the future begin.*"

Made in the USA
Lexington, KY
17 October 2016